THE
KILLER
IN
ME

MARGOT HARRISON

LER
IN

HYPERION
LOS ANGELES   NEW YORK

First Hardcover Edition, July 2016
First Paperback Edition, October 2018
1 3 5 7 9 10 8 6 4 2
FAC-025438-18236

Printed in the United States of America
This book is set in Adobe Caslon Pro/Monotype
Designed by Maria Elias

Library of Congress Control Number for Hardcover: 2015030822

ISBN 978-1-4847-2851-2

Visit www.hyperionteens.com

In memory of Max, who was here for
the beginning of this book but not the end

NINA

1

Sharp spring wind blows from the river as I stand at our town's last pay phone and punch in the number. My hands shake so hard I drop two of my quarters and have to kneel and scrounge for them in the dark.

At last the long-distance call rings through. A woman's voice, almost as deep as a man's, snaps, "Hello?"

Blood thunders in my ears. I don't know if I can do this.

"Hello? Hello?" She's about to slam down the phone.

I use a voice I've practiced, a little lower than my own. "Mrs. Gustafsson?"

Her voice softens. "Can I help you?"

This is it. No turning back.

"Mrs. Gustafsson," I whisper into the receiver, "please double-lock your doors and be extra careful for the next couple of days. Maybe go and stay with relatives. Someone could be watching your house, and I think he means you harm."

Means you harm. I memorized the wording, ominous yet vague.

I can't say, *He wants to come like a thief in the night and kill you before you can scream, and bury you where you'll never be found.*

A couple seconds of silence. When Mrs. Gustafsson comes back, her voice drips suspicion. "Who'm I speaking to here? Cop? Neighborhood watch? FBI?"

Hang up. Just hang up.

"I can't tell you," I say. "Please listen to me. He could be there as soon as Friday."

"You got an out-of-town number. What do you know about my neighborhood? Are you one of Abby's girls?"

I should've used a burner phone. If anything does happen to the Gustafssons, the cops will look at their call record and see my town.

The receiver feels like it weighs twenty pounds as I hang up. The Sunoco sign glares above me, and the bell on the mini-mart's door tings, too bright and loud. I'm probably on the security footage. *Careless. You know better.* My hair's moist with sweat under the ski hat, my bulky sweatshirt sticking to me. My eyes are wet, too.

I should have said more, but what?

She doesn't believe me. She won't take precautions. When he comes for her and her husband, she'll be at home in bed, sleeping soundly, worried about nothing worse than one of Abby's girls prank-calling her. Whoever they are.

I know it's going to happen, and I can't stop it.

. . .

He calls himself the Thief in the Night. He likes to think he's invisible. That's why he doesn't talk, doesn't torture, doesn't interact with them until he has to. Like death itself.

"They" are his victims. He calls them "targets."

First came the old man. Then the homeless guy. The hitchhiker. The lady who ran the campground. The woman in the honky-tonk parking lot.

And now this couple in upstate New York, the Gustafssons.

He found them two Mondays ago when he was in Schenectady for a scale-model conference. He hadn't planned to get into any trouble there (his private code word for killing somebody is "trouble"). But his cyelids felt gritty, the telltale sign he wouldn't be able to sleep, and the left lid kept twitching like it sometimes does. He should've pinched a couple Ambien from his girlfriend back in Albuquerque, but it was too late now. So he slid the battery out of his phone, took a random exit into a quiet neighborhood of little ranch houses, and went hunting.

He looked for a house with no dog, no kids' toys, access through the garage, a master bedroom facing away from the street.

He found one.

He hadn't brought any tools, so everything stayed theoretical. When he hunkered down behind a bare lilac bush and examined the house, he saw it as a puzzle. A mission.

As always, his senses (*my senses*) heightened as he set the scene. He mapped the course of entry, noticing in passing that the man silhouetted against the flat-screen TV was heavyset with a sloping gut. A kid's punch would push the poor bastard over. In a few years, a coronary might get him.

When the Thief came back for the couple, he'd simply speed nature along.

He'd swing back here after the second leg of his trip and chauffeur them to their resting place. The crooked little cabin with the ice-water brook that he'd found on the way here, when he took a wrong turn off the ramp and drove halfway up a mountain.

He spent a few hours there—not planning anything yet, just eating his rest stop takeout and enjoying the desolation. Now he realized it was a good place. It needed someone.

The Thief watched the couple zone out in front of the TV, closing their eyes and ears to reality. Reality is bone-dry, vast, beautiful in its indifference, like the desert where the Thief grew up, or the cold blue sky above it.

Like reality, he's always here, whether they know it or not. Always waiting.

2

After I make the pay-phone call to Mrs. Gustafsson, I can't stop thinking about the house in Schenectady. The garage with a window cracked open; the car sitting inside, unlocked. (He knows how rarely people lock anything.) He was in that garage, but he didn't shatter the glass panel of the door leading into the house. He needed supplies. And the mood wasn't quite right.

Maybe he won't come back.

At nine P.M., I brew a pot of coffee, hoping my mom won't hear the burping of the old percolator. I want to stay awake so badly that I almost text Warren Witter to see if he'll sell me a couple Adderall.

Just a few more pills wouldn't hurt me too much, would they? One more sleepless night? Two?

Thinking about Warren makes me clench up inside. I can already hear the disappointed flinch in his voice as he realizes I've relapsed. *Really, Nina? You sure?*

Warren's liked me since before the pills. Since before *everything.*

About a year ago, I first discovered I could use caffeine in drink and pill forms to rev myself awake every night, all night. No longer would I sleep, blissfully unaware, while predators roamed the world. I would be like *him*—nocturnal.

There were downsides to scoring a victory over my natural sleep patterns. Limited to catnaps in the daytime, I was always either wired or tired, and I once missed a big history test because I passed out under a library table.

That didn't stop me from wanting stronger uppers than I could get over the counter. In homeroom, I overheard Addison Doucette advising Lauren Grayson on where to get a "little pick-me-up" so she could study all night for her algebra midterm. "Ask Warren Witter. His brothers can get him *anything.*"

I didn't believe it at first. Warren's brothers are bad news, but *him* dealing drugs? Back in eighth grade, when we were friends for nearly a year, he was a skinny, quiet kid, his nose always stuck in a paperback with a spaceship on the cover.

Warren hadn't changed much after two years. When I cornered him at his locker and asked about this alleged pick-me-up supply, his face went beet red.

He hid it by bending to adjust his books. "Addy Doucette sent you, huh?"

"Yeah."

"Got a big test coming up?"

I was blushing by then, too. "Lots of tests."

"Yeah-huh. Are you sure you want to get into that shit, Nina?" His eyes looked watery, like I was causing an allergic reaction.

"You're a great salesman," I said.

Warren grinned, and the smile reached his narrow, heavy-lidded eyes, which had always struck me as secretive. His long face had filled out since middle school, with cheeks to balance the cheekbones. Maybe another girl, one who didn't remember how his nose ran all winter in sixth grade and he swiped it with actual cloth handkerchiefs his mom made him bring to school, would have thought his half-shy, half-sly smile was sexy.

"Meet me in the cedars behind the soccer field," he said.

And he sold me the pills, though each time afterward he asked me if I was *sure* I wanted them.

Thus began my beautiful—beautifully convenient, anyway—second friendship with Warren Witter, which lasted until my mom found my stash of Adderall and learned I was capable of keeping secrets from her.

How many secrets, she still has no clue.

But I don't feel like seeing Warren's disappointment right now. And so I gulp coffee and try to murder sleep.

When I read that line about murdering sleep in *Macbeth* during freshman English, I thought, God, if only. Then I realized that Shakespeare means Macbeth's guilty conscience is keeping him awake.

Some people have no conscience, though. And I, for one, would rather do anything than sleep.

. . .

I catch a few fitful hours of rest near dawn—not enough to stop my head from pounding with fatigue the next day, or my eyelids from fluttering shut while Ms. Blenner gets irrationally excited about differential equations. I hate how vulnerable I feel when the world goes fuzzy like this, one big blind spot with me at the center. Anyone could surprise me now.

Open your eyes. Pinch yourself. Coward.

When I do text Warren, during third period, I have a new plan. And a jumbo travel mug of crappy cafeteria coffee.

We meet after school in the cedars on the edge of the soccer field. Warren greets me way too enthusiastically, tripping over his words, but when I tell him what I want instead of pills, his expression darkens.

"Nina," he says, his eyes going to pained slits.

"What? Do you think I'm going to hurt myself?" His expression says, *Yeah, maybe,* so I cross my arms and try to look angry. "You watch too many PSAs. It's for protection."

"Protection, yeah. That's smart." But he still looks doubtful. "Look, if you're worried about something or somebody—maybe I could help?"

It's hard to see Warren as tough when I still remember him as a shoelace in a camo jacket. That jacket fits tighter now, and the T-shirt underneath shows me slopes of lean muscle, but he'll never exactly be a hulking menace.

I like how he's turned out, and I know he feels the same about me, though I wonder why. He needs someone simple and wholesome.

You belong in a Nick Cave song, a cute counselor once told me at summer camp, back before my night terrors ruled out summer camp, flirting, and sleepovers. *Kinda disheveled and pale, with those huge eyes of yours. Like the heroine of a murder ballad.*

Since then, I've learned what "murder ballads" are and how they end—with the pale heroine's eyes vacant and dead. Warren deserves better than that kind of drama.

Maybe he wants to save me. Life in this town is so freaking boring, and Warren's a mystery and true-crime nut. He must be desperate for thrills; I have more than I can handle. I *could* give him a few.

"Somebody stalking you?" he asks, eyes narrow again.

"No," I say. "I'm going to drive to Schenectady to catch an interstate serial killer."

Warren tilts his head and nods, waiting for me to continue with what he must think is a deadpan comedy riff. He doesn't edge away like I'm crazy—good.

"In my secret life, I'm the youngest-ever FBI profiler," I go on. "I need to check out a tip on an unsub."

"The FBI didn't give you a piece?"

"They say I'm too young to pack heat."

Warren makes his index finger into a gun, fires it, blows off the smoke. "A dame like you is never too young."

I grin in spite of myself. "So can you get me one? Maybe a thirty-eight?"

"What makes you think I know about guns, Nina Barrows?"

"You live off the grid," I say, counting reasons on my fingers. "You bring venison jerky to school. Your dad writes letters to the paper about preserving our Second Amendment rights."

It's another of our comedy routines: I rib him for being a woodchuck, which is Vermont for "redneck," and he fires back "bleeding heart" and "tree hugger." Labels that fit our parents better than us, but don't really fit anyone.

He says, "News flash: venison is a sustainable protein. If the apocalypse happens, you'll be lucky to have a hunter on your side. And my dad and I are two different people."

"So you hate guns."

"Not that simple."

"So you like guns. You use them to get sustainable protein, right?"

My boy-relating skills suck. Jocks, preppies, cute hipsters, bad boys—I can barely meet their eyes. Not in a million years could I approach Warren's older brothers, who are twice his size and have a long history of getting tossed in juvie or the state pen. I'm sure *they* could get me a gun, no questions asked.

Warren's still the boy who invites the unpopular girls to dance. Who doesn't ask the weird girl too many questions when she tells him weird things. Who might help her.

A double murder could happen this week a hundred and sixty-six miles from where we stand, and I can't let it. Not this time.

"I have a deer rifle, but that and a thirty-eight pistol are about as much alike as you and Kayla Pinkett," Warren says.

Kayla leads the pep squad. Bouncy ponytail, bouncy C-cups. "Ouch," I say.

"Hey, I didn't mean it in a bad way."

He looks genuinely apologetic, and I feel a stab of something I can't identify. He *likes* me. What's wrong with him?

"Anyway, lucky for you, Nina, we live in a sportsman's wonderland where guns can be sold freely to anyone over sixteen," he says. "Your best bet is Tim's General Store on Route Twelve."

"I'll still need to learn to use it." I know how guns feel in your hand and how it feels to pull the trigger, but the intermediate steps are a blur. For the Thief in the Night, using guns is automatic, not worthy of concentration.

"You've never touched a firearm, have you? You're such a tree hugger, I bet you've never even shot somebody in a video game."

I don't feel like playing our game right now. "Can you help me, or can't you?"

"If you come by our place Friday afternoon, I'll take you to the range. Show you the stance, give you pointers. Wouldn't want you to shoot any innocent bystanders."

The Witter place is creepy. It stretches up a hill and down into a long ravine, full of primo body-dumping sites.

But Warren's safe. I know from the way he twitches when he looks at me, his eyes trying to suss out what I'm thinking. (*Could she, just maybe, think it's hot that I know about guns? If I help her with her stance, will we end up touching? Like, a lot?*)

If he were a killer, he wouldn't wonder or guess. He wouldn't care what I thought or felt. My story would be his to write.

"You'll have to drive," I say. "Meet me here at three."

3

When Warren and I finish talking, the buses are already chugging around the school driveway. It's a woozy April day, no leaves popping yet, just soggy crocuses, the earth finally smelling like warm growth and rot as mud season draws to a close.

I get off the bus downtown and walk the rest of the way, thinking about gun stores. Warren is right: we're a gung-ho gun state, and a .38 is easier for me to get than liquor. My heart still pounds when I think about holding one. And what I might do with it.

I keep an eye on my surroundings. Our state capital is a small town, but not too small for strangers, and I notice them with every step, especially the guys: old men and young men and boys horsing around, hauling crates, looking at their phones, lighting cigarettes.

One young guy looks at me and half smiles. When I start climbing College Hill and glance back, there he still is, ten feet behind me.

He's pale with fuzzy black hair and a plaid shirt, probably a student headed for a lecture.

Still. He looked. He smiled. He has threat potential. I glance back every thirty seconds, not too often, and close a fist on the pepper spray in my coat pocket.

I also carry a Swiss Army Knife. Better than keys if you're going for the eyes.

If Plaid Shirt happened to be the Thief—which he's not—my being armed wouldn't worry him. A weapon, as far as the Thief is concerned, is something to take away from your victim and use against them. Weapons make people overconfident unless they're trained cops or soldiers, which his victims never are. Confidence makes people stupid.

With all the Thief has taught me about being on the other side, the hunter's side, I shouldn't be so scared. But I know my natural role is prey, not predator.

This dude is gaining on me like he's late for a lecture or a hot date. My eyes sweep the street.

Jazz floats from an open apartment window. A gray-haired couple feeds a parking meter fifty feet up the hill. He could pull me into an alley, and they wouldn't notice a thing.

Someone might see from a window, though, and the Thief doesn't like risks. If he killed me here and now, it would be a nineteen-, twenty-point kill. Twenty points is the top of his scale, a number he's never reached.

Victorian rentals, tin mailboxes, and robin-mobbed lawns

fly by. This is not the Thief—can't be. I know where the Thief is, more or less. I've monitored his progress since he cased the Gustafssons' house.

The Thief lives in New Mexico, two thousand miles from Schenectady. After the scale-modeling conference, he headed north to visit a friend with a cabin in Ontario. He cached his two rifles in a deep trench off I-90 before he crossed the border, along with his newly bought supplies. Eight days ago, he was driving to Canada, dirt under his fingernails. He could still feel the cold of the earth from digging the cache, the satisfying heft of his shovel.

Schenectady is a detour from his route home, but he will return. He wouldn't have made that cache otherwise. Like me, he can't stop thinking about the Gustafssons' ranch house.

But he's been sleeping better than me. Since he reached his friend's cabin, he's been going to bed early, exhausted from hiking and fishing and whatever other manly men stuff they have on the agenda.

On Sunday evening, he called his girlfriend, Eliana, who has a silky curtain of black hair, an elegant nose, and a desk job with benefits. The kind of girlfriend a nice, steady, attractive guy would have.

She doesn't know him like I do.

They talked about Eliana's four-year-old daughter, Trixie. "She's been bugging me about wanting to furnish the dolls' attic. I told her attics don't need furniture," Eliana said.

"Sure they do," the Thief objected. "I'll stick a busted couch and some clutter up there."

"Yeah, if you're around, hon. Putting major miles on that Sequoia, huh? I thought this was gonna be a two-week trip."

"I'll be back a week from Tuesday. Promise."

Every time Eliana gets weird about all the traveling he does, the Thief uses that tone of voice. If he were home right now, he'd touch her face. She'd melt toward him, and he'd draw her into his arms.

He moved into Eliana's house a year and eight months ago. Trixie's real dad is out of the picture. The Thief made the kid a dollhouse; he reads her stories about talking foxes and hedgehogs. Those two are the best things in his life, and he can't, won't, lose them.

He's careful. He's always got modeling and carpentry stuff in his Sequoia, so he can tell Eliana he's delivering to a distant client. Crafting minutely detailed models of historical sites is the Thief's passion. He builds cabinets and beds and bureaus for clients all over the Southwest, and insists on delivering everything himself.

I have two logbooks. One with dates, where I record his movements, and one where I note down every single thing I know about him.

I know his name, and my research probably would have told me his street address. But when I found the Web site for his home business, I couldn't click the link.

Some crazy superstitious part of me thought that if I saw his photo, he'd see me, too. Memorize my face. Know me.

Yesterday, the day I tried to warn the Gustafssons, was Tuesday again, a week after the Thief left for Canada. If he plans to be in Albuquerque *next* Tuesday, he'll need to return to Schenectady by Friday or Saturday at the latest.

The Gustafssons' house is on a dark block of ranches leading to an intersection where a sign reads 890 VIA CHRISLER AVENUE. I've found it on Google Street View.

Friday, then. Day after tomorrow. I should've gone home with Warren today, made him take me out to the range, convinced him to lend me a handgun.

For what? It's not like I'm going to step into the Thief's path and yell *Stop!* My phone call to the Gustafssons was a waste of time.

The Thief is a soldier, a woodsman, a tinkerer, the kind of person who survives a zombie apocalypse. I am a nervous honor student.

And now that I know what he's going to do, I'm his accomplice.

My whole body goes so hot and tight that I barely notice the brick college buildings appearing over the hill. I nearly crash into a kid with red dreads coming the opposite way, who calls, "Hey, bro, how'd last night go?"

He's not addressing me—and I turn to find Plaid Shirt. I'd forgotten all about him.

"Not bad," Plaid Shirt says, fist-bumping the kid with dreadlocks and grinning. "Went home with that girl with the tongue piercing."

I'm staring at them, yet neither gives me a single glance. My body goes lax with relief.

Like the Thief, I pass as normal, just another person on the street. No one suspects. No one knows.

4

When I get home, the first thing I notice is the security system: not armed. The second thing I notice is the windows. Mom's cracked open two in the living room and one in the kitchen, letting in the smell of earth.

Mom thinks open windows are just part of enjoying warm weather, even at night. She has friends who don't lock their doors.

I start to text her a reminder about arming the system, when something catches my eye—a raffia handbag on the coffee table. It's not mine, and it's not hers, so—

A stranger's in the house.

I put down my phone, gingerly, and tiptoe into the living room. That's when Mom and seven other women lurch from behind the couch and surge from under the kitchen island and bellow, "Surprise!"

I scream. Not happy-scream, really scream.

The women are wearing goofy party hats and glittery feather boas and are all talking at once, too fast, like they started drinking Mom's white wine before I arrived. When they see I'm still standing there with my hands over my mouth, my eyes panicky wide, they flock around and make reassuring noises.

"You look like you've seen a ghost, kiddo."

"Did you forget it was your birthday?"

I let my hands fall and force out a laugh. No, I didn't forget—just assumed that Mom would make me filet mignon and aioli fries to go with the bakery cake, like she usually does, and we'd have a quiet evening together.

I dodge explanations by hugging Suzy Wolfsheim, the tough-as-nails assistant state's attorney and my favorite of my mom's friends.

People are more likely to trust you when you hug them—another thing I've learned from the Thief.

Mom knows I don't have many friends, so she invited her own. At least she knew enough to pick the outrageous ladies who make raunchy jokes and laugh too loud, not the hippie-dippy ones who give "birthday blessings."

In the corner hides my only age-appropriate friend, Kirby Blessing, taking in all the middle-aged outrageousness and looking more comfortable than I feel. I can still tell she didn't put on that sparkly hat of her own volition.

She grabs me with arms strong from shooting hockey goals, and swings me around. "Happy sweet seventeen!"

Everybody in Kirby's family is always hugging and ruffling

hair—and not just as a way of making people trust them. Part of me likes it, but I still stiffen until she lets me go. "Can't believe I freaked like that. Sorry."

Kirby tilts her head, her heavy ponytail swinging, and asks so only we can hear, "You sure you're okay?"

"Yeah. I just—well, I couldn't sleep last night."

"Oh, shit," Kirby breathes. She grasps my arms again, like I might fly apart.

"It's okay!" I keep my voice low; luckily, Mom's friends are busy admiring our new soapstone woodstove. "I didn't do anything."

Her blue eyes hold mine, alarmed and reassuring at the same time, like my mom's. "But I saw you with Warren. Today, outside."

Kirby thinks I'm craving the pills again—a natural assumption, since we made friends at my addiction support group. I was forced to sit in that moldy church basement once a week for three months, while Kirby only came to pick up her younger brother, Pierce. I thought she was just another tough-talking, sporty girl with tons of friends, somebody who'd dismiss me as a freak, until the night I emerged from that basement feeling like I *would* fly apart, and Kirby put her arms around me and said, "Hey, it's okay. Cry if you want to."

I don't cry in front of people, but that night I did. And I didn't hate Kirby for seeing it, because she'd dodged my defenses as nimbly as she does on the ice going for a goal. She senses what I'm feeling deep down, sometimes better than I do myself.

19

Which is why I have to be extra careful around her. As far as she knows, the cravings for uppers are my only secret.

"Warren and I were just talking," I promise her, as Mom marches out of the kitchen bearing a sheet cake from the culinary school with seventeen lighted candles.

Kirby releases me, but she doesn't look satisfied. The lights go off, and everybody chants, "Make a wish, make a wish, Nina!"

Suzy Wolfsheim says, "Wish for a speed machine," which is a joke because I still can't drive over fifty without feeling a panic attack coming on.

Kirby says, "Wish for us both to get into Middlebury with financial aid," which is something we talk about—her and me at the same college, roommates. I'm still trying to figure out how to tell her I can't sleep in the same room with anyone, even my best friend.

So many things I can't do.

"Wish for world peace," somebody yells.

Mom says, "Wish for health and good fortune."

I wish for the Thief to stop. I don't care who makes it happen or how, whether he ends up shot dead by a cop or sitting in a maximum-security prison. I would even accept him deciding he just doesn't want to hurt people anymore.

Yet as I formulate this wish, I imagine myself standing over the Thief's faceless body with a gun in my hand. I can't help it—that's what I see.

I blow out the candles on the first try.

. . .

"So, how *is* Warren Witter?" Kirby asks as the party thins out. "And what were you guys doing in the woods?" She waggles her eyebrows suggestively at me.

"God no. Not what you think."

The second those words leave my mouth, I want to exchange them for a nice, laid-back, he's-okay-but-not-my-type kind of no. As far as Kirby's jock friends are concerned, Warren is a weirdo who lives in a "compound" surrounded by ten feet of cyclone fence while his dad stocks canned goods and water purifiers for the apocalypse. As far as Kirby's concerned, he's the bad influence who sold me drugs. But I know him better, and I should defend him.

Kirby smirks, then to my surprise, says, "Well, you could do worse. He's kinda blossomed. Hot *and* smart."

I punch her shoulder. "How would you know he's smart?" I never told Kirby about the hours Warren and I spent in middle school bonding over books, star charts, weird science facts, and anime.

"I saw him coming out of Dr. Reardon's office. She was talking about the SATs and National Merit Scholarships, and he looked like he'd just won Megabucks, so he must've qualified."

"He *is* wicked smart," I allow, remembering how Warren used to talk about going to NYU's film program. "He'll probably get in everywhere—he just needs major financial aid."

"And maybe to stop being a freaking drug dealer."

"I don't think he does that anymore." I don't know if it's true, but I hope so.

"You should ask him to do SAT prep with you. Perfect excuse. But you're not going to college with *him* unless it's still Middlebury, 'kay?"

She goes on like that, mapping out our next five years. Kirby and the Thief, they're both great planners.

Me, I can't see past what might happen to a couple in Schenectady on Friday.

And my options? Buy a gun (that terrifies me). Drive to Schenectady (in my mom's car, too nervous to gun it to sixty). Stake out the Gustafssons' house.

And wait.

· · ·

By the time the last guest leaves, all I can think about is that I need to sleep tonight, need it desperately, and that I don't want to. I almost grab Kirby and ask if I can come over later to work on trig. But that won't solve anything.

Mom and I load the dishwasher. Then, instead of disappearing into her home office like usual, she makes me sit down at the dining room table. "Big birthday, Nina. Do you feel different?"

"No," I say like I do every year. My mom gets new-agey about "milestones," though I've told her a million times I don't think anyone changes much from sixteen to seventeen, or even from twelve to twenty. They just reveal new sides.

"I can see the difference in you," Mom says, her face tightening with emotion, framed by the stylish-middle-aged-lady haircut she finally submitted to this year. It's classier than her flowing hippie locks, and more appropriate to her job in the state attorney general's office, but it makes her look older. And seeing that difference in *her* scares me.

First on Mom's birthday agenda is the same gift I get every year: a check. This year, she slides my second, special present across the table—a fat snail-mail envelope, the kind Kirby wants from Middlebury.

This one's from the Arizona Division of Children, Youth, and Families.

I knew this was coming. My mom lived in Arizona when she adopted me, and it was an open process, which means, she's reminded me a million times, that I have the option to contact my birth parents, and at any time they may decide to contact me.

I've always just nodded. And then, to deflect her attention, I've asked her to tell me the story again—hers and mine.

Sixteen and something years ago in Arizona, Mom was dating Dory Biedenkopf, and it was Dory who wanted a baby. Dory worked with child services, and when she introduced Mom to me, ten months old, Mom fell in love with my "big bronze eyes that wouldn't let go." Lesbian couples couldn't adopt, and Mom, with her lawyer job, looked the best on paper as a single parent. So Mom and Dory put off moving in together while my mom jumped through the state's adoption hoops. It took long enough that they drifted apart, and Dory fell in love with somebody else. My mom and I moved to Vermont and lived happily ever after. Dory's new girlfriend had three kids, and *she* lived happily ever after, too. They still have marathon phone convos a few times a year.

That's how Mom tells the story. Yet now that I'm older, I can't help wondering if I ruined my mom's one chance at love. Oh, she's dated, sometimes for as long as a year, and most of her exes stay her good friends. But could Dory have been the One?

As for my birth mom, the woman who couldn't be bothered to keep me for more than ten months, I try not to think about her.

But now, it seems, I have no choice, because the letter in the fat envelope tells me this mystery woman wants to contact me.

Once I get my breathing under control and decipher the legalese, the situation seems pretty mellow. Per the adoption contract Mom's lawyer wrote up, my birth mother has to initiate communication through the state agency until I turn eighteen. She can't just show up on our doorstep.

The worst part is how closely my mom is watching for my reaction.

"Okay," I say. "Well, that's cool, I guess."

When I was seven, I went through a phase of fantasizing about my biological parents. Was my mom a nurse? A soap opera star? A scientist? Did my dad drive a bus? Did he have scratchy cheeks like the daddies in books? Did I have brothers and sisters?

As suddenly as it came, my curiosity vanished. Now all I feel as I gaze at the documents is embarrassment, because they could make my mom uncomfortable.

"You know," I say, "I think I might wait. It's not gonna hurt her if she doesn't know anything about me till I'm older, right?"

My mom touches my hand. Her face looks pretty good, and her abs are better than mine, but every time I see her hands, I remember she's fifty-six. Old enough to have lived a whole life before I came along.

"Nina," she says, "this is totally up to you. But I want you to know that if you do start communicating with your birth mother, you don't need my permission, and you have my blessing."

"You're not worried she's gonna turn out to be way cooler than you and steal me away?"

My mom knows my sense of humor, and the corners of her mouth quirk up. She's tan from hiking and biking every weekend, and her eyes are uncomplicated blue. Unlike me, she has no trouble looking people in the eye. "No," she says.

"You know what's the last thing I need? A new insta-mom telling me what to do."

Mom laughs, and I know we're both remembering last fall, when she had to come down hard on me over the pills. My mom prefers being the good cop, and neither of us liked it one bit when she was lecturing and interrogating me.

I knuckled under, though. I had to kick the habit for my own reasons, and besides, I couldn't hurt her.

She thinks I'm a good person. I don't want that to change.

My mom's smile fades. "I didn't want *any* parents when I was your age. I wished I was an orphan."

She doesn't say the next part, but I already know: she regrets not hugging my grandma before she died.

But what does her mom have to do with my birth mom? "Look," I say, "this chick *gave me up*. That's the only thing I know about her, and it's a big thing, wouldn't you say?"

"She's still part of you, Nina." Mom pats my hand. "Some

adopted children say the biological parent is the missing piece that helps them understand themselves."

"I understand myself fine," I say.

"Take it at your own pace. Those forms say she can't contact you directly until you give her permission."

"Okay, okay." I take the envelope to make her happy.

That's when it hits me in a real-world way, the shit I'd be in if I drove to Schenectady day after tomorrow. I'd need to "borrow" her car, put a gun in the trunk—and maybe miss school on Monday, assuming I came back at all.

And if I don't come back—if he makes me disappear like the others—my mom will be alone. Without answers.

5

The Thief is on the cabin porch with his friend, each palming a Corona. They're worn-out from building a new tool shed, so the Thief listens to the first spring peepers and plans his trip home.

Trixie has a birthday in a week: that's his deadline. As an excuse for doubling back on I-90, he'll tell Eliana he hit the model-making supply store in Syracuse. The reason he's driving all the way up to Schenectady is a blank spot in the middle of his thoughts, but it's a blankness filled with anticipation.

"Schen-ec-tady," he sings to himself while his friend is getting two more beers. A meaty name, hard to pronounce and spell. He'll have no problems with that when this is over. He'll make the place his own.

. . .

On Thursday evening, I stand at the pay phone again, wind from the river whipping the hair that escapes from under my baseball cap. The brim's pulled low to hide my face from cameras—a trick *he* uses—and my clothes are baggy and dark.

It's almost night, but every car that pulls in makes my eyes dart, looking for someone who might notice me. I hold the receiver with gloves and don't let it touch my face.

"Schenectady Police Department; do you have an emergency?"

"Not yet," I whisper.

"How may I direct your call?"

They'll know where I'm calling from. But if I bought a burner at the mini-mart, they'd probably be able to trace it here anyway.

"I'd like to report a possible prowler at five-four-one-eight Maywood Street," I say, lowering my voice into a husky drone. "My grandparents live there—Ruth and Gary Gustafsson. They tell me they've seen a suspicious guy checking out their house—a stranger—but they don't want to report it. They think it's nothing. I'm worried that—"

The operator cuts me off, sounding bored. "You want to file a report, ma'am?"

"No! I'm out of town. I was just wondering if somebody could drive around the block and, you know, make sure they're okay. Especially at night."

"How many times has this individual been seen in the vicinity of the house, ma'am?"

"Once." Technically true. "But he was crouched *in* their backyard looking into their window."

"And this was when?"

I'm not a TV detective who can order round-the-clock protection. The cops have plenty to do, even in Schenectady. I lie: "Two days ago."

"We could send an officer to the house, ma'am. But we need to hear from your grandparents first."

"I already told you. They don't want to report it."

"Do your grandparents have a live-in caregiver who could make the report?"

"No! They're not that old."

The operator's voice gets gentler, her words coming more slowly. She talks about security systems and neighborhood watches and asking neighbors to keep an eye on elderly people.

I just say, "Thank you, thank you, thank you," hang up, and get the hell out of there.

. . .

I lie in bed staring at the ceiling, listening to my mom brush her teeth.

He could still change his mind. Decide it's not worth the trouble. It's relatively daring, this mission he's set himself, grabbing people from a well-populated street. The Gustafssons could wake up while he's breaking in and call the cops. Or, if they're like half the people around here, they could have a Glock on the nightstand and blow his head off. This time next week, the Thief could be history.

Would I still be afraid to sleep then?

6

Ten minutes before midnight. Ten minutes before Friday. My eyes close.

. . .

I'm at a rest stop, watching cars stream past on the interstate like a moving necklace of light. Spring is in the air: freshly turned earth, pungent cedar chips. When I drove this way from New Mexico it was much colder, and you couldn't smell a thing.

Stop. This is not me. This is the Thief, his thoughts in my head. *I'm not him.*

He likes to move from desert spring to northeastern spring, from one climate to another. He likes to *move*.

God, how he loves this part of the night. Stretching his

legs, pouring coffee that's been sitting on the warmer for hours, no one in the world to check on him. He loves his Eliana, but spend every night with her? She knows enough to give him his space.

The only store open in the rest stop is full of crap plastered with Yankees and Baseball Hall of Fame logos. The other customers look tired and doughy, faces like moons.

Not him—he's lean. Traveling light.

The girl who checks him out is slender, too. She's maybe eighteen, tops, with a little heart-shaped face and sandy-blond hair in a ponytail, and he bets she lives on a farm, because this is farming country. The late shift is her way of getting out of morning milking.

Her name tag says "Jaylynne," and he starts chatting her up. He pretends he just came east for the first time and asks her dumb questions.

Does it snow up here? Yup. Are blizzards worse than tornadoes? Uh, no. She starts out cautious, but then her eyes open wide into his and her smile sneaks out. The kid still has braces.

He's never taken a girl like this.

Suddenly, his careful preparations for tomorrow night seem *too* careful. Boringly so.

Two fat sheep vanish from the flock, whoop-de-fucking-do. Everybody will assume Mr. and Mrs. Unlucky got mixed up with the mob and whacked. The Thief will score major points, but only with himself, because no one will care enough to mount a major search effort.

It's different when you take a young, pretty girl. Posters go up everywhere. If they get wind that this disappearance is related to another one, the spray-tanned cable anchors go wild. Girls start locking their windows and doors at night, anticipating the rendezvous they don't want to have with you. Nobody knows your face or name, but everybody knows there's a wolf circling the flock. A thief in the night.

It's like being a supervillain. Satisfying to your ego. But, he has to admit, also cheesy as hell.

Besides, getting famous increases the chances of getting caught. His soon-to-be stepdaughter cannot grow up knowing he did *things* to girls just like her.

Still...

He calls Jaylynne's attention to the junky figurines of famous ballplayers lining the shelves, and she rolls her eyes and says, yeah, they're made in China. The Thief tells her about his scale models and how much more detailed they are. Her eyes stay on him, like she's glad just to talk to somebody new.

He tells her he's bringing a replica of a '63 truck-stop interior to a buyer in Tulsa. Some girls edge away when he gets going on his models, their eyes broadcasting "Nerd alert," but Jaylynne keeps listening.

He asks, "Can you get away for two minutes? Wanna smoke?"

Jaylynne calls another girl to cover the register, and out they go.

The forest is right behind them, frogs peeping so the whole place sings, and it smells damn good. Not like the desert, with its layers of dry and dead under the prickle of sagebrush, but musty with moisture, a mixture of squirmy living things and rotting dead ones. With everything growing so fast, things must decompose fast, too.

He could lay her down here—"dump" is the wrong word—and she'd be part of the spring woods forever. But he doesn't know the terrain. There could be a farm right beyond the belt of trees, someone to find her. Someone to hear.

Or he could load her in the Sequoia and take her to the place he found outside Schenectady—his country cabin. He could give her to that place, and let the old sheep in the ranch house live out their natural days.

He's never taken anybody more than fifteen or twenty miles from where he found them. Feels only fair to leave them where they'll be at home.

But he can break his own rules, can't he? Isn't not having rules the whole point?

Jaylynne doesn't want to smoke a whole cigarette, so they pass his back and forth, maybe four feet apart. "Hey," he says. "Want to see the truck-stop model? I think it's the best work I've done. Almost don't want to let it go."

She hesitates for an instant. "Okay."

Jaylynne seems to relax a little when she sees he's got an SUV, not a van. The gate lifts, gentle as you please, and he stows his coffee on the Sequoia's roof, sweeps the tarp away, and shines the flashlight on his model.

Jaylynne is impressed, or pretends to be. "It looks just like a real little world."

She keeps her distance, maybe three feet from the bumper. Cautious girl. Not dumb.

He points out the chrome around the barstools and the tiny posters on the walls, advertising brands that no longer exist. "Look at this one. That's Doris Day, big star way back when. You look like her."

Jaylynne must want to think she looks like a movie star—who doesn't? Just as he anticipated, she takes a step closer to peer in.

Two steps. She bends to see better, and surely he's out of her peripheral vision now.

His eyes scan the parking lot. Empty. His eyelid twitches.

Arm around her throat, hand on her mouth, a whisper in her ear. *I don't want to hurt you.*

That's all it will take. He's got a good ten inches on her. She'll kick, but not hard enough. She'll decide it's better to give him what he wants and hope things don't end badly.

"Ew. I don't get why they teased their hair back then."

She straightens up, backing right into him. He slipped behind her while she was distracted.

For an instant she doesn't push the Thief away, and he doesn't grab her. Something in him won't move, just stands there smelling her hair. Guava shampoo.

That instant is all it takes for a family of moon-faced travelers to emerge from the rest stop, loaded down with forty-ounce cold cups. They're headed for the very row of cars where the Thief's Sequoia stands, the mom grumbling at the kids to stop begging for candy.

Abort.

Jaylynne darts away from him, like a pinball from a flipper, and says, "Jeez, you scared me."

"Sorry." He uses his *aw, shucks* smile. "Didn't mean to crowd you."

The noisy family holds its course.

He grabs the hot cup he left on the roof of the Sequoia and rattles his keys. "Hey, kiddo, thanks for the java. Back on the road for me."

Maybe he spooked Jaylynne, because she's already retreating, her white arms flashing in the darkness. "Thanks for the smoke, mister. Drive safe!"

"If I ever visit the Baseball Hall of Fame, I'll stop by."

He watches Jaylynne go and thinks of how she'll get those braces off, maybe go to college, have kids of her own, complain about her husband.

She could've stayed in the spring woods forever.

He shouldn't be greedy. Shouldn't be arrogant. This isn't about glorifying or gratifying him as an individual. He serves death, the vacuum, the unknown.

Always waiting. Always there.

7

The birds start up at five thirty, warbling and trilling and practically yowling in the dark. I crouch on my rug with my head tucked under my arms, listening to the world wake.

The sun is what I've been waiting for, but its warmth makes my skin feel old and creased every which way. My eyes ache from staring at darkness.

Pictures are stuck behind my eyelids. Baseball figurines. Blond ponytail. She was about my age. A girl like me.

My head aches from having him in it.

We've always been close, but it feels like we're getting closer. Like I *am* him. Is it because I'm tracking him, or is this just what happens? Will I wake up one day and have him still in my head? Will I go to school and look for a victim?

Six thirty now, creamy sky between the spidery maple branches.

Down the block, Kirby is waking up. Warren is waking up, too. Jaylynne from the rest stop is probably coming off her shift, trudging to bed and letting herself slide into unconsciousness, just like I am now.

She's not even thinking about the weirdo with the tiny truck stop in his car, I bet. Never knowing what she escaped. Never knowing what we shared.

. . .

When the alarm chimes, I stay awake just long enough to tell my mom I have a cold and can't make it to school today— please, just this once; I'll get all the assignments; no, there aren't any tests; jeez, please lay off me.

She does.

The next time I wake up, my eyelids weigh too much, my mouth tastes bitter, and the light is all wrong.

Too red. Too bright.

Words in my head. *Baseball Hall of Fame.*

I rub my eyes and focus on my all-white cat, Sugarman, basking in the patch of sun on my mom's college trunk. That means—

My gaze flies from Sugarman to the clock. 3:10 in the afternoon.

I was supposed to meet Warren at three for gun practice. He's going to think I stood him up. I grab my phone to text him.

I've got text alerts, but before I can read anything, that

name squirms to the surface of my mind again. Where's the Baseball Hall of Fame? A few clicks tell me: Cooperstown, New York, sixty-something miles from Schenectady.

If the Thief was on I-90 near the Cooperstown exit last night, he's in Schenectady today. Assuming his plan hasn't changed, he's there right now. Preparing.

I let the phone thump on the bed. Splash water on my face, slap deodorant under my arms, wiggle into my jeans. Downstairs in the kitchen, I grab my mom's extra set of car keys.

No point in texting or calling Warren now. For this I need face-to-face.

Lucky thing my mom walked to work today.

Forget target practice. Forget stupid cowardly pay-phone calls. I'm going to Schenectady tonight, and if getting a gun means I have to bat my eyes at Warren Witter and tell him lies, so be it.

· · ·

By the time I park my mom's Legacy in the school's lot and jog around the playing field to the woods, it's 3:42. In our usual meeting place, I find no Warren, just a grubby sophomore couple getting each other's shirts off.

I get back on the road and head for the Witter homestead, where I haven't been in three years. My signal vanishes on the winding dirt road, and I take a wrong turn and practically drive up the mountain before the pin pops up on the map again. Six-inch-deep ruts rattle my transmission.

Mud aside, it's a perfect afternoon, the sky bright blue

between the leafless trees. Warren can probably drive like a pro, not to mention shoot a gun. What if I asked him to come along to Schenectady?

I'm still floating dangerously out of control, into that night place. Every time my mind drifts, I smell the cedar chips in that rest stop parking lot, hear those peepers, see those moon-faced tourists. I feel my hands itching to *grab* and hold tight. Pieces of the Thief's life have become bitter tastes on my tongue, sand grains stuck under my fingernails.

Warren will ground me. In the time it takes to drive all the way there, he'll make me back into *me*. But that means getting him to come along in the first place, and he doesn't do anything without asking why.

The fabled Witter compound isn't really that imposing. The cyclone fence stands about four feet tall, revealing the ordinary, dirty-white farmhouse on the other side.

Deep baying fills the air as I pull up. Footfalls pound the dirt road, and now I'm looking at four enormous paws pressed against my windows, two on my side and two on the passenger's. A shepherd mix and a pit bull mix, their barks starting and ending in long growls.

Belle and Gaston, named by Warren when they were adorable puppies and he was six. I remember them, but they don't seem to remember me.

I punch Warren's number, but the call fails. Should I make a run for it?

The dogs grow hoarser, telling me they mean business. I'm ready to give up and pull out when a human voice makes its way through the racket.

"Belle! Gaston! Down! Come, Belle! Leave it!"

The voice is so deep I almost expect one of the scary big brothers, but no, it's Warren.

The muscle-bound monsters romp around him, then submit to being led back inside the fence. Warren taps on my window.

His face is lit up like he's a kid peeking under the Christmas tree. I feel awful already about what I'm going to do.

Why does he like me so much, anyway, after the way I bailed on him when we were kids?

I power down the window, check the dashboard clock. 4:16. The drive to Schenectady takes three hours with good traffic.

"Where the hell were you?" Warren asks, but he doesn't sound angry. "I sent you, like, three texts...."

"I'm so sorry, Warren. I didn't mean to stand you up."

Warren nods too quickly. He's gripping the cuffs of his army jacket, trying to play it cool; it's not working.

"You can get out," he says. "I sent Belle and Big G back to their pen."

I open the door into a muddy ditch. "Were they auditioning for *Cujo*?"

"They wouldn't have hurt you."

"That's good." Maybe I should make my mom get a dog. *He* avoids houses with dogs. "I didn't come to shoot your guns, Warren. Not this time."

The color of his cheeks keeps deepening. "Are you sure? Tierney and his friends might want to use the range tomorrow, so we should get on that."

"I'm actually going to ask you a favor," I say, "and it's a big one."

"No more pills, Nina."

"Bigger than that."

His brows are crescents over a straight mouth. Warren's so readable, always has been. But even when he can't read me back, I know he's trying to decode me in his smart, skeptical way.

"It's going to sound crazy," I say, "and you can't tell your folks. My mom doesn't know I'm here."

He blows a strand of brown hair straight up. "I can deal with them. Tell me what it is."

"You drive fast?"

His face falls. "My truck doesn't really go above sixty. It's a piece of junk."

"This does." I flip my hand at the Subaru like it's an Aston Martin. "I need to go to Schenectady tonight, and it's kind of a bad area, so I was hoping... Well, that's why I wanted a gun."

"I told you I can't just hand you a deadly weapon." One hand digs into his hair. "Jeez, Nina."

"I'm not asking for a gun now." I lower my voice to a humble almost-whisper. "If there's any possibility you'd come with me to Schenectady... I hate asking you. But I might need help."

"Sche—what? Where the hell is that?"

"It's in New York. I said I'd meet my—my... biological mom there, and if my real mom finds out, she'll..."

I was going to say, "She'll tear me a new one," but my voice falters, and the words get lost in my throat. My eyes swim as

41

I think of who might actually be waiting in Schenectady for me, for us, for the Gustafssons.

I think those tears are why Warren gets in the car with me.

. . .

If he had Friday night plans before I came along, he doesn't say so. He runs into the house to tell his mom something—she doesn't text, he says.

Soon we're on Route 4, flying toward Schenectady at seventy-five. I drove to the interstate on-ramp, but when Warren saw how my hands started shaking, he took over.

We're still circling Lake Champlain, sun gleaming on bare maples in every direction. With luck, we'll be in Schenectady by eight.

Warren doesn't have a concealed-carry permit for New York, but he still took a handgun-shaped thing out of his backpack, swaddled in a sweatshirt, and stuck it in the glove compartment. I feel more reassured than I want to.

The Thief won't come after us. Not right out on the street—he's too careful.

I let my tired brain focus on the wrong things. How the sky looks smooth as an eggshell. How we soar over the hilltops, wind rushing through the cracked-open windows. How Warren has demolished the Twix bars I bought. The way he eats junk food, his wiry physique is a miracle.

He sees me looking. "My mom still thinks white sugar is the devil and high-fructose corn syrup is his handmaiden. So I stock up when I'm out."

I grin at him. "I remember how you lit into our leftover Halloween candy."

"Who still has a cupboard of candy corn in June? I was doing you a favor." He stuffs another wrapper in his backpack. "I didn't know you were adopted, Nina. Why didn't you ever tell me that?"

I bite my lip. "You know how kids were back in elementary school. *Where's your dad?* I was enough of a freak without people going around saying my mom wasn't my mom."

His eyes are narrow on the road. "I still wish you'd told me. We were friends."

Were. "Well, I can tell you now," I say, and rattle off the boring details of my real adoption story—anything to keep Warren from reminiscing about the two of us.

The only parts I flat-out lie about are my birth mother's location and my mom's attitude toward her. "She's, like, prejudiced against this woman. She doesn't even want me to meet her before I'm eighteen."

"Your mom's right," Warren says.

I glare at him, surprised to find myself offended on my birth mom's behalf. "Why? Don't you think I have a right to know where I came from?"

"I just mean . . . it's weird. If your birth mom gave you away when you were born, that's one thing. But you were ten months old. Once you're bonded to your kid, you don't *stop* being bonded."

"Thanks for your expertise, Dr. Phil. Because it's not like you know this woman or anything about her life."

He blushes, and his hands fidget on the wheel. "So, but

you do, right? You've been talking to her? Or e-mailing, or something?"

Does he think I'm so messed up I'd surprise my bio mom with an unplanned visit, or is he trying to trap me in a lie?

"Of course we've been e-mailing." I feed Warren a few made-up details, trying to imagine my birth mother. In my head, she looks like Mrs. Gustafsson. She has a gruff voice, bad spelling, a Hotmail account she barely knows how to use.

I half expect Warren to say, "That's such bullshit," but instead he says, "When my brothers were riding me really hard, I used to wish I was adopted. Them and my dad I could do without. But my mom—I wanted to keep her."

"Your mom's cool." Warren's mom is a little weird, a little old-fashioned, and I could never tell if she liked me. But the way she looks at him, you know he's the center of her universe.

"Yeah, well, somebody in the family had to be."

I wonder if his three brothers still "ride" him, whatever that means. I've never seen Warren with a bruise, but he had a darting, furtive way of moving in middle school, like he was ready to dodge a cuff upside the head.

His oldest brother used to terrify me on the school bus when I was little; the crown of his head brushed the roof. The middle one had a scary laugh. It's the youngest of the three, the smart-mouth, I really don't like.

Like Warren's reading my mind, he says, "I've been meaning to tell you. I'm really sorry about Rye being an asshole that time."

I laugh. "That was three years ago." And then realize I've just admitted I remember.

"I should've said something then." Warren's knuckles whiten on the wheel. "I was just a stupid kid, Nina. I was embarrassed."

"It was so not a big deal."

I was at Warren's place that Saturday in March, the weekend I still think of as the Bad Weekend, the two of us shooting and editing funny videos on my laptop. We were trying to clicker-train one of the barn cats to play the piano when Warren's brother Rye sauntered into the living room and started playing with the cat, chanting, "Here, pussy, pussy" and cracking himself up. When I bent over to open the woodstove, he stage-whispered to Warren, "Damn, squirt, you tapped that yet? That's one nice ass."

"It was a big deal," Warren says now. "I mean, you were just a kid."

"So were you." I shrug like I'm way past that, though I still remember my skin prickling with humiliation as I wondered if my jeans were too tight.

I didn't want to be a thing, reduced to part of my anatomy. But Rye put those words in Warren's head, and maybe they'd already been there. If Warren didn't think I was hot, maybe he thought I was a lesbian, like some kids at school insisted. Or ugly. Or a sister. Which was worse, being a thing or being nothing?

We spent two hours trying to train the recalcitrant tabby with tuna, both of us pretending it hadn't happened. For those

45

two hours, I thought being objectified by Rye Witter was the worst thing that could ever happen to me.

Then I fell asleep that Saturday night, and when I woke up, everything had changed.

I acted cool toward Warren afterward, but it wasn't because of his brother. It was because I couldn't trust boys after they hit a certain age, not anymore, and I didn't ever want to feel that way about him.

Soon I started thinking I couldn't trust myself, either.

8

After we make a stop at Whitehall for real food, the car won't start again—just shudders and clicks. We have to get it jumped and driven to the closest twenty-four-hour garage, five miles out of our way. Warren and I wait, drinking bad coffee (me) and more sugar water from the vending machine (him), till the mechanics finish up another job and can handle replacing the Legacy's starter. Night falls outside, and I jiggle my leg and watch the clock.

My phone buzzes twice—Mom.

Warren frowns when I let the second call go to voice mail. "You're not telling your mom anything?"

"Of course I did. Texted her before I left." With a story about spending the night at Kirby's cousin's horse farm, though my mom knows I don't do sleepovers and don't take the car out of town without asking.

"If she's calling, she wants to hear your voice." Warren points at the TV, which is playing a cop show with closed captioning. "Now, that is *not* how you hold a gun."

"Do you check in with *your* mom every time you go anywhere?" I don't like the snide tone of my own voice.

"If I'm gonna miss dinner, yeah. She likes company, and my dad and brothers are usually MIA."

He says it so casually I feel a rush of tenderness for him, which I hide by checking my e-mail. We're already in TV prime time now—how long will this take?

"You worried we're gonna be late?"

"No, my birth mom says it's absolutely fine," I let myself babble. "She's a night owl. Like me. Maybe it's genetic. She'll be up late—I'll text her instead of ringing the doorbell, so I don't wake up the rest of her family. She just put on another pot of coffee."

Warren nods after each sentence, like, *Okay, I get it,* but knowing he isn't believing a word does nothing to shut me up. I have to convince myself, too.

By the time we're on the interstate again, soaring past Saratoga Springs, I'm getting sick of the way Warren taps his feet to inaudible music and fusses with his lank hair. He's probably just as fed up with my silence, because he stops trying to make conversation as we navigate our way into downtown Schenectady.

We roll up to the Gustafssons' house at 11:53.

When I point it out, Warren doesn't say a word. Just slides up alongside the curb and turns off the engine.

"Are you sure the number's right?" he asks then.

"Yeah."

My whole body hums with the excitement of being here. But I see why Warren has doubts. The lights are out at the Gustafssons', even the porch light, and there's no car in the driveway. The garage door is down.

It can't be too late. We're barely into his hunting hours. I step out, stretch, and get my bearings.

"She said to text her, right?"

"Yeah." I forgot. I grab the phone and pretend to text, but my eyes won't stay on the screen. I need to *see* this place.

At first, everything comes at me from a different angle, and nothing looks familiar. The little ranch house with its neat lawn is like a million others.

Then I spot the rusty wheelbarrow adorned with an age-stained McCain '08 bumper sticker. *This is it.*

I turn left at the mailbox and walk just far enough to catch sight of the overpass and the green sign in the distance. 890 VIA CHRISLER AVENUE.

My memory of this place is three-dimensional, full of sounds and smells. Now I'm walking in it, *me* and not the Thief, and I fizz with tension down to my fingernails. The air smells different from Vermont: distant smokestacks instead of wood smoke. Traffic hums on the interstate.

Warren is out of the car, tenting his long arms over his head, and I motion at him to get back in.

"Why?" he asks.

"I'm waiting for her to text back. We don't want to raise a ruckus."

"A ruckus? Seriously?" Warren rolls his eyes and leans on the car. I'm glad, in a deep and cowardly way, that he didn't follow my instructions.

The Thief could be in that house. Lurking behind the garage, or just inside the grassy alley.

Despite what I told Warren, I can't wait out here. I haven't planned what I'll say when Mrs. Gustafsson comes to the door in her bathrobe and slippers and snarls at me. But let her come. Let her snarl. *Please* let those things happen.

A cold dread sinks into my limbs and shortens my breath as I stride up the cutesy flagstone path and the concrete steps. Lace curtains cover the window in the door—the Gustafssons care about keeping their place nice.

He's chosen this place, these people. I'm in his way.

When I find the doorbell, my stomach drops like I'm climbing the top loop of a roller coaster. This is much worse than calling a stranger from a pay phone.

My gloves are back in the car, so I wrap one hand in my scarf, then close my eyes and press the bell.

And wait.

The second ring resonates through the silent house, a soft ding-dong like a dove cooing.

My cat killed a dove last year. I found it under the Douglas fir, beheaded and disemboweled. Doves represent peace. Doves hurt no one. Yet I cuddle my little dove killer, I stroke his cheeks, I feed him treats, I let him sleep on my bed.

I put my ear to the door, my heart pounding as if the Thief could reach out and stab me through the wood.

Nothing.

If he's in there with them, he'll lie low. Two targets is more than I've seen him handle; he won't go for three. Not with houses on either side.

If he's not with them, where are the Gustafssons?

After the fourth ring, I walk around and peer through the garage window. Still open a crack. A thin spear of light splashes paint cans, but I can't see if a car's there. The only way to know is to hoist the window open and climb in.

He imagined it. I could do it. Slither through the window, silently open the house door, or break the glass. (Did I remind Mrs. Gustafsson to lock that door when I called? I have a feeling I didn't.) Creep up the stairs, check their bedroom.

But if I did all that, I'd be the intruder. I'd be the Thief.

Not tonight. I let my breath out slowly, close and open my eyes (*you're awake*), then tiptoe away from the garage and back to the Subaru.

Warren must've got bored waiting, because he's back in the driver's seat, listening to talk radio and eating his next course—Funyuns.

I take out the key, silencing a voice ranting about the hidden messages in zombie movies. "Don't run down the battery. We might have to wait here a little while."

"Why?" he asks between crunches. "It's, like, midnight. Where is she?"

"I don't know."

"She texted you back, right?"

51

I nod, then shake my head.

His eyes have narrowed to slits, that familiar expression: *Stop BS'ing me.* "I thought you weren't supposed to ring the bell 'cause you'd wake up her family."

"They're not here. Nobody is."

"I don't like this," Warren says after a long pause, looking right at me.

I'd rather let him stew about my lying than tell him the truth, so I don't answer, just pull my heels up on the seat, chin on my knees. All the possible scenarios crowd into my mind, blunt and relentless as a cable-news ticker: *The Gustafssons listened to my warning and left the house for the night. The Gustafssons happen to be on vacation. He's already been here and taken them somewhere. He's already been here, but a neighbor called the cops, and he's in custody. He's here now, inside, with them bound and gagged or dead. He won't come. He doesn't exist. There's just me, and I'm here. I'm here for some reason I can't tell Warren because I don't know why myself.*

"So you want to just wait?" Warren asks. He sounds deeply skeptical, but also curious, like he's giving me the benefit of the doubt.

I nod, hoping he's right.

The Thief is going to do this, and he's going to do it tonight. The army trained him to follow through. He may abort a mission, but he'll never go AWOL.

When I close my eyes, I can almost see the place where he plans to leave them.

He's been carrying memories of that place in his head for the past week, cherishing them like an unwilting flower. I don't know where it is, only that there's a cabin or shack, and a brook trickles in the silence of the deep, dark woods.

It's the perfect place. It will honor them. It's almost as special and remote as his place in the desert, the old mine where he left the homeless man.

If the Gustafssons are already there, there's nothing I can do.

My head feels like somebody jammed a beehive into it; the dark, quiet street seems to yell at me, to mock me. *Nothing. Nothing. If you break into that house, you'll be him.*

But it's only midnight.

"I know this sounds crazy, Warren, but this could be my only chance. I have to give her time. I need to be sure."

"Sure, yeah, Nina." He clears his throat. "How'd Mrs. Gustafsson sound when you called to say we were gonna be late?"

My throat closes. "How do you know her name?"

Warren points. "It's on the mailbox."

I breathe again. Still, he's starting to sound like a detective on a cop show. Collecting clues, building a case against me.

"She sounded totally fine, like I said. She said she'd be up."

"Maybe she fell down or had a stroke."

"She's not *that* old, Warren." I don't hide my irritation.

Why didn't I pound on the door? Old people sleep soundly. I should've knocked loudly enough to wake the neighbors, to wake the dead.

I could still do it. Let Warren think what he wants.

No, Warren isn't the problem. My fist will stay suspended above the door as I imagine the knocks reverberating to the cellar. I need silence, invisibility. The suburban night is too peaceful for me to disrupt.

Warren drums his fingertips on the dashboard. "So we're just gonna sit here?"

Fighting back my own impatience and the ragged curtain of fear that keeps descending, I reach for his hand and trap it so he'll stop spazzing.

Warren draws in a deep, fast breath, doesn't pull away. He doesn't come closer, either, or meet my eyes.

Touching him distracts me, too, in a good way, making my heart skip a few beats. His hand is bigger than I expected, dry and reassuring. This hand pulls triggers; it kills bucks, probably skins them, too. He can keep it steady when it matters.

He's such a *good* person under the snark. Straight-shooting and loyal in a traditional way. Long ago I made a resolution to keep him out of this, to keep it all away from him, yet here we are.

I could put his hand on my heart, kiss him, let him push me back against the seat and hold me, and all this would go away for a while. He came here because he cares about me. But if he knew what's in my head, he'd never touch me again.

Warren's hand opens into mine, and I press his palm with my thumb before letting it go. Touching him makes me feel safe, even if it sends the wrong message about why I'm letting him help me.

"Warren," I say, "I know how this looks. So all I can say is—thank you."

9

When I close my eyes, when my head grows heavy and my mind drifts toward sleep, the smells come first.

The musty, mineral odor of a dirt road after the rain. The clean bite of spruce trees.

He always notices smells.

Next, the sounds. A wall of spring peepers to my left sing in unearthly unison, making it harder for me to hear what I need to hear.

I am on high alert. This is a crisis.

My ears strain for scrambling feet, darting pebbles, tiny landslides of wet earth. The telltale sounds of a big, ungainly body making its way down the bank, toward the woods and the brook.

This is the place. I can feel the presence of the shack or cabin, just up the road.

Words, incredulous words, are reverberating in my mind. *The bitch got away.*

The bitch is Mrs. Gustafsson. I am not me.

These are not my thoughts. This is him. *Him.*

I am not the Thief, I remind myself frantically. Still I see through his eyes and hear through his ears—*there, at your ten o'clock, about four meters*—as he detects the sounds of the fleeing woman and glides after her, silent on his rubber soles, the .38 pistol in his hand.

Her gun.

It was on the nightstand, her side. Right out in the open and loaded.

She was still half-asleep when he picked it up; she never even reached for it. He held it to her husband's temple and said, "I'm gonna ask you both to get up and put your hands behind your head, sir, ma'am. Nice and easy, now." He made his voice authoritative and reassuring, like a fireman come to lead them safely from a burning house.

Everything had gone as planned. At eleven on the dot, he broke in through the door from the garage, nabbed their car keys from the peg, and glided to their bedroom without rousing them. A lightning raid, just like he learned to do on his tour when they broke into the homes of suspected insurgents.

The couple acted meek and confused, offered to give him cash and their wedding rings. He told them he was special forces and it was a matter of national security that required them to duct-tape each other's mouths and get downstairs to their Hyundai.

Did they believe him? Of course not. Still, they seemed impressed by his all-black attire and swift, powerful movements. To them, he's no ordinary burglar, but someone who dropped into their lives from a Hollywood action flick. That's probably why they were docile when he taped their hands and made them get in the trunk.

They don't mind being part of my story, he thought as he drove out of the city and up the winding dirt roads. *It's a good story. This is the most excitement they will ever see, even if it's the last.*

Then the banging started inside the trunk. Maybe the sheep weren't so docile, after all.

Once they reached the place, the Thief secured the man first, hauling him out and trussing him to one of the pine support pillars that rose from the cabin's floor. He didn't think the woman could free her feet or get far on her own.

He was wrong.

Now he scrambles down the soggy bank toward the woods, cussing to himself as the damned peepers drown the noise of her flight. His eyelid twitches, his vision blurring for a fraction of a second.

She won't get far. He can track, and he happens to know the nearest inhabited house is over a mile in the opposite direction to where she's heading. But still, points will be taken off for this. It's sloppy. Humiliating.

He pauses at the edge of the woods, letting his eyes adjust so he won't need his flashlight. And there it goes—a splash.

He pins the woman with the flashlight beam as she stands in the brook. She struggles up the opposite bank, but mud slows her down, and a couple of long strides bring him to her.

With her mouth and hands still half duct-taped, her pale blue eyes wide, and her long gray hair coming loose, she no longer looks to him like a person. More like a cow going to the slaughter. But then, maybe he'd look the same in her situation.

The Thief wonders if he's defiling this woodland spot that presses on his senses with its fragrance of spruce needles. All around him, he can feel green leaves rising in tightly folded spears, about to pop.

But a mission is a mission, even if he has no commanding officer but himself. And he doesn't want to prolong her struggles, her suffering.

He forces her to her knees, ignoring the words she's moaning through the gag—prayers? bargaining? curses?

He holds her and says, "Shh, shh." She shakes her head violently when he puts the muzzle against her temple, and that stops him for a second.

Why does she want to live so much, knowing she's still going to die one day? He doesn't understand it. Someone could come up and put a gun to *his* temple right this second, and he wouldn't care.

Or would he? Even an ant struggles when you try to kill it.

He presses her face to the earth and pulls the trigger.

The shot is a crack across the sky, assaulting his sensitive ears, because, dammit, he didn't switch her pistol for his suppressed .22LR. He is a fool.

It's okay, though. The summer cottages in these woods are still empty—he checked—and the only other houses are the kind inhabited by ancient, hardscrabble folk. Maybe they think he just executed a varmint, if they weren't too deaf to hear the shot at all.

He forgot to bring supplies to burn the cabin down, just in case. But he can still dispose of the remains.

Now it's just the peepers and his own harsh breathing. Time to lug the woman up the bank.

As he does his grunt work—most of missions is grunt work, when you come right down to it—the Thief imagines the look on the man's face when he sees the corpse of his wife dumped beside him on the plastic sheet. The Thief isn't looking forward to the other man's despair, but he has to anticipate it so it won't distract him from his work.

Which will be arduous tonight.

He'll finish the man before he opens the case and gets out the tools. There's no need for the target to know what's going to happen to his remains, which is grim necessity.

The Thief doesn't want those remains found. Ever. For covering his tracks, for leaving everything as he found it—including the Hyundai, which he'll park on the other side of town before hiking to his own vehicle—for all that, he will grant himself a clean sixteen points. Deducting two for his screwup with the lady.

Her fraying gray braid hangs over his shoulder. *Almost there.* He wishes he could drag her, but he can't leave marks.

These two people whose first names he's never bothered to

learn will disappear. The night woods will close over them like the ocean after a shark attack, and the other small fish will be left to wonder what lurks beneath.

At last—the cabin. His back is killing him; he needs a warm bath with Epsom salts. He needs the desert air and Eliana's coconut cake, the one she always bakes to welcome him home. Her lips brushing his neck, her sexy voice asking him what took so long.

He steps through the doorway, and the man's muffled moan cuts through the air like a scythe.

10

A man's hands tangle in my hair, gripping my shoulders. With a muffled cry, I push him away and jab my elbow as hard as I can into his side.

I'm no sheep. I won't let you kill me.

"*Ow!* Nina, wake up. It's just a dream. You were freakin' dreaming, okay? What's wrong with you? Oh, shit, Nina. C'mon now."

Not the Thief's voice.

The car door opens, and the dome light blinds me. Warren stands beside my mom's Legacy in his bulky army jacket, rubbing his ribs like they hurt.

He catches his breath and starts talking again. "Nina, if you don't calm down in the next five seconds, I'm gonna call nine-one-one. I don't have a choice. You might be having a seizure."

A seizure? My throat feels rough, like I've been—screaming? Crying? The rest of me feels fine.

"Is it the pills?" Warren asks. "You been taking some new pills, Nina?"

"No." I can't seem to speak above a whisper. "Warren, we have to find a . . . Toyota Sequoia. Black. It's parked on a quiet street, where nobody would notice it. Walking distance from here. We have to find it now."

"No, we don't." His voice has gone gentler. "You were just dreaming, okay?"

"But he's coming back there."

My shorted-out brain scrambles to put the pieces of what I learned together. "He's going to dump their car in town and walk to his. His car is probably eq-equidistant from where he'll leave the Hyundai and this house. He plans logically like that."

"What are you talking about? *Who* are you talking about?"

My cover story floods back to me. How on earth do I get from there to here?

"Please just do this one thing for me," I say. "Find the Sequoia. I-I can't tell you why."

Warren fingers the car keys. He doesn't quite keep the sarcasm out of his voice as he asks, "What about the lady we were waiting for? Your bio mom?"

"She's not coming back." My eyes fill with tears; he can't doubt the realness of those, at least. "I think he took her."

"The guy in the Sequoia?"

I nod. Could I say we're looking for my birth mother's psychotic son, just released from jail? Her abusive husband? No, I'd just be insulting Warren's intelligence.

"This town probably has dozens of black Sequoias," he mutters.

"But not that many," I say, "with a New Mexico license plate."

. . .

Warren starts playing talk radio again. This time I'm glad, because the endless stream of strangers' chatter keeps him from asking me questions. At two A.M., he switches to NPR. Then to an oldies station.

We scour the town—exploring leafy streets with big houses, then gliding past shuttered dry cleaners, check-cashing joints, doughnut shops. In the distance, a gigantic columned building looms on a hill—a courthouse, I think. The Beach Boys croon about sun and fun. "Try that strip mall we skipped before," I say as my eyelids drift closed.

I wake with a jolt to sunlight and a clamor of shrieking birds. The car is parked in a Denny's lot. Warren lies slumped in his seat beside me.

I grab his shoulder and shake him. "You let me fall asleep. Why didn't you wake me?"

Warren blinks like he's still fighting his way through dreams, and they aren't good ones. "We combed the whole grid four times, Nina. Sheesh."

"The light will make it easier to check all the alleys."

He pulls himself upright. "Nina, listen. We're *not going to find* that Sequoia."

"You think it doesn't exist."

"I think you're confused. You were gonna meet your birth mom, and suddenly you have a crazy nightmare and we're chasing a bad guy. I hate to ask, Nina, but...do you normally take meds stronger than Adderall?"

"No." I close my eyes, fatigue wrapping me like mummy bindings, the sunlight a distant, hostile glare. Warren is right: all night I've been telling lies on lies. If I were him, I would've ditched this town and headed home hours ago.

But I'm not Warren. And the Thief may not have reached the Sequoia yet. What he planned to do with those bodies in the cabin must've taken a while. It involved a bow saw.

He could be hiking across town right now, every part of him aching from the exertion. He could be one of the bleary-eyed young men strolling into Denny's for coffee.

But even if the Sequoia pulled in right now and I could point to him, so what? He's eliminated the evidence, and he doesn't take trophies. He'll have ditched his tools like always—that's why he has a Home Depot frequent-buyer card. I can describe the dirt road and cabin, but not find them on a map.

Warren already thinks I'm crazy. So will everyone else.

Sixteen points for the Thief. Zero points for me.

"Okay, Warren."

"Okay what?"

"You're right. Let's go." Home. Back to fighting sleep and being paranoid about strangers who might be following me.

I keep my eyes closed and lean back as we pull out of the lot, trying to forget that cabin, that burbling stream. I've blocked worse memories.

I'm just starting to drift when Warren's voice jerks me upright. "Holy shit, Nina. That's it!"

"Where?"

My eyes snap open on a busy intersection. Tall office buildings—as tall as they get in Schenectady—block the sky. I catch a glimpse of a black SUV, two cars ahead, as Warren hits the gas and blows through a red light.

We careen down the street, swerving around a bike. The rider glares at us.

"New Mexico?" I ask breathlessly. "Did you see?"

"Yeah, when he turned out of the side street. Red-and-yellow—hard to miss."

"Did you see the driver?"

"Are you gonna tell me why I'm chasing him?"

Why *are* we chasing him? What can we possibly do? Carjack him and make him take us to the remains?

"Soon," I say. "Try to get his plate."

If I can link a plate to the name I already know, I'll have proof I'm not crazy, at least.

Ahead of us, the light flicks to yellow. The SUV swishes through it, and so does the next car, but the third one stops.

Warren tries to pull into a side street, but it turns out to be an alley, so he pulls back into the lane, swearing. The light is red now, as a gaggle of uniformed Cub Scouts and their leader navigate the crosswalk.

Horns blare at us, and Warren mutters to himself, too low for me to hear. As the light finally turns green, he says, "This car chase thing is harder than it looks in the movies."

"Where's the interstate?"

"Couple miles from here. You think he's heading there? North or south?"

"South. You saw him?"

I can barely get out the words. *Saw him. His face.*

"A guy, yeah. Didn't catch specs."

Warren bolts to the next light, both of us keeping our eyes peeled for the red-and-yellow plate. "Was he old or young?" I ask.

"Young, I guess. White. Slender. Don't distract me, okay?"

Warren swings into the right lane, the interstate one—we both know the city grid too well by now. My eyes flick from car to car, but there's no Sequoia.

A broad stream of weekend traffic tugs us toward the entrance ramp. I strain my eyes to see the cars ahead of us, squinting as sunlight glares off bumpers.

"I think he lost us," Warren says in a low voice.

We shoot into the concrete slot and onto the interstate, headed south toward Albany. Toward Albuquerque. But it doesn't matter now, does it?

"You mean we lost him." My heart sinks like a stone. "Or do you think he saw us and bolted?"

"Nah, he didn't see us. He got lucky with that light."

"Just a little faster, okay?"

He steps on the gas. "I'm practically going ninety."

We pass car after car without a glimpse of the Sequoia. Warren's lips move like he's reciting a prayer or a curse. When we reach the suburbs of Albany, without a word to me, he slides into the exit lane and around the clover leaf, heading us back up the Northway. He takes the tight curve heart-stoppingly fast, driving one-handed, and all I say is "Thanks for trying. You were all Fast and Furious back there."

Warren snorts, while reality settles in my stomach like a meal turning to heartburn. The Gustafssons are dead, and there's no one I can tell, no report I can file, no investigative journalist or crusading blogger I can call.

Concrete ramps crisscross a sky as flat and gray as my future feels. My mind is with the Thief, imagining him racing southwest, flipping on his radio, looking forward to crashing at a motel and taking his hot bath.

On Tuesday, his girlfriend will greet him with kisses and cake.

Somebody's talking to me, soft but insistent. Asking questions.

Warren. He's still here.

I turn to find him staring at me, his narrow, dark eyes cop-suspicious. "Please look at the road, okay?"

Warren rolls his eyes way up, then back to the asphalt. "What I was trying to say," he says, "is, that was pretty fun and all, and I like having an excuse to drive recklessly as much as the next guy. But now it's time to tell me what the hell we were doing."

WARREN

11

Four hours of driving around a dark Nowheresville, U.S.A., passing the same neon signs and statues and parks and bus shelters and mini-marts till they gave me a headache. All that time, I didn't ask what we were *really* looking for.

If my brothers knew about tonight, they'd laugh their asses off. They'd say I'm whipped. They wouldn't understand that this isn't about sex and that I wouldn't have driven to Schenectady for any cute girl who gave me a smile. This is about Nina—her and me.

Other girls have asked me for favors; that's kind of what happens when you deal drugs, even study drugs. Some have cried, and a couple have not-so-subtly offered something in return. It may sound hot, but their desperation was palpable, and I got very good at talking them into treatment, until eventually I realized the extra income wasn't worth the guilt.

I wouldn't have explored Schenectady for any of those girls. But Nina helped me survive middle school, the most hellish era of my life, and I'm not about to forget that.

. . .

It started in spring of seventh grade with the book report for Ms. Mullins. I'd stayed up all night reading *The Man Who Japed*, by Philip K. Dick, an old book I'd found at a library sale, and now I couldn't seem to explain its convoluted plot. It didn't help that every time I said "Dick," the whole class snickered, and Ray Welles, the class comedian, sang out, "Who you callin' a dick, Witter?"

By the time I finished, Mullins's voice was hoarse from shushing the class. "What does 'japed' mean, Warren?"

I'd read the whole book, yet my mind went blank, and sweat beaded under my collar.

Mullins made me fetch her enormous dictionary and read out the definition. When I was finally allowed to sit down again—amid mutters of "What a dick" and "Dick move, Witter"—a tiny, rolled-up note waited on my desk.

I'd never gotten a note at school that said anything good. I almost threw it away unopened, but curiosity won out. Standing at my locker after the bell, I deciphered a message written in silvery-purple ink and scrunched, adult-looking cursive: *Your book sounds good. Can I borrow it? NB.*

The class had two NBs, but I knew Ned Bissette hadn't written this. The paper wasn't perfumed or anything—just a ratty scrap from a notebook—but everything about it said *special* and *girl*.

I slipped the note into my cherrywood box at home, where I collect wheat pennies, and tried not to think about it. Because she had no dad, Nina Barrows was vulnerable, a semi-outcast like me. Maybe a popular girl had bribed her to lure me in with fake friendship overtures that would tempt me to do something mockable. Paranoid, yes, but this was middle school.

The Dick book stayed in my backpack. Next English class, I sat behind Nina and one row over. She wore a deep blue sweater that was almost purple, like her ink, and a sparkly clip like stars against her black hair.

I set the book on my desk, covering the author's last name with two pencils. I probably would have continued to do this every class until the semester ended, not daring to speak a word, if, when the bell rang, Nina hadn't turned and smiled at me.

Next thing I knew, the hardcover was in her hands, pressed against her soft ultramarine sweater, and I was looking right into her strange, beautiful eyes. How'd I never notice them before?

"I liked it," she said a week later, returning the book. "I like how the main guy, he thought he was being good and going along with the rules. But part of him wanted to break them."

Something swelled in my chest. I was the guy in the book, sticking to the straight and narrow—because my mom needed to have *one* kid who was never arrested—while something deep inside me yearned to raise hell.

How had she known? Did she want to raise hell, too?

We didn't talk much about ourselves, Nina and I, even when we started hanging out after school. Books were safe, movies were safe, making silly videos with our phones was safe. The other kids could look at us and see two nerds doing nerd things, not a guy with a desperate crush on a girl.

I was still petrified the first time she invited me home. We'd been to a comic-drawing workshop at the library, and she lived just up the hill. But was this a date? A study date? What if her mom was there? Would I see her room? If she sat on her bed, should I sit down with her?

Nina's mom worked most afternoons, it turned out, and we played with her cat and watched old movies—never on the same couch. Teasing each other about hot actors and actresses, most of whom were now old or dead, was the closest we got to romance.

We memorized every smart-ass high school movie ever made and thought we were so freaking mature and superior— *middle school dating, what a joke.*

I knew I couldn't tell anyone I just liked being near Nina. For now, that was enough.

By the time I got up the courage to invite her to *my* house, it was winter of eighth grade, and I used the excuse of cutting the Christmas tree. We went out to the woods with my mom, who seemed to like Nina. "She's quiet, but you can tell she's thinking," she said.

A few months later, though, when she picked me up from Nina's house, my mom gave me a strange warning. "That girl isn't going to stick around here after high school, Warren. She's not the type."

"I *know* that." Nina and I had extensively discussed our futures, which included film school in New York or LA for me and some fancy advanced degree for her so she could work at the American Museum of Natural History.

Then I realized my mom thought *I* would stay "around here." She didn't want me to be disappointed when Nina flew away somewhere glamorous and never returned.

After that, I didn't talk to Mom about Nina. But I did invite her over one more time, during mud season, which is when everything went to hell, thanks to Rye.

Then again, maybe I'm giving Rye and his dickishness too much credit. Because that was when Nina started acting weird, and not just to me.

For a few weeks after that disastrous Saturday, we still talked, but Nina didn't invite me over, and gradually she stopped sitting next to me. When I approached her, she smiled and said hi, but her eyes darted away.

Looking back, I know it wasn't just about me or us. Nina developed a waxy paleness and deep circles under her eyes that spring; she missed a whole week of school. I should have asked her what was wrong. But self-centered eighth-grade me thought if she wanted to avoid me, two could play at that game.

I told myself I was making a heroic display of pride, when I was being almost as big a dick as my brother.

Two years later, when Nina came to me for the pills, we were like strangers. She wore dangly earrings and a red scarf that day, and I wanted to wrap my arms around her.

I wanted to say, "Do any japing lately?"

I wanted to ask if she ever finished *East of Eden*.

I wanted to tell her, "Don't do this. You're smart enough already." I wanted to warn her about the headaches, the nervousness, and the other side effects I'd only read about, because I refused to try the stuff myself.

It was her choice, I finally told myself as I took her twenties and doled the pills into a sandwich baggie. Free market, supply and demand.

I profited from her bad choices, over and over. I was secretly relieved when she told me her mom had found her stash, even though it meant I might not see her anymore.

Now I realize that whatever happened to Nina in eighth grade, it's not over. And study drugs were only the beginning.

12

"So?" I say now. "Please don't tell me that dude we chased in the Sequoia was your biological father."

She's lied so much. I try to imagine myself cold and silent like early Clint Eastwood, hard-nosed like Philip Marlowe. Accepting no unlikely stories from dames in distress. But I just feel lost.

Nina is scrunched down in her seat, looking out the window. The wind grabs a tendril of black hair and whips it over her eyes, and I resist the urge to smooth it back. She looks so fragile, so defeated, and I hate how that sight hollows out a space in me. I want to put my arm around her. Last night she almost seemed like she would have let me.

Until she went batshit and attacked me in her sleep.

She says in a small voice, "My birth mom doesn't actually live here. She's in Arizona."

"So." I try to keep my own voice level. No accusing or whining; I'm a detective or a shrink, getting to the truth. "The whole thing was a lie."

She doesn't answer.

"Whose house were we at?"

"The Gustafssons'."

"I know, but who the hell are they? To you, I mean."

"Nobody." Even softer: "I think they're dead."

. . .

It takes all three hours of the drive home, with lots of stops and starts, for her to talk.

I gather this much: Mr. and Mrs. Gustafsson live in that house—or lived. They didn't answer their door last night because the driver of the Sequoia abducted and killed them. So she says.

Does she know the Gustafssons? No. Does she know the driver of the Sequoia? No. Wait, maybe she does. "In a way. I knew he'd do this."

"What do you mean, 'in a way'?"

She looks out the window. "You wouldn't believe me."

I promise her I *would* believe her, though I'm not sure.

"It doesn't matter. It's over now."

She just keeps repeating that, in a dead voice that reminds me of the traumatized final girl at the end of a horror movie. Her face is turned from me, but I suspect there are tears.

"If people got killed, it matters a lot," I point out, getting impatient.

Stop being an asshole, Warren. Nothing happened in Schenectady. Nobody got killed. Nina's been lying to me since yesterday afternoon, maybe without knowing she was. She could have a serious mental illness—a psychosis—and I've been enabling it by obeying her orders, by chasing the Sequoia, by asking these questions. She needs meds, maybe hospitalization. Doctors, her mom. Not me being all up in her face.

"I don't want to get you any more involved. It's dangerous."

Her head's bowed so her hair covers her face, and I can tell she believes what she just said. Behind her, white pines file past under a sky full of fat-bellied rain clouds.

What's wrong with you? I plead silently. *Why can't I help?*

I'll have to call her mom, tell her what happened, find out if Nina's already getting treatment. It's a betrayal, an ugly one, but the alternative is watching her spiral deeper into her own terrors. Or abandoning her—again.

I shouldn't have sold her those pills. *Dick move, Warren.* If only I could take it back, all of it. . . .

· · ·

"Thank you," Nina says when she drops me off. "Thank you, Warren."

Like last night. Only this time she isn't holding my hand.

I watch her switch over to the driver's seat, watch her drive away. I calm my dogs. I go inside, fall on my bed fully clothed, ignore my mom's questions about how I just *disappeared* yesterday.

I can't call Nina's mom yet. I'll need rest for that. Right now I can't seem to convince myself there's no alternative.

When I wake up, it's dark and I can hear the radio downstairs.

And I remember something.

Write it down this second, or you'll forget. I grab a piece of notebook paper and a pen and scribble the sequence of letters and numbers in my head: DP6K62.

The Sequoia's license plate. I didn't exactly *try* to memorize it, but numbers stick in my brain. The two might be a three, but I'm sure about the rest.

. . .

I don't call Nina's mom on Saturday, or on Sunday, or even on Monday.

I can't do it. I don't *want* to do it. All I can see is the expression in Nina's eyes when she thanked me for driving to a stranger's house and chasing another stranger's car. Like I was the only person she could trust.

So I keep making excuses. On Sunday and Monday, I even go online and search "Gustafsson" and their address. Aside from an old article about animal abuse at the slaughterhouse that Mr. Gustafsson manages, no news items come up; no one has murdered them.

I have AP English with Nina, but I sit in the back row

and don't look at her. I keep blinders on in the hallway and avoid the woods behind the soccer field. A new kid asks me for painkillers, and I text him my brother Gray's number and say I'm out of the business.

I started selling because I wanted to save enough for a non-beater car. Now I just want to apply to college without a rap sheet.

An awful thought keeps nagging at me: Did I help make Nina this way? Crying out in her dreams, seeing killers on sleepy streets? Could this have started with a drug interaction, or the amphetamines loosening her grip on reality?

I research "stimulant psychosis." People get it when they're abusing or overdosing, and I didn't see Nina pop a single pill on our trip. Unless—maybe in the restroom?

It rains all week. Mud sluices down our road; the brook jumps its banks. Downtown, sewer water pours into basements. I hope Nina's house is okay.

I remember how her hand felt in mine, and how she breathed softly and evenly as she slept beside me—in a Subaru, fully clothed, ten minutes before she woke up screaming and trying to brain me with her elbow. But still.

I keep on researching. Just in case.

. . .

It takes me four clicks to find out the New Mexico DMV doesn't trace plate numbers for free. You have to pay a private-investigation firm and assure them you have a legit legal reason to want the driver's name and address. Nobody checks up on whether you actually do, and the PI company promises you the specs within a day.

Maybe my dad's right when he says we might as well all be crapping out on Main Street, because privacy doesn't exist anymore.

The trace costs barely more than an oil change, but I don't have an online payment account. I could ask to use Rye's—he's got several, most of them untraceable, that he uses to buy fake IDs for him and his friends. To hear him talk, he's a digital con man.

I hate asking my brother for anything, but I'd hate calling Nina's mom more.

I'll think of a story to tell him. I don't need to hear Rye's thoughts on Nina's degree of hotness; his porn-derived standards can't touch her. Nina reminds me of the pre-Raphaelite girls in my Brit Lit textbook with their pale skin and glowing eyes and acres of hair that waft around them like seaweed. (Except hers just hangs.)

Her eyes, I swear, are bronze. A hazel brown that's weirdly pale and luminous against her black hair; in some lights, they look almost amber.

And she's sick, I remind myself. *She needs your help.*

Enough of being pathetic. What's happening with the Gustafssons of Schenectady these days? I haven't bothered to check in on *them* in a while, so I do.

Shit.

13

On Friday, I catch Nina in the hall, walk right up to her, and practically pin her against her locker. "We have to go to the cops."

Her eyes widen like she has no idea what I'm talking about, and she inches away from me.

I snatch my phone from my pack, wake it, and hand it to her. "You *knew*."

Starting Wednesday, the headlines have been all over the Schenectady papers and TV. "Schenectady PD Seeks Information on Missing Couple."

Ruth and Gary Gustafsson didn't show up to their jobs on Monday, and Mrs. Gustafsson's brother called the cops. The glass in the door from the garage was broken. The couple's Hyundai is missing, but they didn't take their suitcases or their medications. They have grown kids, big families, lots of friends, all of whom say it just doesn't look right.

My browser loads the official MISSING poster. "*Look* at them," I say.

They're both big, gentle-looking people. Mrs. Gustafsson wears a sleeveless shirt that doesn't flatter her in the photo, and Mr. Gustafsson has a comb-over. His arm's around her, and the affection looks real.

I show Nina the bookmarked articles one by one. Mrs. Gustafsson fostered Humane Society kittens. Mr. Gustafsson worked at a slaughterhouse, but his friends describe him as the kindest person they knew. One commenter speculates that an animal-rights group targeted him after a guy on his crew was arrested for skinning a calf alive, but Gustafsson himself wasn't implicated in the cruelty.

Nina's mouth twists as she reads, and her eyes get big and wet.

"Say something," I say.

I was so upset last night, after I found this stuff, that I almost called her. I considered driving over to her house unannounced. Instead, I ended up spending most of the night online, hogging our crappy connection. With Ryc's help, I ordered that trace on the license plate, then jittered through first period wondering what to say to Nina.

Words still fail me. *I thought you were crazy, but now I'm starting to think you're actually an accomplice to . . . abduction? Murder?*

Articles and police alerts are one thing. When I watched the videos, the bottom dropped out of my stomach.

I saw the block we drove on. The house where we parked. It looked different in the sunlight with police tape all over, but I was sure.

In every story, I waited for the reporter to mention a neighbor who noticed a Subaru with Vermont plates lurking outside the Gustafssons' house on Friday night. To say the police were seeking info on the mystery car.

Nothing.

The cops haven't mentioned a lead or a suspect. Foul play remains just one possibility. Nobody can even put a date to the Gustafssons' disappearance—except, I guess, Nina and me.

Or just Nina. Technically, they could have vanished Friday, Saturday, *or* Sunday. How can I be sure she was with me when it happened? It sounds ridiculous, but how do I know she didn't go back to the city and *make* it happen?

"I didn't expect her to look so sweet," Nina says, still staring at the MISSING poster. A tear rolls down her cheek, and she rubs it away like she's not sure what it is. "The only time we talked . . . we got off on the wrong foot, I guess. She thought I was a prank caller."

"Talked? To who?"

She points to Mrs. Gustafsson. "She had a right to be suspicious. I called her out of the blue."

"You *called* her?"

"I tried to warn her. I used a pay phone."

I grab the phone like it might burn Nina, my gaze darting over the kids rummaging in lockers up and down the row. Did anybody hear that?

If they did, they couldn't care less. They probably can't even pronounce Schenectady or find it on a map.

"You've seen all this stuff already," I say, suddenly realizing it. "All these articles."

She nods. "It's just different now—talking about it with you."

I lean in too close to her. With her splotchy cheeks and startled, red-rimmed eyes, she looks like a stranger.

"Who is he?" I whisper.

She shakes her head like she's confused.

"The guy you think did this. The guy you know 'in a way.' Who is he?" As I say the words, I realize what "in a way" might mean. "Is he somebody you don't know in person? Did you meet him online?"

She's edging away from me again, fresh tears welling in her eyes.

I follow her. "You have to tell somebody, Nina."

"I can't."

She grabs her backpack and runs, leaving me staring at the Gustafssons' happy faces as the bell sounds.

14

I've always liked playing detective. Those old-time PIs Sam Spade and Mike Hammer knew how to handle the worst situations—sometimes with fists, sometimes just with a smart-ass remark. And when they encountered a situation beyond repair, they'd light up a smoke or take a swig from their flask and think, *What a screwy world. Can't change it, might as well live with it.*

My dad, by contrast, believes in changing the world. That's why he's off at a Green Mountain Libertarian Caucus meeting on Friday night, leaving Mom and me to eat dinner alone.

When I reach for my water glass for the tenth time, trying to keep the food from sticking in my throat, I catch her staring at me. My mom never asks me what's wrong—I just see my pain reflected on her face. When I was little, she used to cry whenever I skinned my knee or got a splinter, and after a while I learned to put on a tough act so I didn't have to see her fall apart.

"I'm okay, Mom," I say. "Just a little stressed. You know. Finals. College plans."

She makes a *pshaw* gesture. "You'll get in."

"To UVM—sure." I consider broaching the subject of applying to schools with better film-production programs, maybe even out of state. But this is no time for that conversation.

Instead I ask, "If you know about a crime after the fact and you don't say anything, do you think that makes you an accomplice?"

She flinches, probably thinking Rye's made some nasty confession to me, and I add quickly, "This has nothing to do with *anyone* you know. It's something in a book we're reading for school."

Mom relaxes. She doesn't wear makeup, and her cheeks are raw from the winter; sometimes it hurts me how pretty and fragile she looks. "Legally, I think that does make you an accomplice."

"If you knew I killed somebody, would you tell?"

She grins at me and spoons up soup. "Never. To my grave."

"Aw, stop it. You would."

"That's why I'm glad I know you'll never kill anybody, Warren."

I narrow my eyes and try to look villainous. "Can you be sure? How well do you *really* know me?"

She meets me with a smile as trusting as a first grader's. "Some people I might have doubts about. But not you."

. . .

When I check my mail that night, there's a message waiting from the New Mexico PI I paid to trace the Sequoia's plate. My heart pounds as I open it, though I tell myself this doesn't mean anything. For all I know, the guy we chased was a random innocent.

The Sequoia is registered to Dylan Patrick Shadwell. He's twenty-three—will be twenty-four on August third. He lives at 7348 Piedmont Drive NE, Albuquerque, New Mexico. My own quick search reveals a Facebook account for friends only, a bunch of listings and five-star ratings for his custom furniture-making business, and a Twitter account he doesn't use.

His profile pictures show an outdoorsy type, facing away from the camera toward a mountain vista. As far as I can tell, his record is clean.

. . .

On Saturday, they find the Gustafssons' Hyundai.

It was parked behind a defunct auto-parts store in a gravel lot with no security-camera coverage. The police are combing it for evidence, the TV reporters say.

I almost call Nina a few times. I can't stop thinking about her saying she knew the killer "in a way," and then not denying it when I asked if she knew him online.

There are chat rooms where you can connect with sickos, and it's not *that* hard to stumble in by mistake. She could've been looking for a discussion of Nick Cave or H. P. Lovecraft, and boom, she's talking to a psycho.

Things like that have happened. Charles Manson built a cult of pretty young women, and he didn't even have the Internet.

I can't exactly see Nina as a Manson groupie, but now this idea's in my head, I can't get rid of it, either. So on Sunday evening, after a short and nasty struggle with myself, I hack her e-mail.

It's way too easy—her password is her birthday and her cat's name, just like it was in eighth grade.

Her in-box is full of messages from the school, her mom, Kirby Blessing, iTunes, and me. A few things from girls I don't know, but no IMs from sinister strangers, and certainly nothing from Dylan Shadwell.

In fact, only one message catches my eye. *RE: Staying at Hacienda Zamora.*

If Hacienda Zamora is a hotel, it's nowhere around here. I click.

Dear Ms. Barrows: We understand your concerns about finding safe lodging for your daughter. Rooms at Hacienda Zamora are key-card-locked, and front-desk personnel are on duty 24/7. We would need from you a letter attesting to your taking full financial responsibility for your daughter during her stay with us. . . .

I skim down to the quoted text. Nina wrote to this place pretending to be her mom: *I am considering booking a room for my seventeen-year-old daughter this June. . . .* She must have wanted to make sure the hotel wouldn't turn her away when they saw she wasn't of age.

Except Hacienda Zamora isn't a hotel; it's a bed-and-breakfast, specializing in weddings. And it's located twenty minutes north of Albuquerque, New Mexico.

. . .

When I ambush Nina at her locker again on Monday, after the last bell, she doesn't even try to get away. She just lowers her head and asks, "Want to go outside?"

We sit on a rotting log behind a clump of cedars. The girls' track team is pounding around the soccer field in their shorts and sweatshirts, and I hear a couple of them griping because the soggy ground is ruining their shoes.

I'll start slow—not mention that I know she might be planning some kind of crazy trip to New Mexico.

Nina says, "I wish I had a smoke. That's what people do out here."

"You don't smoke."

She gives me a look, like *How well do you know me?* "Actually, I have."

"Well, I don't." And then, awkwardly, I say, "We need to talk."

"I wish you'd forget I ever told you anything. That was just me being weird." Nina shakes her head. She's wearing a turquoise pullover with ribbon around the neck, and her own neck looks fragile, like someone could come along and snap it.

"Well, yeah. I mean, 'weird' is definitely a word for it. But Nina, I *can't* forget. You know stuff you shouldn't—I mean, unless—"

"Unless I had something to do with it." She laughs, short and brittle.

You don't. Please convince me you don't. "Those people could still be *alive*," I blurt out before I can stop myself. "You could be the one to save them."

"They're not alive."

"How do you know?" I lean toward her, but she's staring at mushed-down dead leaves. She seems way too sure about the Gustafssons.

And how can anyone be sure except the person who took them? The idea makes the world go gray and tilt, like I'm going to be sick, bile pressing itself up into my throat.

It's an effort for me to look at her, and maybe an effort for her to look back. I can tell she's clenching her jaw so her lip doesn't quiver.

I fight the nausea. "The Gustafssons were, like, sixty, Nina. Were. Are. They couldn't fight back."

"Stop it," she says in a low voice. "Stop it."

"Do you know what happened to them?"

She nods, and her face starts to crumple as she fans dead leaves with her left Converse. Above our heads, the golden-green maples are leafing out. The sky is baby blue, and the air feels sticky.

"They found the Hyundai," I say—feeding her scraps of info to get her to spill, detective-style. "Will they find anything in it?"

"I don't know." After a minute, she adds, "Probably not. He's careful."

"Who's *he*? The guy in the Sequoia?"

"It doesn't matter. I don't have proof it's him."

"No e-mails, chats, nothing like that?"

"No."

Mating birds warble like crazy in the trees. Clumps of tightly curled, emerald-green fiddleheads pock the forest floor. The world is too spring-feverish for this conversation.

Nina takes a deep breath. "I think they're in garbage bags, under some junk, in an abandoned cabin in the woods. The Gustafssons, I mean." She glances up, and the golden light turns her face sickly yellow. "I don't think they're in one piece."

I shiver. Please let that not be true, even if it means she *is* crazy. No one deserves that.

"You could tell the police. Do it anonymously. Just so, you know, the Gustafssons' family would know what happened to them."

"Maybe," Nina says, in a closed way that tells me she's already considered this and ruled it out. Because an anonymous tip might be traced back to her? Because she doesn't want the killer to be caught? Because she doesn't really know anything?

"What do you know about *him*? You know—the guy?" My hand dips discreetly into my backpack for the crappy tablet I borrowed from Rye. "What's his name?"

"I don't know." Lip caught between her teeth. "Well, okay, yes. I know his name. It's—Shadwell. Dylan."

My heart pounds against my army jacket. "You know where he lives?"

"Albuquerque."

The biggest city in New Mexico—an easy guess.

She goes on, "I know his house number starts with a seven, but not the rest of it or the street."

I'm suddenly drenched with sweat under my jacket. I would make the world's worst detective.

"Can you describe the house?" I almost whisper.

Nina gives me a hard look. "Why? It won't prove anything."

"Please."

"Okay." Nina closes her eyes, like darkness helps her remember. "It's Spanish-style, two floors, small. White stucco with red tiles. There's a front porch with a juniper bush next to it, and the yard is just rocks except for a strip of shrubs."

"Xeriscaped," I say. "Because it's so dry there."

"Whatever. There's a little window high up, in the living room, that's shaped like a flower." She opens her eyes. "Is that enough?"

Sweat drips down my nose, and I brush it away as I swipe the tablet. The image from Google Street View is loaded and ready.

I wouldn't have called the window a flower. To me it's more like an amoeba, or just a random-shaped ornamental window.

Everything else is the way she described it. I brought the tablet so we could both see the details.

Nina snatches the tablet from me, shaking so hard she almost drops it. "I've never seen it before twilight," she says. "In the sun. Like this."

I expect her to ask how I got the address, or why I didn't show it to her right away. But she just keeps staring, her face two inches from the screen, like I've disappeared into thin air. Like nothing exists anymore but her and that house.

"So you've seen his house," I say finally. "Nina, is this Shadwell guy, like, related to you? Or a friend of your mom's? Have you seen him do bad shit before?"

She puts down the tablet and gazes into the distance. "I have. But it's not like you think. And I can't explain."

"Try me."

"It won't help." A softness flits over her face, like she's considering telling me. Then her jaw stiffens again. "Even if you believed me, it wouldn't change anything. They're gone."

And now I play my last card. "Would it change anything," I ask, "if your mom knew you were planning a trip to New Mexico?"

Two seconds ago, Nina was acting like she'd lost the will to live. Now I've never seen her so alive with anger. Two pink spots appear on her cheeks, and her eyes go wide, fixed on me. My pulse races and pleasure centers click on in my brain, until I realize what I'm seeing is her excited about hating my guts.

"How do you know? What did you *do*?" And then, in a lower voice, she says, "I know I brought you into this mess, but why can't you just *stop*?"

"Because you did bring me into it. And now I'm here." I clear my throat—then, gingerly, reach out to touch her hand where it grips the log. She shudders but doesn't pull away.

"Whatever you tell me," I say, "you can trust me not to tell anybody else."

Part of me knew I'd never make that call to her mom.

She shudders again—then, to my surprise, opens her hand and clasps mine. Her palm is clammy, but her fingers feel wiry-strong. "You're going to think I'm crazy. Crazier."

I repeat, "Try me."

NINA

15

I don't know Dylan Shadwell. He doesn't know me.

But he's with me every night as I drift off to sleep. Always has been, as far back as I can remember.

Maybe it's better to say I'm with him, dreaming my way into his life. I can't try to stop him, only watch what happens through his eyes, and hear it through his ears, and taste it with his tongue, and feel it through his skin.

It starts with shifting, pulsing pictures as my thoughts fray into unconsciousness. I fall out of myself—can't stop it—and now I'm looking through a hole in a frosted-glass window. Everything *he* thinks and experiences in the present moment is sharp-edged and vivid; the rest bleeds and blurs in the background. I know his hopes and fears only when they crowd their way into the now.

He's been with me so long, it took me years to realize I was the only girl who closed her eyes and saw pieces of a life that wasn't hers.

And he wasn't always like this.

. . .

My first memory of him is also my first memory of me.

I'm four, staring at my night-light, a strangely terrifying white bunny chomping a plastic carrot. Pink eyes leer through the dark, ready to swell to monster size when mine close. Mommy's room is just a few steps down the hall, but she says big girls don't run from what scares them.

Instead of running, I pray: *Let me close my eyes and wake up with Mommy.*

My prayer is half answered. I close my eyes and wake up somewhere else.

The bunny-light is gone. It's daytime.

I'm gazing down at a mean-looking, red-striped turtle sitting on a rock, enclosed in a glittery glass box. Every detail is perfect, yet I know I'm not here. I can't control my body, only watch it do things.

I reach into the box with a hand that's bigger and browner than my real hand, a hand with scars and blunt, bitten nails. A boy's hand. I feel the pinch of cold raw hamburger between my fingers as I set it in the turtle's bowl.

This *is* my hand, only I am somebody else. A boy. Somebody who doesn't run from what scares him.

The turtle lashes its flexible neck to snatch the meat. Its

eyes are dead. The boy who is me yanks his hand back, and we feel a rush of excitement—*that turtle could take my finger off.* The turtle is a hundred times scarier than my bunny night-light, yet I'm no longer afraid.

A chuckle rises in my throat. A deep boy's chuckle. Then come thoughts:

Turtles can live fifty years. T. Rex will outlive me if I die when I'm thirty-four like Dad did. Turtles don't off themselves. Too smart.

So the boy has a dad. His dad is dead. I can't imagine knowing a dead person. The boy feels older than me, but not grown-up.

T. Rex is the turtle's name. And the boy's? He doesn't like his first name, so he gives himself a new one every few months, naming himself after cartoon superheroes, wrestlers, ninja warriors.

It will take him a while to become the Thief.

. . .

In the early years, I never saw him hurt an animal, a younger kid, even an insect. Nobody hurt him.

Of course, I saw only a sliver of his life.

Ordinary stuff. I watched his hands—my hands—carefully paint a model orc to add to the battle scene in his bedroom, or position one last playing card to finish a magnificent castle. I savored the fake-flavor explosion of Doritos as he slumped on the couch watching a scary movie my mom would never have let *me* watch. The boy lived in a trailer, somewhere dry and hot. He had all the things I wasn't allowed to have, like junk food and hundreds of cable channels. He had a young, pretty mom who wore tight jeans and smelled like cigarettes when she kissed him good night.

Their family had been bigger before the Bad Days. There'd been his dad, an aunt and uncle in California, and a baby he remembered in a car seat beside him, maybe a cousin. Occasionally, the boy would think tenderly of that baby, like when he built a dollhouse for a friend's kid sister: *I'd have built her an even better one.*

He didn't think about the Bad Days.

He did think about his father, who was dead. He remembered strong hands hoisting him into an apple tree. Sun shone through the leaves. The boy noticed a white sheet dangling from a bough, just limply hanging, and everything about that sheet was suddenly so *wrong* that he shoved the memory to the back of his mind.

I took it all in stride. I let the boy, who was six years older than me, give me a new vocabulary. One day when I was seven, I called my mom a douche bag.

"Who taught you that, Nina?"

"Kids at school."

This seemed to upset her, so I came clean and told her the truth: I saw a boy every night. No, not in my room. No, not in my dreams, either—or was he? I still wasn't clear on what was a dream and what wasn't. But I knew I never saw the boy during nap time—only when I went to bed between sunset and sunrise. When I did see him, it always lasted for about half an hour.

I expected Mom to be shocked and disbelieving, but instead her voice went calm and soothing as she said, "It sounds like you have a friend in your imagination."

Imaginary friends were normal, I learned, and they could be boys or girls. What seemed to interest Mom wasn't that I was seeing through someone else's eyes each night, but that he was a *he.* "It makes sense for you to be curious about boys, Nina," she said.

And so my confession became a longer conversation where Mom explained to me that sometimes women love other women and prefer their company. She was like that, and that was fine, and because she was like that, and because her surviving family was mostly female, too, I had not known a lot of boys or men in my life so far. She told me it was perfectly normal for me to fantasize about having a dad, a grandfather, a big brother.

Everything was fine in this conversation, everything was okay, so I just kept nodding. But I'd seen how Mom's face looked when other parents made comments about our family: *Oh, I'm so sorry, Nina. I didn't realize it was just you and your mom.*

Their tone of voice said it wasn't fine at all. Something was missing from our family—some*one* was missing. If I kept talking to Mom about my night boy, she might think I'd imagined him to fill the gap.

And that might make her sad, so I decided to keep the boy to myself. Separate. Mine. I never mentioned him again.

I passed through a phase where I thought the boy could see me in his dreams, too. I tried to send him telepathic messages; I arranged my posters and stuffed animals in new ways to keep him interested. No message ever returned. Maybe the boy didn't see me like I saw him, or he went to sleep too late to find me awake. Maybe he wasn't real.

But he did some things I couldn't have imagined.

One night when I was nine, the boy took the top sheet off his bed and rolled it into a long, skinny rope. He knotted one end of the rope to his bedpost and looped the other around his neck. Then he braced his feet against the footboard and pushed till the sheet cinched around his windpipe and he saw nothing but blackness with starry flashes of white.

I couldn't breathe, only silently scream at him: *No. No! What are you doing?*

He didn't hear me. Just a second more, he was thinking. *Prove you have the stones to do it, just like he did. Just a second more.*

Then his feet were scrabbling against the footboard, and he breathed in huge gulps, tearing the noose from his throat.

Dammit, he thought. *It's way harder than I thought.*

In a flash of light, I saw his dad's smiling face. The apple tree. The sheet.

The whole thing mystified me until a few years later, when I watched a TV show about a convict who hangs himself with a bedsheet.

Could the boy's dad have hanged himself that way? From the apple tree? Or in jail, where a sheet is all you have?

Suddenly, I understood better why the boy's mind sometimes went cold, rotating around a nameless, faceless fear. *It's coming for you. It could happen any minute. The most you can decide is when.*

As he got older, the boy started taking his mom's car out on long night drives in the desert. The stars blazed overhead, the road was a straight ribbon, and he smoked American Spirits and played oldies stations.

One station played the Kinks and T. Rex, and another played jangly sixties pop songs in French, and that's how I came to love old music. At first I thought the boy loved it, too. Later I realized it was just neutral background for him, white noise that didn't interrupt his thoughts.

But, oh, he loved smoking. He loved making that tiny flame blossom, fostering it, controlling it, inhaling till his lungs burned, and tipping the ashes out the window. He loved feeling in control.

He loved watching the neon of truck stops and gas stations floating through the dark. He loved the black silhouettes of mesas on the horizon.

And he loved knowing anything could happen on a highway at night, and he'd be able to handle it. Anything.

That dark thought kept revolving in his mind: *You will die. The most you can decide is when.*

When he was eighteen and I had just turned twelve, the boy joined the army. For two years, my nights teemed with sweaty guys in camo striding down dusty streets. It was usually morning there, because of the time shift. These visions were blurrier and quieter than usual, as if distance muffled the transmission.

The boy didn't kill anyone over there as far as I know. He was jittery with fear and anger (at his own fear) most of the time, though, and a spot grew in the corner of his eye, a presence he couldn't blink away.

It was the sheet dangling from the apple tree, turning dappled sun to shadow. White as bone. His own death might not happen today, but it waited for him, perhaps just around the corner.

I will decide when.

Then, the spring I turned fourteen, the boy came home.

. . .

It was Saturday night, the night of the March day in eighth grade I came back from Warren's house, wishing I would never see him again. I remember everything about that night: the whole-wheat mac-and-cheese with broccoli, the book I stayed up reading, my mom taking a long bath. I remember hearing a text alert and not picking up the phone, because it would be Warren. I remember laying out my outfit for Monday a whole day ahead and thinking that I'd look *very* mature in this cardigan with pearl buttons, and no high school boy would dare mess with me. I remember lying in bed willing myself to fall asleep.

. . .

Without warning, I'm standing in shrubbery, looking in someone's window.

An old window with cracked panes. The shrubbery is cedars and junipers—northern trees like ours. *He's close to me.*

But the boy isn't thinking about where he is or where he's been. He's watching an old man alone inside the house, making instant coffee.

The boy goes around and knocks on the door. He tells the old man he's just gotten out of the service and is hitchhiking to the bus station in Oneonta, and might he have permission to sleep on the old man's property? He'll leave it just like he found it. He gives a name he makes up on the spot.

His voice is formal, a little stilted. He's trying not to drawl like the desert rats back home, because he's a soldier now. A warrior.

Someone who can tighten the sheet around his own throat—or anyone else's. Someone who watches in the night, unseen. Someone in control.

The old man says the boy shouldn't sleep outdoors on a crisp night like this, not after serving his country. The old man invites him in.

I see and hear their conversation in a watery montage, because the boy isn't paying close attention to it. Whenever his eyes go to the cast-iron skillet hanging above the stove, though, he focuses so sharply I nearly pass out.

It makes him dizzy, looking at that skillet. It's perfect.

Eliminate the target with his own weapons.

Usually the boy's thoughts are a humming murmur, but now they become sharp-edged objects crowding into my head and taking up space. *Not another soul for miles. Too good to pass up. They won't miss him for weeks. Months, maybe.*

No photos in this house. No grandchildren. A hermit.

Hasn't he lived long enough? Why not? I could take him like a thief in the night.

The boy's inner voice isn't snarky or snide. It's flat, assessing the terrain like he's a soldier on a mission.

Maybe he *is* a soldier on a super-secret mission. Maybe the old man is a terrorist in hiding, or an aged war criminal. It doesn't seem very likely, but—

No, something's wrong here. Nothing makes sense, and suddenly I feel like I don't know this boy, this young man who's practically part of me. *Why not?* That's not how you think about killing a terrorist.

For the first time ever, I try to open my eyes and stop the dream.

I imagine my own hand, my real hand, clutching a handful of the comforter. I imagine reaching out to grab my cat, Sugarman, who was purring against my hip when I dozed off.

I don't have a hand to reach. I'm a pair of eyes spinning in blackness, dizzier and dizzier, and when I return to the light, I'm standing over the old man and raising the skillet a second time.

Blood trickles down the old man's cheek. I missed the look on his face when he grasped what was happening.

That look is the worst part, I will learn. After the realization that *You're going to kill me*, after the surprise and terror, come the dull eyes. Once their eyes go dull, it's generally easier to finish the job.

It doesn't feel easy this first time. Inside, I'm screaming— *Help! Murder! Stop!*—even as I heft the skillet's weight and bring it down *three, four, five*. As I wait for the crack. You don't just hear it, you feel it.

Like an eggshell. Only duller, more resonant. A skull is much harder to shatter.

The spittle at the corner of the old man's mouth. The

blood-matted hair. The half-open eye rolled to white. If I had a body right now, if I were me, these sights would make my throat close with terror and empathy.

The boy feels nothing like that, just the noose tightening around his own throat. Then he feels something being released, and everything goes white like heaven and he's floating and soaring, looking down on the world, lighter than air.

The soaring and floating last only a few seconds, but it's worth it. Down he comes.

He's been sloppy with this first kill, sloppier than he'll ever be again. Lucky the blood is concentrated on the tattered rag rug. After the old man stops breathing, the boy sits with the body, watching the clock move on the wall.

A body without life is different. It's special. The boy respects it in a way he's never respected a living person. Though he's kept his work gloves on, he brings two fingers of his right hand to the old man's forehead and says, "This was your time. Go with God." He has no idea if he believes in God, but it sounds good. Ceremonial. Final.

He wraps the corpse in the rug and hoists it on his shoulder and stows it in his car trunk.

And with the trunk's *thunk*, I wake at last.

. . .

That Saturday night I crouched in bed with my eyes wide open, muscles locked, struggling to shake what I told myself was a nightmare.

He couldn't have done that, not really. I *knew* him.

The images wouldn't go away. My room melted into the old man's kitchen, his flowered wallpaper creeping up my walls. The world pulsed—*in, out; here, there; my room, his room*—till my stomach twisted and I curled up in a ball. Sugarman growled and sprang off the bed.

I knew the boy, but now the boy was the Thief, and I'd been inside the Thief, so close that he still seemed to be in the room with me. Through his eyes, I looked down at me on the bed and Sugarman on the rug: lumps of flesh. Future corpses. He'd hunt us like the cat hunted mice, pupils swallowing his eyes.

The Thief's muscles were my muscles, flexing as he lifted the skillet like Tupperware. He was so strong, and I'd always loved being inside him, feeling sinewy and invincible. Till now.

Something lay huddled on the rug just beyond Sugarman, a dark mound. *Rag rug.* Could the old man's lifeless body still be here? Hadn't I wrapped it in that rug, lifted it, gotten rid of it?

No, it was just a pile of clothes I'd tossed aside as I built Monday's outfit.

Inside me, the Thief laughed at my cardigan and pearl buttons. Rye Witter laughed. Everyone laughed. Clothes couldn't keep me safe.

Breathe. Breathe. Bow your head, be small, don't look. Maybe he's coming. Looming above you with the skillet ready to arc through the air. How many swings would it take to crack my skull?

He was so close to me. I'd *let* him be close.

Would I ever see his face? Would I see it soon?

I lurched into the bathroom and went fetal on the mat, my

shoulders shuddering, not sobbing but whining a little with each breath.

It's a dream; it's always been just a dream.

Suddenly, I had to check on my mom, and I crept to her door, taking underwater strides on my tiptoes. She was a hump in the covers, still breathing. No one had slipped into her room and stabbed or strangled her.

I didn't wake her. When she came downstairs at dawn, she found me on the living room couch, rigid as death and clutching the fireplace poker, watching the front door.

"Nina, my lord!"

I couldn't tell her. I could *never* tell her. My mom lived in a world where horrible crimes could be explained by horrible childhoods. Her boss, the attorney general, believed in rehabilitation, and she came home from the courthouse and told me stories where killers wrote earnest pleas for forgiveness, and victims' relatives were forgiving.

"I thought I heard somebody downstairs," I said.

She pulled the poker from my limp hands.

• • •

That's how it's been for the past three years.

A dream every night. More bodies: the homeless man, the hitchhiker, the campground lady.

When I went back to school after the Bad Weekend, I could see how eager Warren was to make things okay between us. I could barely remember why they weren't okay. Since Saturday afternoon, my world had split from his, and I was caught in a dark maelstrom that tore people like Warren apart.

For all his enthusiasm about guns and hunting and kick-ass video games, Warren was the kind of person who *always* sympathized with the hero over the villain. When a movie hero did something "gray"—like a detective roughing up a suspect—I could see him fidgeting. Heroes could not also be bullies. Lines were not supposed to be blurred.

For me, there were no lines anymore. And I worried I'd do or say something that crossed his.

One of the last conversations we had was about *Pee-wee's Big Adventure*. Warren asked if I remembered the scene where Pee-wee Herman saves the animals from a burning pet shop. He hates snakes, he's *not* going to save the snakes, but at the last minute he dashes in and comes out draped in snakes, his face twisted with comic repulsion.

"He doesn't want to care about them, but he *does*," Warren said. "That's why Pee-wee is the perfect movie hero. He does the right thing even by reptiles."

He was eyeballing me too hard, and I suddenly wondered if Warren was Pee-wee and I was the snake. Was this his weird way of saying he still liked me, even though I never sat with him anymore? Had he noticed when Maddy Penner called his sweater "gay," and I laughed?

Well, he wasn't going to make me feel worse than I already did.

"One of those snakes should've bitten Pee-wee," I said. "No, seriously. I think that would be a *lot* funnier."

Warren just looked at me.

"Because," I said, "whether you're nice to them or not, that's what snakes actually do."

. . .

For a while, I thought the solution was to embrace the bad. To keep the good at a distance. I let Warren drift away, and I went through what my mom calls a "dark teen period." It involved wearing black, reading every book I could find about war atrocities and serial killers, and sneering cynically at my mom's view of the world, which I characterized as "sickly-gooey sweetness and light."

Books taught me the Thief was no anomaly. All through human history, people had been robbing and raping and killing and doing unspeakable things to their enemies. Suddenly, it seemed like a miracle that nothing bad had ever happened to me. The only way to be safe from bad people, *really* safe, was to strike first.

I begged Mom for a home security system—*yes, right here in Vermont; it can happen anywhere.* And when I realized she wasn't going to give in, I struck first.

I didn't plan it. I just came home from school one day and found a kitchen window halfway open, practically inviting somebody to break in. So I did.

I'd learned a few quick-and-dirty tricks from *him.* I checked to make sure our neighbors weren't home. I put on latex gloves from Rite Aid, snuck around to the back, slashed the screen with kitchen shears, and climbed in.

So easy.

I longed to take our twenty-inch TV so we could replace it with a plasma, but it was too heavy. The set of silverware was an heirloom. So I settled for throwing pillows and newspapers on the floor and overturning a vase of flowers. Sugarman watched, flicking his ears, and strolled out through the mutilated screen.

I unhooked the cute little speaker dock Mom bought to play her music while she cooked. I started feeling queasy as I shoved it in my bag, and worse as I pedaled my bike to the "dump site"—a sandy spit in the river. As I tossed that maybe ninety-dollar gizmo into a swift current, my stomach lurched.

I was a criminal now. The speaker was crap, but it was Mom's. Even if somebody fished it out of the river, it would never work again.

And then I realized I was feeling the same way Pee-wee did about the snakes. The same way Warren did about me. The same way the Thief did *not* feel about his victims.

Whether I liked it or not, empathy weighed me down like a stone around my neck. Empathy for people and snakes and sometimes even for inanimate objects just because they were connected to people.

The police weren't impressed with our burglary. They called it a "crime of opportunity." My mom bought me the security system, but I didn't feel triumphant—just empty.

I hugged her as if we'd been through something terrible. And I stopped telling her she was too sweet and naïve. After all, who did we have but each other?

. . .

After the second year and the fourth murder, I started reading the signs. The Thief was an addict now, and when he was jonesing, I could tell. I brewed pots of coffee, stayed up all night. As long as I was awake from sundown to sunup, I'd never have to see him in action, never have to know what he'd done.

It was a brilliant solution, I thought, except soon I needed stronger stimulants than coffee and NoDoz. I tried faking ADHD, but my mom was skeptical. So I ended up buying Warren's wares.

Months of topsy-turvy sleeping ensued. I developed an eyelid twitch in the wee hours, which creeped me out, because I knew *he* had one, too. But by doing all my sleeping in two daylight blocks, from sunrise to seven and during the late afternoon, I could avoid *him*. Feeling awful half the time, deceiving my mom, and acquiring a nervous tic were small prices to pay.

Except there was another problem. I missed him.

. . .

Maybe that was why, one week last September, I let the pills run out and didn't call Warren.

For five nights in a row, I ignored my schedule. I slept and slept, and it felt so good—not just because I desperately needed the rest. It felt good to be back at *his* place, to check in on Eliana and Trixie. It felt good to see him working on his latest model, to watch his familiar big hands handling tools. It felt like coming home.

Until the fifth night, when he traveled. And his urge blindsided me.

. . .

The Thief thinks he knows about girls and women. He knows how to make them smile and move closer to him. This is how he thinks:

Sometimes there's a chick sitting alone in a bar, and she's not young anymore, not old either, and you just know she wants a guy to sit down next to her. There's something about how she leans to one side, like she wants to lay her head on your shoulder and just rest.

A woman like that, you can make her trust you.

One night in a honky-tonk in the Texas Panhandle, the Thief sees a woman like that.

He doesn't sit down next to her. Too obvious. He gets his single Coors and hunkers down at a table in the back. When he figures the woman is about tired of being lonely in this redneck hot spot, he slips outside and smokes, leaning against his Sequoia with the darkly tinted back windows.

When the woman comes out, headed to her car, he doesn't go to her. He plays a long game.

He leans on his hood, trying to look bored and kinda cocky, and takes deep drags on his cigarette, burning his lungs and liking the pain.

When she puts her key in the lock, he asks, not moving, "Hey, miss. Can you tell me the best route from here to Amarillo?"

"You're way off track," the woman says, no give in her voice.

"I was out visiting the family of a buddy of mine, ma'am. Friend from the service, died in an IED attack, God rest his soul. His mom and gramma, they're all alone, so I wanted to check on 'em."

The angles of her face soften, and she leaves her car and comes closer to tell him about roads, turn-offs, landmarks.

Her black hair is blowsy and overdone, and she has smoker's wrinkles but good features. He especially likes her royal-blue tank top; it's loose—classier that way—and made of something shiny he wants to touch. She reminds him of his mom, and he feels a pang of tenderness for her.

(Sociopaths do feel. That's something I've learned. And that it doesn't matter.)

He's still confused, he says. Takes out his map, spreads it on the hood. All the time watching in the corner of his eye for someone else coming out of the bar; that would be an automatic abort.

She asks for a light, and he gives it to her. They bend over the map together, him shining a flashlight on it, and he works her around closer to the driver's side with her back to the woods. Feels her teased hair graze his arm.

If anybody comes out, he'll abort. If anybody comes out, this wasn't meant to be.

The Thief has power, but he doesn't pretend to have absolute power. He listens to the signals the universe gives him.

He swaps the flashlight for the Beretta 85F so quickly she barely has a chance to gasp. Then he's pressing it against the silky top, whispering that he won't hurt her, she just has to get in the car. "Open the door. It ain't locked. Nice 'n' easy. Don't cry. Wouldn't hurt a nice lady like you. Just need some . . ."

He mumbles the last word (*"money"? "comfort"?*). It doesn't matter because she's inside and he's pushing himself in after.

He doesn't make her suffer. He finishes it right there in the parking lot on that muggy night, quick and clean as he can make it, cinching the cord around her neck till the pencil inside the loop breaks. A method he's been wanting to try, just out of curiosity, but he doesn't think he'd do it again.

Unnecessarily brutal. His eyelid twitches while he holds the cord taut, like his body's rebelling, but he's used to it.

Bulging eyes, grasping hands, a broken nail. The dangerous scratches she leaves on his bare arms. The deep rattle in the throat as she fights for air. The surge of adrenaline as he realizes someone could rap on the car window *right now*.

Then, when it's over, the usual soaring, floating sensation. The sweet fever of accomplishment. He's never been so daring before. He took her fast, clean, practically out in the open. He'll give himself fourteen points out of twenty for this, and that's conservative. He's a perfectionist, according to his former CO.

He reaches into the back for the ratty sleeping bag he keeps there, along with plastic sheeting, duct tape, and his modeling and carpentry tools. He tosses it over her still form (*sacred form*, he thinks) and turns the key and pulls out of the lot. It's that easy.

He scoped out his dump site well in advance, last time he passed through the Panhandle, though he didn't know who he'd put there. Now he does, and that feels good, a key fitting in a lock.

His whole life he's been fascinated by out-of-the-way

places, abandoned spots off the main roads, choked with scrub pines and brush, with nobody but coyotes to see how the full moon hits the outcroppings. Places like his desert cabin back home.

As he follows the winding map of country roads in his head, bringing this empty shell to its final resting place, he thinks of her silky tank top. Imagines it under his hand, soothing and tickling his work-roughened skin, promising the kind of comfort Eliana gives him.

He thrusts thoughts of his girlfriend away.

Does he dare touch the silk now? Nah, it's wrong. It's disrespectful, and he respects death more than anybody.

The silk is soft, though. Just like her still-soft skin.

. . .

On TV, people puke their guts out when they discover a murder scene. That's how you know they care.

Maybe my stomach is cast iron, or I'm missing a gene. I woke that night hugging myself and gasping for breath, but I didn't puke. Something sank to my bowels like a stone, paralyzing my limbs and freezing my tears before they fell. I knelt before the toilet bowl, imagining how it would feel to retch and hurl.

Trying, trying, trying to get it out. But all I'd seen and known was stuck inside me, part of me now. Nothing budged. My stomach didn't even churn.

. . .

The next day, I went straight to Warren and re-upped. I returned to my precious schedule of sleep and pills. But I couldn't stop myself from checking the Amarillo papers on a school computer.

Six days later, there she was.

A picture from her glory days, when she was a Miss Texas contender with a greasy, blinding smile and ginormous teased hair, but unmistakably her.

Kara Ann Messinger of Hereford, 35, mother of two, has not been seen since she left Dubie's Doghouse on Route 519 on September 12 at approximately 12:30 A.M. The state police welcome tips from anyone with leads regarding her whereabouts.

This was a real woman, and I'd had my hands around her throat. Cinched the cord. Killed her.

No, not me. I was an innocent bystander. Or a not-so-innocent witness, because what good is a witness who can't lead the cops to the killer or at least a body?

Three days passed, and Kara Ann Messinger remained unfound. I tried to remember the roads the Thief had taken from the bar to the dump site, but all I could visualize were yellow lines in headlights, blurred by his excitement and my terror. Finally, using the Sunoco pay phone, I called the state troopers' tip line and left a message saying I'd been in the Dubie's Doghouse parking lot that night, and I'd seen a woman who looked like Kara Ann Messinger enter a black Sequoia with New Mexico plates. A young man was with her.

That was as far as I dared go, and I didn't leave a number. What if they found and questioned the Thief? What if he knew somehow who I was, what I'd done?

Nothing happened. The Thief's life went on as usual. The story faded from the news.

Of the five victims before the Gustafssons, Kara Ann Messinger was the only one whose image I saw outside my sleep. Maybe she was the only one ever reported missing. The old man in Oneonta wasn't, and the other murders happened in places I can't identify, just dark houses or bars or gas stations. Lighted islands in the night. The Thief is clever at hiding corpses, each in a different desolate place. Only one in his home state. No "hunting grounds" for him. No media limelight.

Now, though, I knew he was real.

. . .

After I saw Kara Ann Messinger, I made a special lunch date with Suzy Wolfsheim, my mom's friend—and mine—the assistant prosecutor for Washington County. We sat in a vegan café drinking dairy-free lattes with dandelion extract, and I told Suzy about the "screenplay" I was writing.

My story, I said, was about a girl who sees murders in her dreams, murders that happen in real life. Should she go to the authorities?

"Like *Medium*," Suzy said. "I loved that show!"

"I'm wondering, though. What would happen? I mean, assuming she didn't have a track record as a psychic."

Suzy practically choked on her dandelion faux latte. "Most people who claim to have a track record as a psychic...don't. Without corroborating physical evidence," she went on, "you're just another wing-nut. Even *with* physical evidence in a single case, most of the cops and state's attorneys I know are, shall we say, very cynical about 'psychic visions.'"

She explained to me point by point what the cops would say to my heroine, and then what the state's attorney's office would say. By the end of our lunch, I knew how many nuisance calls law enforcement agencies take from people who claim to be psychic or to have special insight into a crime. I knew how they treat those calls. I knew that, without hard evidence, I would be dismissed quicker than you can say *hypnagogic hallucinations*—the science-y term for things you see when you're half-asleep.

And even if I could lead the Texas state troopers down the country roads to Kara Ann Messinger's last resting place, I knew their first question would be: *How were you involved in this crime?*

. . .

So I did the only thing I could. I packed up those pills I'd bought, hid them under a bunch of hideous scarves in my closet, and started sleeping again.

This time, I vowed, would be different. I would not be a passive witness. The Thief was my enemy, and I needed intel, evidence, ammunition to put him away. I could only track him by watching him at night, by letting him in. I'd get inside him and hunt my prey like he was hunting his.

Being in his head is my secret weapon. I know how cautious he is, how little it takes to make him abort a "mission." If we ever met, I'd never overpower him physically, but I just might have the advantage of surprise.

I started logging the Thief's movements, plotting his course on the U.S. map above my bed. I got the idea from the giant map he keeps on the wall of his workshop. He's too careful to mark his kills there, of course, but he likes to trace the routes with his finger.

After a few weeks, I got lucky and caught him driving to his favorite spot in the desert, the abandoned mine north of Albuquerque. I mapped the whole thing and drew rough pictures of the site, including the entrance to the cave where I think he buried the homeless man.

Now, if only I could *go* there, maybe I'd find something.

But that was the same week my mom went looking in my room for a scarf to wear to an awards dinner, and promptly discovered my hideous-scarf stash and the pill stash within. And my life got more complicated.

"I stopped taking them. I don't *need* them anymore," I told everybody—Mom, the therapist, the guidance counselor. The first was true; the second, not entirely. Once I started going to the support group, I realized I actually *could* use support, though I got more from Kirby than from the twelve steps.

And I couldn't ever relapse. I had to sleep. Next time he dumped a body, I told myself, I'd memorize the turns in the road. I'd call the troopers and lead them straight to the site.

Instead, I got Ruth and Gary Gustafsson's address. My one chance to *prevent* a murder, and I blew it.

Doubts? I've been through them all. What if the lady I saw die in Texas wasn't actually Kara Ann Messinger? What if my mind tacked her real face to a dream? What if there is no Thief?

Crazy? I wish. That possibility rocks me like a boat on a

tranquil lake, swaddles me like a comforter. *Please, let me be crazy. Let it all end and start with me.*

Yes, maybe there is no Thief, just a twisted, wayward fantasy in a sick brain. Neurons misfiring, connections out of whack. If only I had proof positive, I'd take meds, do electroshock therapy. Anything to stop this ache, this helplessness: *You have to do something. You can't stand by and watch.*

But now the Gustafssons are gone. I knew it before it happened. He isn't going to stop.

I have just one lead: that possible burial site in the desert. And anyone who stops *me* from going after him is my enemy.

WARREN

16

When I drive up to Nina's house on Tuesday, she's sitting on the porch in the tepid spring sun reading *In Cold Blood*. It's on our AP English schedule for the end of the semester, so maybe she's getting a head start.

It's not like she doesn't already know how it feels inside a killer's head. Or think she does. The whole time she was telling me the story of her life with the Thief, she wouldn't look at me. I just kept nodding and holding her hand. No judgment, no questions—not yet.

I lay awake for hours last night, everything she'd told me swirling in my brain. There were so many possible explanations: hallucinations, repressed memories of childhood trauma, plain old guilt and complicity. Nothing was resolved when I drifted off. But when the birds nesting in the gable woke me, I had just one thought: *I have to help her.*

So I get right to it, my words coming out in a rush. "You want to go find Dylan Shadwell. In Albuquerque. And do what?"

Nina sways in the porch swing, making the ropes creak. The wind chases fluffy clouds. "You don't have to pretend you believe me."

"I'm not pretending." I try to find the right word, one that won't be a lie. "I'm . . . giving you the benefit of the doubt. I'm suspending disbelief, because I want to know what happened to the Gustafssons, too. So will you tell me your plan, or not?"

After a long moment, she says, "I'm not going to knock on his door and ask where he buried them. I know how dangerous he is. Better than you ever will."

So she's not going to thrust a shotgun in a stranger's face. Good. Her tone still makes something tingle on the back of my neck, and I want to swat it like a blackfly.

"What *are* you going to do? Show up and try to sell him Girl Scout cookies?"

Nina grabs her backpack. Out comes a notebook. "I've been weighing different plans. Will you promise not to have me committed if I tell you?"

"If I was gonna do that, you'd already be in a straitjacket."

That almost gets me a smile. More importantly, she opens the notebook and starts talking.

Plan One: We go to the Schenectady PD, both of us, and lie. We say we happened to drive past the lot where the

Gustafssons' car was found at the very instant Dylan Shadwell stumbled out of it, bleeding and carrying a suspicious package. We trailed him to his car and got the plate number.

I shake my head. "I won't commit perjury." *Or accuse someone I don't even know.* "It would make more sense to go back there and search wherever you think he hid the bodies."

"There are about ten square miles where they could be. Even if we could dig them up, there might be no forensic traces of him, so it wouldn't do any good."

Finding the Gustafssons' remains would do their relatives some good, I almost say. But she's not thinking about the victims anymore, just the killer. "Why don't you just call in an anonymous tip and make them search his place?"

"I tried that once before, remember? With the Texas murder. He's got a clean record, and he's careful. He always dumps his tools somewhere different from the—you know."

"The remains?"

She nods. "Anyway, who's going to believe he drove out of his way just to kill those people? *You* don't, even."

Nina calls Plan Two "the voice of God." "It's dumbass. But I wrote it down anyway."

"Tell me this dumbass plan." When we're just tossing around ideas, being with her is *almost* like it used to be.

She'll send untraceable letters to Dylan Shadwell in which she describes his career of terror with details only he could know. She'll warn him to stop.

Nervous, pent-up laughter bursts out of me. "Are you going to say you're his guardian angel?"

"It's not as stupid as you think. He believes he's sort of . . .

on a mission. Not from God, but from the universe or fate. He brings people death, and they never see it coming."

I can't help saying the first thing that comes into my head. "If you think you can scare him into not impersonating the Grim Reaper, you know nothing about criminals, Nina, let alone psychopaths."

"What do *you* know about them?"

Plenty—about garden-variety criminals, anyway. When I was little, I used to watch my brother Gray steal from the collection plate, my mom's purse, pretty much any source of loose cash. After nights lying awake imagining my brother in prison orange, I wrote him a letter pretending to be an angel who was sad to witness his life of crime.

My three brothers spent the next nine years calling me "our little angel" and making limp-wristed harping motions. After I agreed to start selling their pharma overflow, they elevated their mockery to Oscar-winning levels, swooning sarcastically at my virtuousness. I was terrified my mom would grasp their meaning and realize I wasn't the Good Kid after all.

"Criminals," I tell Nina, "always think they're right and the world is wrong. You can't guilt them out of crime. That's true of a two-bit thief—or a drug dealer like yours truly—and I'm guessing it's true of a serial killer."

Her face is red. "I don't think of you as a criminal. Anyway, how do you . . . change them, then?"

Change a criminal? With me, shame and the fear of getting caught kicked in. With small-timers like my brothers, repeated applications of the stick (jail) and the carrot (honest paycheck) seem to work.

But the person who stalked and killed the Gustafssons, if there is such a person? "Some people can't be changed," I say.

Nina nods, but not vigorously. Like she's wishing there was another solution to all the sickos out there, a humane trap-and-release system.

I don't believe there is, so I jump to the next plan.

Plan Three is another digging-up-evidence scheme. Nina is pretty sure this guy buried at least one body in New Mexico, way out in the desert, and she thinks she can find it.

"It's underground," she says, "a kind of cave—an abandoned mine. Linking the remains to him would be the problem, but this other killing happened back when he was sloppier. So there's a chance."

I'm already reading over her shoulder, checking out Plan Four. Bait a trap. Become a potential victim.

"No way," I say.

"You're right. It would never work. He doesn't let victims just come to him, not anymore—he chooses them. It's important to him."

"That's not the point." I want to say that if this guy *is* a psycho, she shouldn't get within twenty feet of him. But that might imply that I no longer have disbelief to suspend.

Besides, my skeptical mind says that if she searches that cave in the desert and finds nada, maybe she'll start realizing she can't trust her visions. It's the only option that seems both harmless and potentially effective.

"Plan Three wins," I say. "Hands down. You think so, too, right? That's why you're planning this trip to Albuquerque. To find that cave."

"Exactly." She nods eagerly. "The B-and-B I wrote to—I still can't believe you hacked my e-mail, by the way; that was an unbelievably shitty thing to do—"

"I know." I spread my hands in surrender. "But you wouldn't have told me anything otherwise."

"You practically blackmailed me—don't brag about it. But I guess it felt good to tell somebody. So, anyway, the B-and-B is in this tiny town called Algodones. Close to the cave."

I nod, feeling a blush creep over my face. *It felt good to tell somebody.* I was right—Nina needs someone on her side. Maybe even needs *me.* "So you can just forget about this other plan, right?"

And I point to the last item on her list:

Plan Five: Kill him.

17

What kind of girl invents a psychopath? And then makes plans that range from guilting him into walking the straight and narrow to gunning him down like the Man with No Name?

This girl, who's training her eyes on me—bronze irises, long lashes, the calligraphy strokes of her black brows. This girl with her delicate neck, her fragile wrists. She's not tiny, but I could bring her down, and I'm well aware of my physical limitations.

Nina couldn't have abducted the Gustafssons by herself. Or could she? Sometimes unimposing people perform amazing feats—lift overturned cars, win marathons, kill their whole families with axes.

Dylan Shadwell could have done it, easy. His Facebook pic shows him standing on a mountain summit in profile, tall and wiry-strong.

But all I really know about Dylan Shadwell is that he happened to be in Schenectady that morning.

"Plan Five is a last resort, yeah," Nina is saying. "But, see, I've been...watching him since it happened."

I try not to let the doubt show on my face. *Disbelief suspended.*

"He's been watching the same news videos as you. He's never had this much media attention. It gets him keyed up, knowing he's the mystery man they all want, and then he can't settle down. I think he's already jonesing for the next kill. And I can't just let it happen. If we'd been an hour earlier to the Gustafssons' house..."

If everything she told me is true, and we'd been an hour earlier, we might be dead, too. But I don't say that, just let her keep talking:

"A couple days ago, you were trying to make me feel like a piece of crap because I didn't go to the police. Well, it worked."

That gives me a stab of guilt. "I just needed you to start talking to me."

"I did. I am." Her gaze says, *Now I've told you, will you try to stop me?*

"So you're going to drive to Albuquerque and try Plan Three. And if it doesn't work, Plan Five is on the table. Nuclear option."

Nina looks straight at me, no blinking. "Yes."

Is that why she asked me for a gun? I try not to show I'm rattled. "And you're not worried about being arrested for the murder of a guy because you had psychic visions about him?"

"It's a *last resort.*"

I swallow hard. *Don't pretend you believe her, but don't flip out and tell her she's nuts. That won't help, and you're here to help.* "Your mom's never going to let you take a huge road trip for no reason. Alone."

Nina's face lights up like she's back on solid ground—proud to tell me about her plans. "There is a reason. It's a trip to find out where I came from."

I just stare at her.

"My birth mom—I didn't lie to you about being adopted. She lives in Arizona, close to the New Mexico border. We've been e-mailing. I *did* lie when I said my mom didn't want me to see her. She's cool with it, so I'll arrange to visit Becca for five days—that's her name, Becca Cantillo. My mom will think I'm staying for a week. The other two days, I'll go to Algodones and check out the desert site."

She *has* planned this out. "That birth mom makes a pretty convenient excuse, huh?" I say.

Nina doesn't answer, her eyes following a car as it rambles down the quiet street.

A slowing car—the Legacy I drove to Schenectady. "Shit, your mom?" I ask as it crunches into the driveway.

"Why 'shit'? My mom likes you."

"Oh-kay." I can't say that seeing her mom just reminds me of my earlier plan to call her up and spill everything about

Nina. I kept quiet, and now I have to face Ms. Barrows right after hearing her daughter discuss killing a stranger in cold blood.

I get up and make a show of brushing myself off to leave. "I have homework."

But before I can escape, Ms. Barrows opens the front door from inside, brandishing a giant pizza box and shouting, "I got us American Flatbread! Warren! I feel like it's been years since you came around."

"It has."

We shake hands, Ms. Barrows looking me in the eye like a politician. She works at the statehouse, so she's well aware of my dad and brothers, the town gadfly and the county pariahs, but she's never seemed to hold them against me. "Why don't you come in? We've got plenty to go around."

What the hell. Yes, it's too late for me to tell Nina's mom everything. But if I'm going to stop Nina from going to Albuquerque to kill someone, this woman is my best ally.

"Sounds awesome," I say. And become the perfect guest.

I help set the table and pour the ice water and portion out the pizza—excuse me, the *flatbread*. Luckily, I'm hungry enough to act enthused about fancy pizza with smelly cheese and roasted parsnips.

As we munch on the dense crust, the long blue dusk falls outside, and Nina's mom turns on the lights. Their house feels quiet and neat, like a church or a funeral home, so I keep up my nervous jabbering, filling the silence, while Nina stares at her plate.

Nina's mom tells me to call her Kathleen instead of Ms. Barrows and asks how my dad's campaigning for the Libertarian gubernatorial candidate is going. Nina looks bemused, then bored—she hates politics. But I don't shut up.

It's my secret weapon: I'm good at talking to people's moms. My dad and brothers rarely make it to the dinner table, so I've carved out my niche as the one who compliments Mom's meat loaf and listens to her complain about the rude lady who runs the general store. And the truth is, I'd miss those dinners if I left home.

My mom might miss them even more—which is why it's an *if* for me, not a *when*.

Nina just shakes her head as her mom and I debate the future of renewables. I've done my research, and Kathleen seems impressed.

After about twenty minutes of enviro-geeking, with Nina looking the whole time like she wants to stick a fork in her gut, I manage to steer the conversation to the American Southwest.

"How long till it's basically an apocalyptic wasteland?" I say. "With the whole water shortage issue..."

"Tell me about it," Kathleen interrupts. "I lived near Phoenix for twelve years."

"I've always wanted to see the desert. It looks amazing on film."

"Everybody should see it at least once."

Before I can casually bring up the subject of Nina's road-trip plan, Nina says, to my surprise, "Warren's, like, a real filmmaker now. He made an amazing video for the Lonesome Chuckettes."

The Lonesome Chuckettes are a local girl band—Woodchuckettes, get it?—who sing sad country songs. I met one of them at the cable-access station where I get my cameras and mics, and she talked me into forty hours of free labor. Now she's pestering me for a second video.

"I'm just messing around," I say, shaking my head. "I have to borrow most of my gear. Can't even shoot DSLR yet."

"No, it's really good. He's got almost four thousand hits on YouTube."

Maybe she's trying to change the subject from Arizona, but I can't help blushing. I never told Nina about the Chuckettes video. "That's not really a lot," I point out. "I'm planning another vid for them that'll be way better."

And then I have an idea.

"A ton of stuff gets filmed in New Mexico," I say. "They've got tax incentives. I hear the film program at their state university is awesome."

Kathleen beams at me—maybe she's relieved to know I'm college bound. "You should apply there! You are applying to film schools, aren't you?"

"Uh... of course." It's no time to bring up my leaving-home dilemma, so I turn to Nina. "If you go out to Albuquerque on your road trip, maybe you could snap pics of the campus for me. You know, this summer."

Kathleen swings to face her daughter, her mouth hardening. "What road trip this summer?"

Nina looks like she just found a fingernail in her flatbread. She may never talk to me again. "It's in the early stages. I was going to work out the details before I told you."

"You told *me* you were going to explore Route Sixty-Six," I say innocently. "Tucumcari. Amarillo. Albuquerque. All the way to Arizona. For a week, right?"

Kathleen's eyes haven't left her daughter. "Nina, is this about...Ms. Cantillo?"

Nina wedges her fork into a crack between the table leaves. "I told you I was e-mailing her."

"Planning a visit is different than e-mailing."

"You *told* me," Nina says, "you'd be fine with me getting to know her."

Emotions flit over Kathleen's face, and I suddenly wish I hadn't kicked this hornet's nest.

"We could fly into Phoenix together," she says, "but I can't take time off this summer. Maybe a weekend in October. I'd love to visit my friends out there."

Nina's mouth is set. "I don't want to just fly there, meet her, and come back. I want to take a road trip. I want the *experience*. I was going to tell you."

Kathleen relaxes a little, like she realizes Nina isn't abandoning her. "Whose car were you planning to take?"

If I told my mom I was taking off for Arizona, she'd bawl me out for five minutes straight. Then cry and tell me she didn't mean to be harsh, the world is just so *dangerous*. And I would promise to stay in town forever.

Kathleen, by contrast, is a model of mellow. When Nina says, "I was going to buy a secondhand Toyota with my savings from working in the library," her mother actually nods.

"I don't want you taking on consumer debt. But tell me more."

Nina's crazy idea is fast becoming a real plan. Why'd I open my mouth?

Nina launches into a spiel about the Grand Canyon and the Petrified Forest and other stuff she supposedly yearns to see. "I don't want to stay with . . . Ms. Cantillo the whole time," she says. "I mean, I'd feel more comfortable if I didn't have to be her guest. I want to do campgrounds and motels."

Roadside motels—another suggestion that would make my mom flip. If I were a girl, she'd probably keep me chained to her waist till I was thirty.

Kathleen doesn't bat an eye. "I know places along the way," she says. "Family-run, good people. I could ask the owners to keep an eye on you. You'd have to check in every day with me. Send me pics. Blog it all so I can imagine what you're doing."

Nina nods, and I wonder how she plans to pretend she's in Arizona when she's really in Albuquerque, digging up bones.

A lonesome stretch of red desert. Sun slanting across the mouth of an abandoned mine shaft. I shake off the images— *Don't you start believing, too.*

There are no bones to dig up. But maybe Nina has to see that to believe it.

"I went out west the summer I was seventeen," Kathleen is saying dreamily. "I drove to San Francisco by myself. One night I was so tired, I parked on the shoulder and slept in the desert."

"Your folks didn't mind?" I hear an edge in my voice.

Nina's mom shakes her head. "They barely noticed I was gone. I had the time of my life in SF. Saw my first live show, kissed my first girl."

"Mom, please. I've heard this story a million times."

"I know. Get your laptop. Let's plot an itinerary, just for fun."

The two of them are A-OK again, best of friends.

"You're going to need to learn to drive on the freeway," I point out, remembering how I drove Nina six hours to and from Schenectady like her chauffeur and bodyguard in one.

"You are a nervous driver, Nina," Kathleen says, brows creasing. "And it's quite a slog."

Then she turns to me, her face brightening like she's had a brainstorm, and says something I could never have guessed she'd say in a million years, wouldn't have fantasized about even in my sappiest moments.

"Hey, Warren! You want to visit UNM, and it's right on the way. What if you two went together?"

I wait for Nina to cross her arms or pop her eyes or push her chair out in frustration. Nothing happens.

I look right at her, and she looks back with a question in her eyes. I'm not sure, but I think it's *Why not?*

18

I don't make any decisions that night—too many new sensations have me feeling brittle and shell-shocked. I just mutter something noncommittal about how I'll run the idea past my folks, while Nina watches me warily.

I can guess what her next thought was after *Why not. If you think you're going along so you can tattle to my mom when I take a desert detour, think again.*

I need to convince her I'll keep her secrets. Because I will, won't I?

At home, I check on WRGB in Schenectady. Nothing about the Gustafssons. Rapes and domestic murders and suspected mob killings are happening all over upstate New York, but no one seems to remember the older couple that disappeared that weekend.

Sometimes I see the Gustafssons' photo in my head as I drift off to sleep, or their neat little house with the stone walkway and the wheelbarrow in the yard. *Don't forget us. Don't let us vanish.*

But who took them? So far, I've heard just one alternative theory—anti-slaughterhouse protestors did it—and that came from an anonymous commenter with obvious whacko credentials. Nina knew they were going to disappear before it happened, and she tried to help them. That much I believe.

As for the rest, I decide, I'm going to maintain an attitude of benign neutrality. Like Switzerland. I won't say I do think Dylan Shadwell is a killer, or that I don't.

But I won't let her do anything crazy. If I come along to New Mexico, maybe I can distract her. Be the voice of reason. Encourage her to look for bones in that cave and cushion her fall back to reality when she doesn't find any.

I open a new window and check out the University of New Mexico's film program. It's not one of the top twenty-five in the nation, but it looks solid, with an emphasis on production.

A professor named Ethan Sandoval is teaching a summer production course with a location shoot. I shoot him an e-mail with a link to my Chuckettes video. He probably won't bother to answer a high school kid bugging him from thousands of miles away, but it's worth a shot.

Not that I'm really going to apply to college in New Mexico—my mom would flip. This is just an excuse for the road trip with Nina. But if I do some crewing out there, while she visits her birth mom in Arizona, maybe I can spin it as an internship when I apply to NYU.

After all, New York is only five hours away.

I go to sleep seeing the red-washed desert in my head like I'm viewing it through a monitor. I adjust my light levels, frame carefully, capture the whole landscape—except for Nina, who's somewhere in the corner of my frame, always half out of sight.

I know she's looking for that cave.

. . .

I arrange a meeting at the town's crunchiest coffee shop with Violet Sadler, the youngest Lonesome Chuckette, to talk about making a video for their "killer" new cut.

"Guess what?" Violet says when we meet up. "We ran a campaign, and we can pay you a whole two hundred dollars this time."

"Is it another song about how a cowboy left a girl alone in a desert dive bar to smoke a million Marlboros?" I ask, pretending we don't both know that figure is insulting.

She pats my arm, her mammoth earrings tinkling. "You know it is, kiddo. Only kinda song I write."

I duck my head to hide my blush. "If you wait a few months, I can get you fresh B-roll of the desert. For atmosphere."

"No kidding?"

It must be synergy, because that night I get an e-mail from Ethan Sandoval, the UNM professor. It's short: *If you shot and cut this by yourself, nice job. We can always use extra PAs on location, assuming they're willing to WORK. Please send your official school transcript and two letters of rec to our departmental admin,*

137

along with a parental letter if you're under 18, and tell her if you want temp housing in the dorms. Best, ES.

This thing, this trip, is becoming real.

. . .

When Nina invites me over for dinner a few days later, she has a surprise for me. Her mom has bought herself a shiny new Prius and dumped the Legacy on Nina as a belated birthday gift.

"Wish I got presents like that," I say. It's an older car, but with only fifty K on the odometer.

Nina ducks her head. "I think she just wants me to be safe. On the trip. *Us* to be safe—if you're going."

I manage not to break out in a huge grin. "I'll talk to my mom tonight."

When Kathleen comes home from the statehouse, she unpacks Indian takeout and solemnly promises me there's dessert.

I glance at Nina, who says, "I told her about your sugar fixation."

She smirks like she's ragging on me, but I'm glowing inside. Nina told her mom something about me. I'm part of her life.

I tell myself I'm only happy because this bodes well for the success of Operation Us on the Road. And now I have the possibility of experience on a real, live film shoot, even if I'm just getting takeout and driving props from place to place.

During dinner, I tell Nina and Kathleen about my possible crewing gig at UNM and the B-roll I'll shoot in the desert for the Chuckettes.

"We could do some shooting up north past Bernalillo, maybe." My eyes meet Nina's, and I catch a flash of gratitude from her. We both know that's where she expects to find the abandoned mine.

So, we can kill two birds with one stone. Me exploring the desert with my camera, her combing it for a corpse. I just hope she'll be satisfied with whatever she finds—or doesn't.

We plan it out. She'll be in Arizona for the first four days, staying at a B-and-B and visiting her birth mom, while I camp out in the UNM dorms back in Albuquerque. After several hours e-mailing back and forth with various harried admins, I've figured out how to get the summer-school lodging rate prorated.

Then Nina will drive back to Albuquerque, and we'll spend our last three days in the comfort of a nice, clean motel, checking out tourist attractions like the Meteorite Museum, Los Alamos, Chaco Canyon, and all the shooting locations of *Breaking Bad*.

Have I memorized the New Mexico tourism site? Indeedy. "I'm obsessed with the Manhattan Project," I insist.

Kathleen's face lights up. "You're the first kid I've ever heard say *that*."

I'm not faking my enthusiasm. The more I read about New Mexico and the more images I see online of crumbling pink hills and blazing blue skies, the more I want to go. I want to know about the ancient Anasazi people who lived in Chaco Canyon. I want to see the sun-burnt pueblos to the west of Albuquerque, and the town of Tucumcari to the east, with its dinosaur statues and twinkling neon. I want to stand on the desert floor and look at the night sky. To me, raised in this gray, flood-prone town, the place might as well be Mars.

I want to get *out*, even just for a week.

I can see my excitement reflected on Nina's and Kathleen's faces. They, too, are imagining how it would feel to stand on a plain and gaze up at thousands of stars.

Maybe, if I can get Nina involved enough in my obsessions, she'll forget hers. Maybe meeting her birth mom in her birth state will click some loose piece into place for her, and her nightmares will end. Maybe the cops will catch the Gustafssons' killer. Maybe, after that cave turns out to hold nothing but sand, we'll edge close to each other in its warm darkness and she'll kiss me.

That sounds like the last scene of a cheesy indie flick. I can't dwell on any of those possibilities, can't let them sprout into spindly hopes. But—maybe.

. . .

I spend hours with Nina surrounded by road maps, laptops, and glossy brochures. Prof. Sandoval connects me with my taskmaster-to-be, an intense student producer named Sasha Charney, who asks me to promise I'm "not one of those slacker interns who spend the whole shoot smoking behind the van." I promise I'm a good worker bee. I set up our road trip blog. I help choose a motel. I buy a snake-bite kit.

And I tell my mom.

She takes it better than I expected. In fact, she's 100 percent behind the whole UNM part, especially when I tell her the dorms have resident advisors to nip keggers in the bud. "You *should* meet kids your age with common interests," she says. "Sometimes I feel like you're so alone here."

But when I tell her about the Nina factor, she says, "I thought that girl stopped being nice to you."

"That was just middle school." It's just like Mom to remember my lowest points as well as I do. "We've been hanging out."

"Hanging out or...?"

"It's not like that. We're just friends." And I smile like I'm fine with that, but I know she knows I'm not.

We meet downtown for a dinner of crappy Vermont Mexican—Nina, Kathleen, my parents, and I—and it's one of the most awkward meals of my life. Kathleen does all the talking. She congratulates my parents on having a well-read, articulate, thoughtful, non-date-rapist son, while my dad's eyes glaze over and my mom goes beet red (though I can tell she's proud).

As soon as he can, my dad excuses himself and goes to talk politics at the bar, where all his friends and cronies hang out. My mom and I exchange glances.

I know my dad isn't treating Kathleen Barrows like she has a contagious disease because she's gay. It's because she's rich and smooth and confident, all the things that make him feel small. Who's *she* to judge his kid?

It's still painful to watch him. When the check comes, he practically leaps on it.

My mom has stayed quiet through the meal; she's shy in public. But I've seen her sizing up Nina and Kathleen, missing nothing.

When we get home, she says, "You still like that girl more than she likes you."

My whole face burns, and I want to yell at her, "Who put you in charge of making sure I don't get hurt?"

But it's not her fault she wants to shield me from harm like an anxious hen on an especially thin-shelled egg.

"I want to go on this trip," I say. "I want to go with Nina, yeah, but it's not *about* her. We won't even be together for most of it."

Like always, Mom sees right through me, probably because she's the only one who bothers to look. She touches my face before I can flinch. "I want you to be careful with that girl."

"Not an issue."

Not in the way she means, anyway. I don't tell Mom about the deer rifle and the ancient .22LR I plan to stow in a box in the Legacy's trunk—one a present from my dad, the other my own purchase. Insurance against anyone hurting either of us, *just in case.*

My mom's eyes go softer. "There was something about the way you looked at her. It reminded me of how I used to hang on every word Ed said to me."

My dad—my mom married him at eighteen, after he waltzed in like a hero and promised to rescue her from her strict family. He played Prince Charming for the first few years, anyway.

My throat goes tight as I say, "Different thing. Trust me. When it comes to Nina, I've adopted a policy of benign neutrality."

It feels good to say it out loud, even if I can't say everything:

that I'll do my best to protect Nina from her obsession, her nightmares, but I won't be pulled in.

"I don't know," Mom says. I can feel her relenting, giving in to the plan. "Nina seems like a nice girl. Smart. Polite. Only, there's something cold in her eyes."

19

We have permission, and soon we have a solid itinerary. Reservations at B-and-Bs, dorms, non-seedy motels. A start date: June eighteenth.

The woods turn into walls of green, tangles of ferns and maple saplings. We cram for finals, and it rains for eight days straight. Basements flood, then roads. Culverts and brooks no longer exist.

I'm still hoping against hope for news from Schenectady about the Gustafssons: an arrest, a mug shot. Something to convince Nina her dream killer didn't do this, so we can have our road trip unhaunted by her fears.

But there's nothing. And she keeps asking me to take her out to the range and teach her to shoot.

I'm leery of giving her the means to kill. Not because I

think she'd pull the trigger on an innocent, but because of the look she gets in her eyes when she talks about Dylan Shadwell. And because my policy of benign neutrality forbids me from confessing my disagreement with Nina on a major point: I don't believe he killed the Gustafssons.

Oh, sure, he *could* have. No denying he was in Schenectady that day. But since when do serial killers travel thousands of miles to pick victims at random? They have hunting grounds, patterns, profiles. They don't drive for hours so they can boast about killing defenseless sixty-something suburbanites. That's hired hit man behavior.

So every day I check WRGB, hoping to hear that the sweet-looking Gustafssons had mob connections or stumbled on a massive meth ring or *something*. I revisit the pre-disappearance article about the animal abuse scandal at Mr. Gustafsson's slaughterhouse, which describes how he escorted some scruffy protestors off the property last fall. It seems far-fetched to say they targeted him, but who knows?

I keep telling Nina we'll have our shooting lesson soon. The rain stops, leaving our town a sea of mud. Finally, a week before school lets out, I drive Nina up the hill to my house, knowing we'll have the backyard to ourselves for a few hours.

I can't put it off anymore. And I want to make sure of something: that she's not lying to me when she says she's never held a gun.

A little voice in the back of my head has been whispering, *What if she went to Schenectady a second time that weekend?*

So, in the backyard, I pass her my little .22LR Sidekick. "First rule: don't point it at me. Or you. Or anyone."

Nina's reaction is almost too convincing. She clasps my disco-era revolver with both hands like it's a viper that's slowly winding itself around her arm.

"It's not loaded," I say, relieving her of it.

She scowls and kicks a clod of mud. "I can do this, okay? It's like driving. You just need to give me time."

"I'm not sure why you *need* to do it."

I try to say it as gently as I can, but Nina still gives me a full-bore glare. "You believe in protecting yourself with guns, right? Better safe than sorry?"

That's the standard local reasoning for having an arsenal. People hunt, of course, but plenty of guys around these parts also think they need an AR-15 to fight off the bloodthirsty, crack-happy invaders who are itching to come up from the city and slaughter their sons and rape their daughters.

I can't remember the last time anything like that happened in real life—and Nina's paranoid enough already.

"Safety and prevention are the name of the game," I say lamely. "That mainly means, when you have a gun, you need to keep other people safe from *you*—understand?"

She nods too quickly. "I'll do everything by the book, Warren. I just hate how scared I am of these things. I want to know I could use one if I had to. Do *you* understand?"

Nina leans toward me on her toes, her eyes gleaming, and I feel the force of her yearning to be strong, unafraid. No longer an easy target when she's driving those Arizona highways alone.

And I say yes.

We start with my .30-06 hunting rifle, because it's easier to hit things with. I tell her to pretend she's competing in the Olympic Biathlon. That steadies her, though she's still wide of the target. I show her how to hold and load the revolver, but save shooting it for our next session.

The next day, the mud's a little drier, and Nina looks so tense about shooting that I say, half as a joke, "Get down and give me twenty."

She just looks at me.

"No, I'm serious. If you carry weapons, if you wanna protect yourself, you have to be strong in other ways, too."

"Like you. Arms of steel." She does a few halfhearted jumping jacks.

"How 'bout this—let's run a mile. Get the blood flowing, and you won't shake as much."

"I always hated PE. But okay."

We take a narrow two-mile trail that winds up a mountain and down again around the pasture, with jutting rocks and fallen trunks in the way. The first time we run it, Nina quits after a few minutes and stands panting and repeating, "Hate PE."

But she picks up the Sidekick like a tool this time, not a vicious animal.

On our third day of training, she runs nearly a mile and walks the rest, complaining about the mud. We start with the rifle and move to the Sidekick, and she pings two bottles.

On the fourth day, I start doing push-ups, and she gets down and imitates me with her knees in the grass.

"You need arm strength to aim." I take her to the woodshed and show her how I split the logs my dad and I hauled out of the woods last fall, bringing the ax down in one quick move.

She tries it, and the log bounces under the blade and rolls away. She groans.

"Fast," I say. "Decisive. Merciless."

On the fifth day, she runs the mountain part of the track without stopping and breaks two bottles with the rifle. She gets the ax stuck in a log and says, "Dammit," hair plastered to her forehead.

"Be patient." Maybe we need Eastern wisdom. I teach her to slither out of a chokehold, something I remember from a long-ago karate class. We end up jabbing each other in the ribs and laughing hysterically.

We take a brief break for finals, but then school's done and we can use the whole long afternoons. Nina says she's started jogging around her neighborhood in the mornings.

"I can tell," I say. She can run the track without stopping now. One day she beats me to the end, though I swear I stumbled on a tree root.

Day by day, her aim is improving, and she starts to look natural with the rifle on her shoulder or the Sidekick in her grip. It gets hot for a few days, and she wears tank tops that show me the definition of her biceps.

"You look kick-ass," I say before I can stop myself.

Nina doesn't answer, just swings the ax and moans when it sticks in the log. "I'll never master this. Never."

She aims the rifle at bottles, breaks them. We work toward twice around the track. I add obstacles to it—orange crates, a muddy trench, a rope strung between the pines—and start calling it a Death Race. This actually makes the run harder for me than for Nina, who weaves and skips with no problem.

On the day she splits a log straight down the middle, she grabs me and does a victory dance. "I'm a woodsman! I can split firewood!"

Her hands on me feel different—less fragile, more sinewy. Embarrassment makes me pull away.

"Well, you're not a sharpshooter," I say later after she shatters a Nantucket Nectars bottle with the Sidekick. "But if something big, like a bear, gets close enough, you'll have a chance."

She nudges me in the ribs. "I'm tons better, and you know it. Thanks to you."

To hide my blush, I go and start setting up more targets. Yesterday my mom watched us practice and then invited Nina to dinner. After the meal, I saw less of that fear for me in Mom's eyes.

"What does *your* mom think is the deal with us?" I ask before I can stop myself.

Nina stands in the grass, her bare arms wrapped tightly across her chest. "What do you mean, the 'deal'?"

"Doesn't it bother Kathleen that we're going to be, like, sleeping in the same room?"

I know it would bother *my* mom if she could bring herself to ask about our lodging arrangements in Albuquerque. Not only is she too embarrassed, but she seems to assume it's Nina's mom's job to guard her daughter's purity.

Nina just grins, probably because she can see the pink

sneaking over my face. "Two rooms would cost a fortune. Anyway, they all have twin beds. My mom made sure of *that*."

"So, what does she think?" I can't stop myself. "That we're friends, like, platonic for all eternity? Hasn't she given you the third degree?"

God, Nina won't look away from me. She must think my discomfort is funny.

"No," she says. "My mom gives me the annual Planned Parenthood lecture and trusts me not to be stupid. The only one giving me the third degree is you."

Is Nina still just at the lecture phase where Planned Parenthood is concerned? Or has she...been there? I try to balance a bottle on the fence, but it slips from my shaking fingers. I haven't seen her with other guys, except occasionally talking to David Chang in English, but what do I know? I'm a pathetic virgin.

"And your mom's not worried that, um, I'll...act like a dick?" Chasing the bottle in the tall grass gives me an excuse not to look at her.

"What does that mean?"

I shrug. Nina likes me for the same reasons her mom does: I'm non-creepy. Trustworthy. The nice guy who uses his words and isn't physically threatening.

"Are you saying my mom should be worried you might jump me or something?" Her accusing eyes are pinning me now.

I sigh. "No."

"You act like that makes you sad. That I trust you and she trusts you."

It doesn't make me sad. I don't want to make Nina feel fear, just *something*. Whatever she felt when she gave me the note in silvery-purple ink.

"Look, I'm sorry," Nina says behind me. "My mom's not like yours. She told me about the birds and bees when I was so young you'd freak if you knew. She doesn't care what we do as long as it's safe and *I'm* safe, and she says you're an 'ethical and responsible young man.' Yeah, stop groaning. This is worse: she won't stop talking about how great it is to see me finally 'interacting with a male.'"

I don't stop groaning.

"Uh-huh. It's like you're an alien species. Anyway, I told her we're friends. Friends who just happen to have a mutual obsession with Route Sixty-Six, Indian pueblos, meteorites, and fictional meth labs."

I set the bottle back on the fence, not blushing anymore, and look Nina in the eye. "Friends."

Nina's brows come together. Then she steps forward and clasps my right hand tightly, like we're soldiers on a mission.

"I haven't forgotten how you helped me in Schenectady," she says. "You didn't believe me, but you acted like you did."

Something hard and cold sinks in my chest, sucking the breath from my lungs. I hoped getting strong was helping Nina fight the nightmares, distracting her. But she has to go and bring *him* into this. And I see the question in her eyes: *Do you still not believe me?*

I don't want to answer it, so I let other words rush out and distract her. "Hey, Nina. Remember that animal-rights debate in Civ class last semester?"

She looks perplexed. "Yeah."

"You talked about slaughterhouses—I remember. How they should be better regulated. When you were researching for that debate, did you ever happen to read about that case in New York, with the guy who flayed the calves?"

She shudders. "I read about a few cases like that."

"Well, the one I'm thinking of happened at Mr. Gustafsson's slaughterhouse."

"His slaughterhouse?"

I go on impatiently, "Where he worked. Remember the news reports? The commenter with the conspiracy theory? Anyway, months *before* he went missing, there was an article about the abuse that mentioned Mr. Gustafsson. People were asking why he didn't report it sooner. I'm just saying—maybe his name was already in your head. Maybe that's why you thought he was in danger."

She drops my hand and steps away. "You *don't* believe me."

"That's not what I meant." This is backfiring badly. "It's just... Nina, you need to consider other possible explanations. When you bring everything back to *him*, it scares me."

Her eyes are wet. "He should scare you. He thinks you can just make people disappear. He thinks all our lives matter less than we think—including his. But you think I just made him up, don't you?"

She looks so angry and lonely that I reach out without thinking and grasp both her arms at the elbow, steadying her. "I know there are people like that in the world," I say. "And about Mr. Gustafsson—I'm sorry. I just had to ask."

20

Our first night on the road, all my joints are stodgy from hours behind the wheel, and I fall into bed expecting to get eight straight beautiful, almost-dreamless hours like I usually do.

Then I'm awake, and it's still dark behind the curtains. I roll over just enough to see the clock on the nightstand through slitted eyes: 3:20 A.M. The other bed is empty.

The bathroom door clicks, light appears around the edges, and water rushes.

So this is how it feels to sleep with Nina Barrows. Okay, in the twin bed beside hers, under a polyester spread with a tacky rose print, with the hissing window air conditioner making the room into a walk-in freezer. This is how it feels.

I turn over and stare into the dark.

She stays in there for forty-two minutes, not making a sound. Then she tiptoes back to her bed, and my eyes snap closed as the springs creak. Five minutes later, when I peek, she's a fetal hump in the covers.

We've come five hundred miles today. We're almost in Ohio. We've dutifully called and texted our moms and posted pics of endless cornfields to our blog. Three more days till we see the desert.

. . .

Until the third day, the road trip sucks. Ohio, Indiana, Illinois, and Missouri are pretty much like home, just with rounded hills instead of mountains, and the occasional nuclear glow of a big city on the horizon.

I have problems staying awake on the flat stretches, so Nina reads to me. We listen anxiously to tornado warnings on the radio. She insists on buying junk food "fuel" for me, teasing me the whole time.

When I speed, she fusses. "We can't get stopped. Not with ... that stuff in the trunk."

She means the guns—safely cased and unloaded for transport, but not legal for me to possess in most of the states we traverse. I've already coached her to play dumb if anyone stops her on the way to Arizona. "Blame your boyfriend, the gun nut." *Wait, did I just say that?*

But she didn't seem to notice my deep blush, just said, "Ha-ha."

Every night I still check the Schenectady news sites out of

habit, but I never mention who's supposedly in Albuquerque. Sometimes Nina goes quiet and I feel like she's *about* to mention him, but she never does.

Until Indianapolis, where I can't help pointing out how *big* people are—in every direction. It's just an observation. Whatever people in the middle of the country eat—maybe those fields and fields of gleaming corn?—makes them larger than I'm used to at home.

Nina's eyes go cold, and she says, "That's what *he* thinks. He thinks America let itself get soft around the middle. Too comfortable. Easy pickings."

I gun it on a straightaway, feeling my back begin to cramp. "I didn't mean it like that. Anyway, if there was justice in this world, *I'd* be huge. Right?"

Ugly discussion averted. She grins and says, "Lucky you've got the metabolism of a hummingbird."

When we cross into Oklahoma, the dirt is red instead of black. The ditches on the median are a mess of jagged fissures, nothing growing there but black-eyed Susans. Charcoal-gray clouds swallow the sun. We stop talking; we just look.

"There's gonna be a tornado," I say, but there isn't. Just wind, wind, wind.

That night I wake at two A.M. to find the bed beside me empty again. The bathroom light is on, door closed. The wind wails, battering the flimsy walls of our motel.

I wonder what would happen if I knocked on the door. Asked if she was okay.

On the fourth day, we cross the Texas Panhandle. The clouds burn off, leaving nothing but glaring sun and endless flat fields of mud and yellowish grass. At the wheel, I spot a watery glitter on the asphalt about a hundred feet ahead.

We drive through it. And the glitter's still ahead of us, making the blacktop buckle and shudder. I rub my eyes, realizing I'm just seeing a heat mirage, more vivid than the ones back east.

Then I wonder if Nina feels this way at night, when she sees things that aren't there in the daytime. When she dreams and wakes and runs into the bathroom.

At a diner called the Sands, we have a late lunch, or maybe brunch—either way, a grease-stravaganza. On this trip, we've decided to observe only two meals: breakfast and snack. We're all about hash browns, pancakes, bacon, waffles, burnt-tasting coffee, sausage you don't want to know the origins of.

Hank Williams Sr. yowls sadly from a jukebox. The waitress calls us both "hon" with a monster twang. When she sees I haven't finished my Western omelette, she asks if I'm sure I want her to clear. "You might as well eat up, hon. It ain't gonna stick to your ribs—you're growing like a weed."

Then she reaches down and tousles my hair. Nina puts her hand over her mouth, while I feel my face go beet red.

Nina's practically tearing up with laughter by the time the waitress is gone. "Oh, my God. Warren, you might need a restraining order."

"She's my mom's age, okay? But stacked," I can't help pointing out.

Nina flicks a butter pat at me. "She's gonna have to fight Violet the Chuckette."

I flick it back. "Shut up. Violet's into bikers. Not me."

But it's true that, when I introduced Violet and Nina at the Golden Dome Café, Violet smiled at us both in a weird, intense way and patted my arm three times during the conversation. Not that I counted or anything.

Before we leave the Sands, Nina makes me pose with her under the vintage sign. She pulls out a pack of Marlboros and says, "Pretend you're smoking one. More Texas that way."

I wave them away; I don't need to explain to my mom that I was ironically *pretending* to smoke. "Where'd you get those?"

"Table next to ours. Somebody just left them."

I persuade her not to put some stranger's smoke in her mouth, and we snap the picture. We both look tan and strong in it, leaning half on the sign and half on each other.

"Don't post that one," Nina says, and I know it's because of *him*. She doesn't want pictures of us online, just in case. The blog is landscapes-only.

If there were no *him*, I wonder if she'd be willing to put us out there for the world to see, together.

. . .

Late that afternoon, a sign welcomes us to New Mexico, Land of Enchantment.

Green has bled out of the landscape. The red sun slants on distant anthills of beige sand, and I wonder why anybody ever put down roots in the desert. It looks sterile, dry, dead, like outer space.

Also streamlined, clean. No wild tangles of brush and saplings to muddy the outlines. You can see every jut of rock.

Sagebrush casts sharp shadows on the flat ground; tumble-weeds lurk on the medians.

We practice saying "Tucumcari," which is fun to say, and I tell her the plot of the old western *For a Few Dollars More*. The whole thing. She doesn't make me stop.

The sun goes down, and the desert turns blue. A glow grows on the horizon. Albuquerque.

. . .

Nina will sleep in town tonight, in the same motel where we'll stay together later in the week. Tomorrow morning, she'll set out for four days in Arizona with her birth mom, while I head into the desert with Prof. Sandoval's shoot. Sasha Charney, my student taskmaster, has been texting me frantic reminders to show up early and get the keys to the departmental van, so I can swing by a mini-mart and stock up enough water to fuel a trek across the Sahara.

For three days Nina and I have done everything together. Now I'm going to be meeting a dozen new people, trying to remember names. I try not to glance at her too often as she helps me drag my stuff into the cinder-block dorm room, because the ache is starting.

She needs this, I remind myself. *Leaving Albuquerque is for the best.*

One last glance at the gun box before I close the trunk of the Legacy. I'm leaving it there—locked, and the key stays with me. Part of me wants to give Nina the little Sidekick for protection, but I've convinced myself that's a bad idea. The chances she'll need to scare off an attacker are low. The chances she might get caught with it in this state where you have to be nineteen to own a handgun, or that she might misuse it . . . I won't think about.

When I'm all settled in, I steel myself for good-byes, but Nina says, "Hey, I could go for coffee and a slice of pie right now. Whaddaya think?"

"Always pie," I say, trying to hide my relief.

Of course Albuquerque has a chain of 24/7 pie joints. The hostess gives us a vinyl booth, and Nina orders peach and I order pecan with a decaf.

"Wait!" she says as I try to dig in, and snaps a pic. "Lean across the table so I can get both of us. I'm sending this one to Kirby."

I strike the pose. "I thought we had a rule about photos."

Nina's dark brows bunch up. "I'll ask Kirby not to post it anywhere. She knows we're on this trip together."

News to me. I scrunch a sugar packet in my palm. "Does Kirby also know about . . . you know? Schenectady?"

Nina looks horrified. "Of course not. I haven't told anybody, and I hope you haven't."

I shake my head, cursing myself for breaking my own rules. Three days on the road and four days in Arizona are supposed to make Nina *forget* Schenectady and whatever she thinks happened there.

I've seen pictures of Nina's birth mom, Becca Cantillo—a big woman with long hair and a wide, weathered smile, standing on a porch covered with bougainvillea and wind chimes. I imagine her home as a spa where Nina will be restored. She'll get in touch with her roots, purging any past trauma that might have made her imagine . . . things. No matter how many times she insists she was adopted before her memories start, I can't help wondering if her nightmares go back to being separated from her mom in Arizona. Back to the desert.

And when we go out to that abandoned mine and find it as empty as Al Capone's famous vault, maybe Nina will finally accept that there's no *him* in her head, either. Just weightless shreds and tatters of childhood fears.

It's wishful thinking, but being on the road *has* made her less jumpy. And now here I am, nudging her back into the obsession zone.

"I'll never tell anybody," I say. "And I'll keep checking on Schenectady news if it makes you feel better."

She nods, though it's more like a nervous twitch. "Not sure I'll have a good signal out there."

She looks so unsettled that I do the only thing I can think of—I take her hand between mine, palm to palm, sweat to sweat. "Just focus on your visit for now. Call me when you can."

Country Muzak croons around us. Nina doesn't pull away.

"Thanks for making this trip so awesome, Warren. I don't know if I could've done it alone."

And then she adds in a low voice, so low I'm not entirely sure later if I heard or imagined the words, "It's still okay if you don't believe me."

NINA

21

Our first night on the road, I close my eyes and I drift and I dream.

He's followed me, of course. I can't escape him.

Tonight he's in his special underground hidey-hole, the place he calls "the mine," where he buried the homeless man. The place he keeps returning to. The place I plan to use against him.

I still don't think of him by his name, though I use it with Warren. *He's* always hated it: the name of a poet, a folk singer, a school shooter. Too many conflicting associations. I hate his name for a different reason: because it gives him humanity.

This is no natural cave. By the light of the camping lantern he's placed on the ground, I can see exposed rock face and masonry, wooden beams. The cavity stretches into two or three rooms in the distance.

The floor is dry and crumbly, almost pure sand. In the room to our right, where the earth looks darker, he buried the homeless man. I remember how his arms and shoulders ached as he dug down to where the soil moistened.

Twice I've climbed down into the mine with him. The dry air feels like it's been trapped for centuries. You enter the mine from a desert ridge, and below the ridge stands the abandoned cabin where he sometimes sits on winter nights, feeding an ancient woodstove.

Take I-85 north past Bernalillo, past Algodones, past the casino . . . watch for the turn-off on your right.

The bench against the wall is ancient, rotting. Its seat lifts to reveal a hollow compartment, the hinges intact. Inside is a steel toolbox, and inside the toolbox are the new Remington 597, his dad's Beretta Cheetah, and a box of ammo.

He takes out the Beretta, examines it in the lantern light, strokes its barrel. He had to ditch the 597 he used on Mr. Gustafsson, and the Glock he took from their bedside table and used on the wife. He needs to transfer his suppressor to the new rifle, test it on the range.

He's been thinking about nailing moving targets, setting up ambushes at stop signs. Using binoculars to pick out cars to bring to a sudden halt.

Like that bottle-green Beemer the college girl was driving. Yesterday he followed her for a few blocks and watched her talk on her phone, too cool for a handsfree. She was pretty and obviously knew it, but she kept moving the phone from her ear to flick her hair back with one finger. It made her look insecure.

Insecure people do what you say when you point a gun at them.

That reminds him of the little girl from before the Bad Days, the one in the car seat. She was always so nervy, fidgety, flighty, crying, and needing to be soothed.

His mind winces in guilt, complicated feelings tearing at him. *She's almost as old as that college girl now.*

So maybe he won't do a girl next. Maybe he'll resist the temptation ever to do a nice college girl, the kind people miss. Too close.

He won't do a kid; that's a given. But a woman Eliana's age? Maybe one with no kids. He made the mistake of doing a woman with school-age kids once, and he still thinks about those kids sometimes. Hopes they're okay.

How long since he's field-stripped that Beretta? He keeps it more for sentimental reasons than practical ones, but it can't hurt to be prepared.

He pulls cloths, lube, solvent, brushes from his backpack and begins breaking it down. It's boring work, so his thoughts drift.

The mine is open to the outside, no locked doors, but well hidden from casual observers—if there are any casual observers out here. How hard would it be to build a secure, locked enclosure—say, in that corner? A prison cell?

Yes, that corner would work. He'd just have to haul his materials in the long way, through the mucky lower passage that floods in August. He'd bring the target in that way, too.

But why? And who?

He did a lot of talking with the Gustafssons. He had to get them in the car. He thought treating them like people would bother him, but it didn't really. Maybe he could keep somebody here for a few days before it was over. Keep *her*.

Great, now he's thinking about girls again. But it's just thinking.

Maybe a girl like Jaylynne from the rest stop, only older. It would be a challenge, talking. But he wouldn't tell her what he was going to do. He would let her think he just wanted money. People are eager to believe the best-case scenario, don't want to know the worst.

He imagines his arm curling around a little girl's shoulders, as if he could shield her from the thoughts in his head. *Forgive me. I love you.*

Twitch.

He doesn't hate women. He just doesn't like how some of them *flaunt* themselves, like their beauty is a charm that makes them immune to aging and disease and death.

If he thought his mom or Eliana knew, thought Trixie might ever find out, he'd do what his father did. Tighten the noose around his neck, and *bam*, that's all she wrote.

It wouldn't be a loss, really. He knows he's no great asset to the world, and eventually his time will be over, just like everyone's. He just doesn't want death to blindside him again.

Fool me once . . .

He puts the cleaned Beretta back in the toolbox, shuts it in the bench, and stands. Zips the rifle in his duffel bag. He'll hide it in the Sequoia on the way to the range, like he did the previous one, because Eliana hates guns.

He climbs the rough wooden ladder he built and finds himself blinking back the light of a new day. The desert stretches for miles below his outcropping, the rising sun a blazing penny above the distant mesa.

It'll take time to improve his marksmanship with the new 597. More time to build a prison. He'll wait and see. The news reports on the Gustafssons have stopped, leaving him to slog through day after day with nothing to look forward to, but he still has the secret knowledge of what he did, and that lasts him a while.

No one even knows he exists. They know the person they call by his name. But the other part of him, the truer part? That part is a stranger.

22

Our last day on the road, I say good-bye to Warren and watch him walk back to his mango-yellow dorm. At the door he pauses, turns to look at me, and I wave, and he waves, and then we just stay stock-still staring at each other till I put the car in gear.

I don't look back again.

I fall into bed at 11:20, aching all over from ten hours plus in the Subaru, my left eyelid twitching like *his* from all the caffeine.

Now, here's the weird thing: when my mind floats into his mind, *he's* sleeping, too.

We share a time zone now. And he's not out driving tonight; I can feel Eliana breathing beside him and the pillow humped under his arm. This is his bed, where he sleeps like other people. I've been here before, but only when he turned in early because he had the flu.

His sleep is shallow. Something makes him turn over and open his eyes, showing me a stucco ceiling. Thoughts form: *Home Depot. First thing after breakfast. Eighty-four by forty-four—wait, no. Forty-two?*

The measurements slip from his mind's grasp, and he sleeps for real. We sleep together, Dylan and I.

And that's how he becomes "Dylan" to me.

• • •

At 6:15, my eyes snap open. The AC churns. Desert sunlight already glares around the edges of the blinds.

I'm wide-awake, a resolution fully formed in my mind. I've been making lots of plans recently, but this one is new, born overnight.

I pull on clothes that won't stand out.

The flamingo-colored cinder-block motel belongs to a middle-aged gay couple who've decorated it with Southwestern kitsch. Downstairs, I pause by the pool, under a teal ceramic kokopelli, and snap a few pics for my mom and the blog. I text my mom, then Warren: *On the road again! Getting an early start.*

They think I'm headed to Arizona. Becca Cantillo thinks I'm spending the next two days in Albuquerque with a nameless "friend" who has family in the city. Before we started on the road, I e-mailed the motel owners, using my mom's account, and reserved the room here for tomorrow night and the next. Then I pushed back my Arizona reservations. Change of plans, I said.

It was easy. I didn't like lying, especially to Warren, but I needed the time.

Time to explore the mine shaft by myself, without someone looking over my shoulder and wondering if I'm *this* close to cracking into a million pieces. Time to see *him* with my own two eyes.

I won't even leave the car, I promise myself. I'll keep a safe distance from him, and I can't be scared with the sun shining like a ten-thousand-watt spotlight. Albuquerque in broad daylight is a far cry from the desert nights I know through Dylan's eyes.

23

His street is quieter than the Gustafssons'. It's a funky little suburban neighborhood; I pass a hippie market and a terraced café before turning onto Piedmont, which is a cul-de-sac. Most of the houses have mature trees and front lawns, but the green stops in back, making room for tawny rock gardens and swimming pools.

The house is easy to recognize: the only two-story one on the block. It's older than the others, too, with its cream-colored stucco and rose-shaped window. There's a Big Wheel on the lawn, and the Sequoia stands in the driveway beside a white Honda Civic.

I park three houses down and wait.

The girl comes out first.

Girl, woman. *Eliana.* I know how her breath feels against his neck. I know her low laugh. Here she is in the flesh, dressed in a stylish A-line dress with a peacock-blue scarf, opening the Civic's door and buckling her little girl into the car seat.

Trixie. Short for Beatrix. Currently obsessed with dinosaurs, stuffed kitties, and pretty hula girls who wear flowers behind their ears. Leaves her colored-pencil drawings on the counter, couch, floor.

Trixie is usually asleep when I'm there. When Dylan thinks of her, it's a memory of her reaching up her arms, her eyes glittering and her smile wide enough to devour him. She calls him by his name, struggling with the *L* sound. Lately she's been calling him "Daddy," and Eliana doesn't stop her.

The driver's-side door slams. A few minutes later, Eliana swooshes past in the Civic, while I hunch low in my seat.

Twenty minutes pass, and the house door stays closed. Of course—Dylan doesn't have a nine-to-five. He can read the paper over breakfast and waltz over to Home Depot whenever.

My sluggish synapses ache for caffeine, but I don't want to miss him.

I must not be paying attention, because the revving motor catches me off guard. I sit bolt upright just in time to see the Sequoia headed toward me.

Shoulders hunched, head down. You're lost, looking at a map.

Then I'm rushing to turn around in the nearest driveway before the SUV disappears.

When I reach the stop sign, he's already two blocks ahead of me. In a second I'll lose him.

The transmission groans as I gun the Legacy down a wide commercial street, reminding myself this isn't a repeat of Schenectady. I know where he lives now, and exactly where he's going.

The Home Depot is mammoth, like everything out here, with acres and acres of dusty parking lot. I make a mental note of the section where the Sequoia turns in, then hunker down to watch Dylan stride across the asphalt to the sliding doors.

I can't see his face from this distance, yet my hands shake uncontrollably. The Thief and I are probably closer now than we were in Schenectady when Warren spotted his license plate.

I've been calling him Dylan. Human, vulnerable. But is "Dylan" only a mask to hide the Thief?

He wears faded jeans and a dark-red T-shirt. His stride is long and confident. He's skinnier than I expected, but tall, with long arms and broad shoulders.

I've caught blurry glimpses of him in mirrors when he brushed his teeth or shaved. But when he looks at himself, he doesn't really see. He knows he can rely on his face, with its strong, symmetrical features, to inspire trust in others. Nothing else matters, except when his eyes zero in on a pimple or shaving nick.

Now I'm looking at him with my eyes, not his. Controlling the gaze feels surprisingly good—so good that when he disappears inside the store, I scramble out of the car, lock it, and follow.

I'm at the sliding doors before I stop. *What am I doing?*

The lady selling hot dogs and nachos from an outdoor stall

is looking at me, so I step through the doors and tense, waiting to find him on the other side.

Instead, I find a blast of AC and a heap of red buckets that don't look like shopping baskets.

I've been to this store exactly twice, inside Dylan's head. (At home, the closest one is thirty-five miles away.) I immediately discover it's less like shopping than visiting a foreign country.

The ceiling soars as high as the Notre-Dame Basilica of Montreal, paned with fluorescents that make me squint. Everything dwarfs me: the three-story display shelves, the jumbo carts, the people pushing them.

I want to scurry for cover like a field mouse on a parking lot. But where is he? Did he start with the first aisle on the right, like I would, or head straight for his goal?

The first aisle blinds me with lights: dangling from chains, perched on posts, illuminating places where vanity mirrors should be. No monster.

Drawn to the glitter, I keep walking like an idiot. If he appears at either end of this aisle, I won't be able to hide.

I need a weapon—something I can hold, cold steel to palm, just to feel safer. But the screwdrivers to my right are all bubbled in plastic.

It takes forever to reach the back of the store, but at last I'm turning the corner into a dimmer, perpendicular corridor. I'll eyeball each aisle from back here, and then—

Crap, crap, crap—I can't breathe. He's standing right smack in my way, back turned to me, tapping on his phone.

What's in the next aisle down? A hall of mirrors, like I'm

in a carnival. They reflect my red, blotchy cheeks and terrified eyes times five, ten, twenty, fifty.

Get a hold of yourself. Nobody's chasing you. This is just an ordinary trip to Home Depot to buy...sponges? Detergent? A water filter? A saw? An ax? Do they sell guns here?

Guns. I know Warren left them unloaded in the locked box in the Legacy. I couldn't demand the key without giving my plan away.

"Finding everything okay, sweetheart?"

A smocked lady with stringy blond hair dangling from a sweatband peers at me, her eyes narrowed like she knows I don't belong.

"I'm looking for...water filters." Something small enough to carry.

"Aisle six, right through the kitchen displays to your right." She stays put like she wants to lead me there, so I fish out my phone and pretend to be texting till she drifts away.

There's a text from Warren, but I'm bathed in sweat and shaking too hard to swipe the screen. *Ordinary trip. Think water filters.*

Something flickers in the line of mirrors to my right, and without warning, there he is.

Behind me, reflected in the mirrors I'm still facing. For an instant his red shirt hovers right over my shoulder, but he walks briskly, a bright blur moving from mirror to mirror as I stand frozen, willing him not to turn and see my face (*would it matter?*), my heart trying to bolt like a spooked horse.

Something roars in my ears as he reaches the aisle's end and disappears. My body is a dry leaf caught in the gutter during a storm. Wet-eyed and shaky legged, I lift the phone and gaze at my wallpaper of Sugarman toying with a catnip mouse.

I wanted to see Dylan Shadwell. Now I have—reflected many times over. *Leave*, says the drumbeat in my head.

He's not following me; he hasn't noticed me. It's this place scaring me, full of sharp things he knows how to use and I don't. Warren wouldn't be cowering. Neither should I, and I still haven't seen Dylan from the front. What if I have to testify against him in a courtroom someday?

I recognized his house and car. If I look him in the face, will I know for sure?

Just one look, one real look into the eyes those seven people saw just before they died. Maybe everything will be in those eyes: T. Rex the turtle, the sheet dangling from the apple tree, the old man bleeding on his rag rug.

First I need to feel the solidity of wood or steel in my hand. Something dangerous.

I cut across the open kitchen displays, feeling that urge to bolt again. *It's okay. He doesn't know me. I'm just another girl.*

This is where he comes to stock up for his expeditions. Where he buys lumber, paint, flooring, and saw blades, and where he buys duct tape, plastic sheeting, gloves, rope, and knives. What's on the list today?

At the end of the water-filter aisle hang serrated utility knives—in plastic bubbles, of course. Useless.

I've lost track of him. I peek into a new aisle, see it's clear, and creep between a lit-up display of fancy drills and one of saw blades, round and toothy as ninja throwing stars. I saw Dylan buy one of those once.

The aisle splits, and I head left. At last, here are hard things that aren't in safe bubbles. Dangling hammers with wicked claws, mallets, chisels.

Blunt force, or a blade? Trying to choose, I realize these could be his thoughts. *Can I slit a throat and clean it up? How long will it take to crack a skull with this hammer that fits perfectly in my palm?*

My thoughts, his thoughts, am I sure I know the difference?

A woman's voice from the drill area, too far away to be addressing me: "Are you finding everything okay, sir?"

She's talking to him. He's here. Everything's frozen, my fingers poised inches from a steel hammer, and I don't dare turn to look. But I have to move. Just a few more steps, and I can see without being seen.

I press my back to the display, knees shaking. Twenty feet away, Dylan holds an electric drill. The blond smocked lady has accosted him, looking as bored as ever.

Something comes loose behind me, and I grab it before it can slide from its peg and hit the floor with a thud. A tiny hatchet. I pick up another one with a blade as long as my hand and swing it, testing. Much lighter than Warren's ax.

Dylan screws in a drill bit and asks something I don't hear because the drill is already whining, the sound boring its way through the air between us and deep into my head.

The smocked lady stays still, foot tapping. When the drill goes silent, she drones, "See, when they released the half-inch seven-eighty, they discontinued the seven-fifty."

"Seems like kind of a rip-off."

His voice. Not reverberating inside my own head. Real.

He can't see me here, but I can't see him well, either. Hatchet in hand, I scoot to the end of the split aisle and tiptoe down the one parallel to Dylan's. Here I can peek through the gap between two tall galvanized-steel pipes.

What if Warren's right not to believe me? What if Dylan's just what he seems?

The shadows under his eyes are too big for his narrow, angular face. He's pale like me, and he's good-looking, but you can tell he doesn't sleep enough. There's an intensity to his movements, a readiness, that must put people on edge.

When he tells the lady he'll think about the drill, his voice is low, confident, reassuring. Like it must have been when he surprised the Gustafssons in bed and promised he'd only rob them.

What the hell am I doing?

Sweat blossoms on my palms, and my heart reverberates in my suddenly tight throat. I back out of the aisle past the line of self-service checkouts, my mind telling me stupidly that I need to buy something or it won't look right. People will notice. He will.

Dylan follows me.

No, he doesn't. He just happens to step toward the cash wrap as I do, but it's okay, because I'm safe in a side aisle again, and *oh, shit, he's still coming this way.*

Steady pace, no glances back. He isn't following me; he's just chosen the same route. The hatchet's wooden handle is slick in my palm as I reach the back of the store and dart sideways, skipping several aisles to choose the last one.

Silver-white lumber rises to the ceiling here, smelling like pine woods at home. There are no women in this aisle, even employees, so I stick out. Burly men push flatbed carts piled high with boards that could crush me.

I look back, and there he is again—sauntering steadily between the towering stockade walls of lumber, just like I am. Well, I'm trying to, but I seem to be trudging in drying cement.

He can't possibly know me. He can't know.

Hatchet. Lumber. Warren taught me to split logs with an enormous ax. The burly men won't let anyone hurt me. But Dylan isn't stopping to look at lumber prices or anything else. He hasn't chosen this path for his shopping needs. He's after me.

I can't know that, can I? To know someone's following you, you have to meet their eyes.

At last, here's the cash wrap, but I can't bolt through the sliding doors. Parking lots are dangerous. *Wait here where it's safe, let him leave. Stop trembling.*

I need to buy something besides this freaking hatchet, something innocent. A home décor magazine? No. A bag of M&M'S? Yes. I'll give it to Warren when I see him, which will be soon. I'll never tell him about this. It'll be fine.

It *is* fine. He wasn't following me, just wandering in the same direction, or he'd be here. I pretend to scan magazine covers, my eyes darting toward the lumber aisle. Nothing yet.

"You in line, honey?" She's right beside me, a large woman with a cartful of louvered door panels.

I shake my head. And as I turn to make room for her,

there's Dylan, ten feet away from me, a coil of black nylon cord swinging from his hand.

He doesn't look at me, just disappears into the next checkout to the left. Now he's even closer, separated from me by a rack of magazines and Altoids, and my breath has jammed up in my chest. I try to cough, but all that comes is a croak.

The large lady's scanning her doors. She's having trouble finding the bar code, has to lug the doors out of the cart and flip them. I want to help, but I'm frozen.

After he checks out, I'll give him five minutes to leave the parking lot. Ten. An hour. Then I'll drive to Arizona and try to forget this ever happened.

The thought floods me with relief, so why are my eyes wet? Warren will never know how close I came to losing it.

"Hey, ma'am, can I help you with that?"

He's here. He's in our checkout lane. The hatchet's in front of me, half raised, before I know I've moved.

The large lady lets go of her second door with a groan. "You sure can, young man. These things are like granite."

I stare at Altoids and gum packets while Dylan passes within inches of me, his hip grazing mine. Grabs the louvered door, lifts it effortlessly to the scanner. "Here we go," he says.

I hold the hatchet poised over the conveyor belt, trying to make it look natural. *What a good Samaritan.* If they were alone in the dark, he'd shoot the lady in the face or strangle her without thinking twice.

I didn't imagine any of those things he did. I couldn't have.

"Can't thank you enough, son. I could've put my back out."

"No problem, ma'am."

Then, at last, he turns to face me. And I can no longer deny that he *sees* me.

He meets my eyes awkwardly, like a shy person who's been pretending not to see you in the hopes you'll notice him first. Almost like Warren might do.

"Nina?" he says.

This is not a dream. The hatchet blade glints against the black rubber conveyor, my knuckles white on the handle. I could turn with one motion and bury it in his neck. Easier than splitting a log.

"Nina," he says, no question mark this time.

The scanner beeps. Maybe it is a dream, because the floor is starting to waver like Jell-O, or else my legs are, and I don't seem to be breathing.

"Sorry. I know this is weird. But you look like—somebody."

I don't look like anybody you know. Shout it, turn, raise, chop—

I don't do it. I raise my eyes. His are the exact same color as mine, the goldish-brown Warren insists on calling bronze.

"How do you know my name?" The words sound heavy and foreign, a language of nightmares that makes no sense in daylight.

His eyes glisten. "You don't know who I am, do you?"

I lie with my head, a tiny shake.

"I'm Dylan," he says, and somehow, suddenly, he's holding my free hand. A solid grip from the fingers that strangled Kara Ann Messinger. The cord in his other hand.

My other hand doesn't drop the hatchet.

"Becca sent me your pics," he says. "That's how I recognized you—but she didn't say you were coming."

"How do you know Becca?" It comes out in a whisper, but I already know the answer. I knew as soon as I looked into his eyes. Tears rise in them now.

He takes a shaky breath. "She's my mom," he says.

24

We sit in a strip mall coffee shop with our bags tucked under the round table. His containing miscellaneous nuts and bolts and fixtures. Mine containing M&M'S and a small, sharp hatchet that I have informed him is for chopping brush at campgrounds.

The girl at the counter talks to her headset. She has a Sailor Moon tattoo on her shoulder. Above her hangs a pink clock with a mirrored face, but the hands don't seem to move.

More evidence I am dreaming.

Across from me sits a killer, but he looks like a harmless, lanky boy propping his long arms awkwardly on the table. I look back at him.

The clock still hasn't moved. Or has it?

I have been listening, not talking. Safer that way.

So far I know that this person claims to have the same two biological parents I do. He is talking about one-in-a-million coincidences. He is apologizing for "springing this" on me when Becca should have been the one to explain.

Explain what? I just keep nodding.

"Are you just in Albuquerque for the night?" he asks me at last. "Or staying?"

"Staying for a few days."

I should have said I'm just passing through, but it's too late. The words are out.

To make up for my slip, I start saying "we" instead of "I." I'm here with a friend, I explain. A girl.

I don't want to think about Warren. He kept probing like a shrink, trying to connect my night visions to my past. If he were here, he'd be saying triumphantly, *See? He's your brother; that's why you've dreamed about him all your life. Your dreams got twisted, is all.*

No, Warren. Babies don't form memories like that. And how do you explain the things my dreams got right?

The counter girl blends a magenta smoothie. The flowers on the bushes outside are the color of cantaloupe. I *think* the clock has jumped forward a few minutes.

"Mom didn't mention me, did she?" asks the stranger across the table.

Becca did mention an older brother, but I assumed he was a half sibling like the two younger ones. "Kind of. But she didn't tell me your name or send a picture."

Tears well in his eyes again.

His hair is a few shades lighter than mine, but it falls in the same lank clumps on the same high forehead. I've never seen anyone who looked so much like me. Does he feel the same way?

"I guess Mom wanted to let you go at your own pace," he says. "Not overload you with instant family. And I went and ruined it."

On certain words, his southwestern drawl comes out—the "desert rat" accent he tried to ditch in the army. He never has an accent when he talks to his targets. He controls what he says to them very carefully.

(*If that actually happened*, Warren says in my head.)

If I didn't know better, I'd think Dylan cared deeply about having a long-lost sister, so deeply he could barely express it without choking up.

"It's okay." I sound like somebody's choking me, too. "I can handle it. That's why I came here."

"You drove all the way from Vermont?" he asks, not taking his eyes off me.

That's the opening for me to talk about myself, I guess. I tell him the absolute minimum.

"Oh, I know that," he says when I say I'm entering senior year, like I've accused him of not knowing his own birthday. "I was six when you went away, and you were ten months. You were already named Nina then—you know that, right? Our mom named you after Nina Simone, the singer."

I nod. Becca told me that, like it gave her a stronger claim on me. Like it mattered that my *real* mom chose to respect her naming choice when I was too young to remember or give a crap.

"It was right after our dad—well, after he passed away."

Passed away. Such delicate language from someone who ends lives whenever he feels like it, as brutally as he feels like it.

"You knew that, right?" Dylan asks, his eyes probing my face. "Mom told you about him?"

I nod.

My father "passed away." It was a "tragedy." Becca had "trouble keeping her head above water" afterward, and that's how I ended up being adopted by a nice lesbian. She used a lot of flowery phrases that revealed no specifics, and I didn't ask.

"Our dad committed suicide," I say. Something Becca didn't tell me; something I shouldn't know.

I want to see how Dylan reacts.

His eyes go wide. "Mom doesn't like to talk about it. I didn't know how many..."

"Details she gave me? Not many." I clear my throat. "She didn't even tell me his name—your name. My birth name. She only used her married name."

"It's Shadwell," he says. "Nina Augustine Shadwell. That's the name you were born with."

"Augustine." I giggle insanely, watching raspberry-colored liquid whip in the blender behind the counter. "Wow."

He smiles, his cheekbones becoming hard points. This is my brother, the multiple murderer. The Thief in the Night.

(If he is.)

I remember sitting on our porch in the April sun, listening to Warren tell me how he tried to guilt one of his brothers out of stealing. Warren's brothers are bad news, but he's not. Me,

I'm used to being the only guilty party in my family. My mom is the most upright, honest, *good* person I know.

But no. If I know even one thing about Dylan, I know he isn't part of my family just because we share some DNA. Families don't work like that.

My phone vibrates inside my bag.

"That's probably my friend back at the motel. Jaylynne."

The name of the girl he almost killed at the rest stop. Why did I say that? What's wrong with me?

He nods like he doesn't recognize it. "She's waiting for you, I bet."

"Yeah, I told her I was running over to buy snacks and—the hatchet. She's probably worried."

Jaylynne's name should have made him flinch, react somehow, but it didn't. Ten minutes have passed; the spell of the unmoving clock is broken. I can't sit here with him another minute, pretending everything is fine.

Do people notice we look alike? Do they assume we're brother and sister?

Dylan passes me a napkin scrawled with an address and phone number I already know.

"I guess you need time to process," he says. "I sure would. And if you don't want to spend any time with me or my family while you're here, I totally understand."

Aren't you sensitive!

My mind speaks in the gruff voice of Ruth Gustafsson, the woman who almost got across the brook and into the woods. Maybe she seemed like a "sheep" to her killer, but she wasn't ready to die.

There's no killer in his eyes right now, only concern for me. I want to claw it off his face and expose the pitiless blankness beneath.

Again that gentle nudging voice in my head asks, *What if you're wrong?*

Dylan's still talking. "But my girlfriend, Eliana—she does an awesome chicken mole. We could make dinner for you tomorrow night. Your friend's welcome to come, too."

"She wants to spend time with her cousins," I snap. My imaginary Jaylynne has family in Albuquerque.

I understand now why the real Jaylynne went outside with Dylan. When he wants to be, he's charming without being pushy. Some girls would see the intensity of his gaze as flattering.

"Of course. No pressure," Dylan says, raising both hands. "It's an open invitation, Nina. Text me if you want to come over. If you don't, totally cool. You came to see Mom, not me. But I bet Eli and Trixie would love to meet you. I've always told them about my sister."

"But you didn't *know* me," I say too loudly.

Then I remember the little girl in his head, the one in the car seat, the small, scared person he imagines protecting. The one who disappeared from his life.

He just looks at me, tiny wrinkles forming at the corners of his eyes. "I knew you for ten months," he says, "and for nine months before that as a bump in my mom's belly. Believe me, that was enough time for me to know you."

It wasn't. You don't.

"I *always* remembered you," he says. "And I've missed you every single night since you went away."

25

I text Mom and Warren two pics of the Arizona desert that I stole from a stranger's vacation collection. *I'm here!* Then I turn up the AC in the motel room full blast, yank the bedcovers over my head, and fall asleep.

When I wake up, the sun is painting the Sandia Mountains bloodred above the roofs. Shadows swath the pool. For an instant, I wonder if it's still the same day.

Everything comes back at once, too fast. The hatchet, now perched on the edge of the desk. The lady with her louvered doors. A stranger saying, *"I've always told them about my sister."* A dinner invitation.

Too much. I'm in deep water; every movement, every thought is a rugged current threatening to sweep me out to sea. This bed is my safety zone.

I was going to drive up north, out to the mine shaft. Now it's too late; I haven't even stocked up on water.

I eat the M&M'S and sit on the bed watching the sky turn violet. When Mom calls, I pick up.

She starts to talk, but I interrupt. "Why didn't you tell me I had a brother?"

Silence. Then Mom says in a low voice, "I didn't know. Nina, what's happening there?"

"Nothing." A sob wells up in my throat, and I swallow it. Why'd I say anything? Now I have to lie. "It's just—well, I guess Becca *kind of* told me, but she didn't really tell me. And then meeting him here, at her house, it was—a surprise. And not a surprise, because it's like I always knew. Did you really not know about him? Are you sure?"

Mom starts talking, her voice firmly in soothing-therapist mode, explaining for the nth time that she never met my birth mother. "Maybe I did know about a brother at some point—but the thing was, frankly, I didn't especially *want* to know. Once you entered my life, the past didn't matter. It's hard to explain, but a baby is all about right here and right now."

I can't blame her for not dwelling on my past—but it's frustrating. "What about Dory? She worked for social services, right? Maybe she met my brother, maybe she talked about him, and I . . . *absorbed* it."

That might explain why the "boy" in my head had a name almost from the beginning, though I could never remember when or how I first heard it. Mom may not recall Dory pronouncing those four syllables—"Dylan Shadwell"—but I loved unfamiliar words and names when I was little. Sometimes I would sing them to myself for hours. Maybe I heard his once or twice, and it stuck.

Maybe I built an image of my big brother from a few careless words. Maybe my night companion was never more than a reflection of what I wanted, and later what I feared.

Which would mean *I'm* the twisted one.

And the Gustafssons? They *did* disappear—but maybe, like that Internet commenter said, it was the slaughterhouse protestors who did it. Maybe they thought Mr. Gustafsson was part of a conspiracy to conceal horrific brutality. Maybe Warren's right, and it was the article about the protest that put Mr. Gustafsson's name in my head. Maybe—

These thoughts are the ocean waves that pour into my nose and mouth as I flail—a swimmer out of my depth, losing sight of the horizon, of everything I think I know.

Mom keeps talking in that same calm voice. "I don't remember Dory discussing your birth family. And I don't think toddlers 'absorb' things like that. Have you asked Becca why she didn't tell you about your brother?"

Good question. But I'm not ready to have that conversation with a woman I don't know.

"I'm okay, really." I cling to scraps of remembered normality, trying to sound like I'm not drowning. "My brother seems really nice, and I'm going to have dinner with him tomorrow." *Am I?* "It was just—sudden."

I let Mom talk on for forty minutes, quoting every adoption book she's ever read, and agree with her that my "distressed" feelings are normal.

After we hang up, I pull the curtains and crawl under the covers again.

· · ·

When I finally drift into sleep, he's already there.

It's strange sharing somebody's mind while he's sleeping. It's a little like hearing Warren's breathing across a motel room, except that Dylan's breathing reverberates inside my head, and it doesn't take long to sync with mine.

He dreams.

He's in Home Depot, buying a length of nylon rope. When he looks down the aisle, it starts growing. The empty corridor stretches and stretches till he can't see the cash wrap at the end. The fluorescents blink out.

He takes a step and kicks something in the dark, and when he picks it up, he feels the curly fur of Trixie's stuffed poodle. It's wet like it's been out in the rain.

Then he's in the upstairs hall of his house, the toy still in his hand. He tells Eliana they need to teach Trixie not to leave stuff around, but she's in the shower and doesn't hear him.

The toy is still damp. He'll toss it in the laundry without looking at it. No. He'll go out to the shed and hide it before anyone sees the blood, then burn it later. Eli never goes in the shed.

His mom stands down the hall wearing a necklace made of crystals. She holds out a nylon rope and says, "You forgot this." Then she says, "If she cries, you just rock her, honey. She's got a dry diaper. I'm going out for an hour or so."

From there, his sleep is like jumping off a diving board into a deep, dark pool where we drown together.

. . .

When I wake again, it's nearly four A.M. by the glowing red clock beside my bed, and I know I have to say yes to dinner tomorrow.

Dylan Shadwell hasn't given a hint of being anything but ecstatic to see me. He did not react to the name "Jaylynne." He recognized me from Becca's photos. He has no reason in the world to suspect I know anything.

Unless.

When I was little, I used to wonder if he visited my head at night, too. All my attempts to communicate with him failed, but . . .

If he *has* been spying on my nightlife this whole time, what has he seen? The map on my wall? The logbook? The cross-country drive? Warren and me scarfing down pie?

Has he sensed how someone lurks in the corner of my mind every night, terrorizing me?

I've learned something from exploring Dylan's head: the fears and hopes that hide in our mental wallpaper are funny things. When they're your own, you can instantly pick them out of the loudest, busiest pattern of surface thoughts and sensations. But a stranger inside your mind might see only a darting, persistent shadow.

For instance, the man by the apple tree—Dylan's dad. I watched him flit through Dylan's mental wallpaper for years before I pieced together how he died. And I didn't know that the little girl in the car seat, the one Dylan thought of so tenderly, was *me*.

So even if Dylan can see inside my mind each night, he may not know *I* know. I need to be sure, though. I'll think of ways to test him while I drive to the desert tomorrow. I need evidence, not just of what he's done but of what I'm up against.

If he *does* know, maybe I'll find out how much of that tenderness for his sister is real, and how much is just a memory.

One thing I know: if I put his secret life in danger, if he even thinks I might, everything will change in an instant.

26

I text Dylan when I wake up, hoping against hope he'll be busy tonight. Eliana seems like the kind of person who rolls her eyes at last-minute guests. Maybe she'll tell him no way, she isn't cooking chicken mole for this out-of-nowhere sister of his, not on such short notice.

But he texts back: *Awesome. Will start grilling @ 7.*

. . .

I do everything you're supposed to do when you explore the desert. Wait till afternoon, when the sun is lower. Lug several gallons of backup water to my car, plus the bottles in my day-pack. Dress light and white, twisting a wet bandanna around my forehead under my visor.

Nothing prepares me for a world without shade.

First I take the highway north, then a dirt county road that winds into the desert, then a side road marked with a sign that has no name, just numbers. The side road's not on my GPS, but it's exactly where I remember seeing it in my sleep.

(Unless you're just telling yourself that, Warren says in my head. *Unless your imagination is bending your memory of those dreams to fit reality.)*

Three and a half miles in, the subroad dead-ends, and I'm left staring at blinding blond sand and dark green bushes till purple mountains close off the horizon.

Only when I backtrack, going extraslow, do I spot the ridge to my right. Even then, I don't see the cabin in its shadow until I've parked a safe distance away and started walking.

It's not much of a cabin—more like a falling-down shack. Also not much of a shadow. But there *is* a cabin, just like I knew there'd be, even if everything looks harder and more weathered in the blazing daylight.

And if there's a cabin, there must be a mine entrance on the ridge behind it.

As I hike toward the cabin, I discover that three P.M. in June in New Mexico is still too hot. The visor and bandanna are like a Kleenex at Niagara Falls. My throat already feels dry, my feet heavy, the wind droning in my ears. My sweat evaporates as quickly as it beads.

You can do this. Just thirty feet more.

The cabin door hangs open on one hinge. I reach for my

flashlight, half wishing I had Warren's little Sidekick. What if someone's camping in here?

The door creaks, nails on a chalkboard. I pause on the threshold, too aware of my prints on the sandy floorboards, and sweep my beam around the single room.

Rot-darkened boards with the occasional dab of plaster. One window, high on the back wall, spills sunlight on the floor.

The floorboards look newer than the walls—I don't remember that. But there's the greasy pipe extending from a blackened woodstove through the ceiling. And that must be the metal-and-Formica chair where he sits on winter nights, enjoying the stove's crackle and the silence.

My heart trips when I see writing on the walls. HEATHER + LUIS 4 EVA, various linked initials, a couple of halfhearted tags.

I don't remember the graffiti. They make it seem less like *his* cabin and more like a hangout, a hookup spot, a dare-you-to-spend-the-night-here kind of place.

Cigarette butts, a Coors can, more wall scratchings declaring eternal love. I heave open the stove's bulky door and shine the beam inside, keeping my back to the wall and one eye on the door.

I find soft gray ash mixed with black chunks from recent burns. Words come back to me from his dream: he was going to hide a bloody toy in the shed where he does the woodwork and "burn it later."

He burns things in this stove, in a place no one can associate with him.

I scoop a few ashes into a Baggie and seal it. I need to get inside that shed. He padlocks it when he's away for a while, hiding the key under Eliana's potted aloe.

Maybe there's nothing in there—he was just dreaming, after all. Maybe there is.

On the cabin's threshold, I pause to make sure I'm leaving everything as I found it—footprints scuffed, door at the right angle.

When I turn, all I see is *bright*. I shade my eyes and wait till sky and earth and road reappear.

Hot wind scours me as I climb the ridge, keeping a nervous eye out for snakes. In Vermont, we'd call this barely a hill. Here it's the highest point for miles.

I have a flashlight and a phone, no shovel. I can *feel* how close the mine entrance is. I'll climb down without breaking my neck, open the hollow bench, and snap pictures of his box with the guns and ammo inside.

That's enough for now. Knowing what I'll find there—our dad's Beretta Cheetah—is *proof.* Maybe not good enough for Warren, but good enough for me.

The reddish ridge dips and bends like the corpse of a brontosaurus that pooped out in the desert. It takes me a few minutes to reach the drop-off facing the cabin, dodging boulders and taking care not to slip on gravel.

This flat, bare place could be where he sits looking at the stars after he hauls himself out of the cave. Which means the entrance should be right below me.

I let my legs swing over the cliff and close my eyes to feel my way like he does, in darkness. His legs are longer than mine. My eyes snap open as I start to slide, and I grab a rock protrusion and lower myself onto the narrow ledge I know will be there.

Below stretches sheer rock face. I can climb back up, but not down. Right before my eyes should be a second ledge and a black crevice less than a foot wide.

But there is no crevice, no overlapping lip of rock to creep under. Just hot red stone—seamed and gravelly where pieces have broken off, but not split open.

This has to be the place. The grooved ledge under my sneakers feels right. The jutting parapet of rock to my left looks right. The distance to the top is right, allowing for the height difference. If it were dark, the stars would probably be right, too.

There's nothing here.

I don't know how long I spend perched on that ledge clearing debris from the creases in the rock, getting dirt and sand under my fingernails, willing a black chasm to yawn before me and invite me into Dylan's private domain. I only know that by the time I pull myself up the ridge, my nails are torn and bloody, the shadows are long, and my throat aches from taking sharp, angry breaths of dry air.

The cabin, the ridge, the stove, the chair, everything is right. But there's no cave. No mine.

No evidence.

. . .

By the time I get back to Albuquerque, it's six, and I have to rush to shower and scrub my nails clean. Throw on a nice summery top, apply lip gloss. Try to approximate presentable, when I'd rather curl up in the dark again.

Whenever I close my eyes, there's the unyielding rock face. And now I wonder why I didn't explore all the way around the base of the ridge. Isn't there also a tunnel somewhere, a back way he uses when he's transporting something, like a body?

But I've been *inside* that crevice in my dreams, and I still couldn't find it. What are my chances of finding the tunnel?

As I pass the pool, I remember the only time I've swum on this trip—at the Missouri motel with Warren. He did laps in a strong crawl, arms churning the water. When he stood up and slicked back his hair—darker wet—I glanced up and quickly back down, my face hot. In the western sunlight with his skin bronzing up, he looked different, like he'd grown into his own skin. I imagined running my hands over those strong shoulders beaded with chlorine-sweet water, into the hollow at the small of his back.

I redden again at the memory. If Warren were here now, if he'd been with me today, he'd think I was certifiable.

Sooner or later he'll figure that out, and he'll grow out of his feelings for me—what else can he do? Why should any sane person want to be with me when there are just two possible conclusions left: either my brother is a psycho, or I am?

27

The walk up the path to the stucco house on Piedmont seems to take five years, my legs heavy, sun beating on my head.

I can't face Dylan again. I can't stand him looking at me like he knows me because we lived a whole ten months together when I was too young to make memories.

Eliana opens the door before I can hit the bell, and just like that, I'm back in the world where there's no incriminating grit under my fingernails. Where I'm supposed to be polite.

She looks older than Dylan, maybe mid-to-late twenties, but she's working her shorts and tan thighs and long, thick dark hair. Her jewelry is arty, her hair sports a dyed-blue streak, and her scoop-neck exposes a tiny tattoo of an anchor.

"Welcome," she says, her smile displaying perfect teeth, and kisses me on both cheeks. Her nails are French manicured.

I could count on one hand the women who do themselves up like this in my hometown.

I feel like I'm seeing her for the first time. It's not that Eliana looks different in Dylan's head, just that he doesn't notice the things I do. He notices her soft hands, her geranium soap, and the edge on her voice when she tells him to please clean up after himself, how old is he? He notices the soothing tone she uses to read Trixie bedtime stories, and how she smells after she bakes his favorite coconut cake. But the nervous energy that makes her whole body vibrate? How she has to have things just so? He tunes those parts out.

Maybe that's just how long-term relationships are.

"When Dylan told me you were here in ABQ, I was stunned," Eliana says, flipping her hair over her shoulder. "It's *so* exciting to meet you after hearing about you for years."

My guess was right: Eliana's not happy with a last-minute guest. But she's the perfect hostess, the perfect girlfriend, so she makes the best of the situation.

What's Dylan been telling her about me? "It's great to meet you, too."

The small talk ends when a knee-high paisley whirlwind blows into the room, grabs Eliana's hand, and twirls her in a circle. "I found Maisie! I found her!" it shrieks. "She fell in back of the TV and broke her back!"

"Trixie, keep it down." Eliana takes the whirlwind by both shoulders so it solidifies into a small girl with stringy hair and enormous dark eyes. "Nina, this is my daughter, Beatrix. Maisie is her stuffed rabbit."

"She's a *hare*," Trixie corrects.

"Excuse me. A hare. Trixie, this is Nina, Dylan's sister."

I kneel to the kid's height. "My friend's little sister is named Maisie."

Trixie retreats behind Eliana's legs, clutching Maisie to her chest, her voice stretching into a whine. "Where's Georgia? You said she was coming."

Eliana sighs, takes Trixie's hand, and ferries her toward the open slider door. "This is Nina, his *other* sister. We're not always good with new grown-ups, are we, Trix?"

Grown-up? That's not how I feel.

"I saw pictures of Georgia," I tell Trixie, who's staring accusingly at me. Georgia is Dylan's much younger half sister—mine, too, I guess. "She's got pretty black hair. So do you."

Trixie holds out her rabbit to me, like I've demanded an explanation for its condition. "Maisie didn't break her back really. She doesn't have bones, just stuffing."

I like this kid enough to be glad she's not biologically Dylan's. Because we've got craziness in our family somewhere.

The slider leads to the back patio, and there he is.

He's grilling marinated chicken breasts and corn on the cob. He wears a clean button-down, tucked in, and he smiles and reaches out his free hand to grip mine. "I'm so psyched you could come."

As we touch, his eyes catch mine and dart away shyly. A maneuver I've noticed myself doing when I don't feel comfortable.

I don't pull away first. I let him do it.

I'm grateful for the distraction of Trixie twirling around the patio, singing a ditty about a fox and a hare. Eliana shushes her and asks what I'd like to drink.

I offer to set the patio table while Eliana tosses the salad, and she smiles with obvious relief and shows me where stuff is in the kitchen.

I already know.

The silverware is to the right of the sink, under the window with potted begonias and a kokopelli suncatcher. The plates and glasses are in the cabinets on the left. Those are Dylan's two stops when he grabs a midnight snack.

But the dark blue and burnt orange plates aren't Fiestaware, like I thought, and they have leaf designs around the rims that I don't remember.

(*Maybe the silverware and stuff was a lucky guess,* I imagine Warren saying. *Memories are malleable. You have to test everything you believe now, Nina.*)

When the table's set, the platter of grilled food is ready to go, and Eliana puts a huge red salad bowl in the center. Maybe she wants to get the meal over with as quickly as I do.

Dylan sits down opposite me and pops a Corona. He takes a swig, and Eliana, busy getting food on Trixie's plate, says, "Please use your glass."

"But we're outdoors." He smiles like a naughty kid charming his mom. His eyes meet mine briefly, with that same shyness. I'm glad he's not staring at me like he did in the café.

"Fine. Be a frat boy." Eliana collapses into her seat, her plate still empty, and her gaze shifts to me. "Nina, I don't know if you've noticed, but you and Dylan have the *exact* same eyes. I've never seen anybody else with eyes that color. It's spooky."

"Walnut-colored eyes," Dylan says, rolling his dismissively. "My...mom calls them bronze."

This serves as Eliana's cue to ask me a million questions about my mom, my road trip, my home, my school, my college plans. It's tough to answer them all while I'm munching on lime-spritzed corn, choking down bites of unexpectedly spicy chicken, gulping water, and keeping my mouth politely closed. The food is amazing, but a *lot* hotter than the faux Mexican we eat in Vermont.

Eliana shaves Trixie's corn from the cob and shoots me follow-up questions like a good hostess. Dylan keeps his head down, shoveling food into his mouth.

Twenty minutes in, I start to think that if this awkwardness is a "real" family dinner, I'm fine with my two-person household.

Except I liked it when Warren joined Mom and me for dinner, those nights we planned the trip. The two of them arguing about politics, him making fun of our steamed kale, making us laugh—it felt weirdly right, like he was our missing piece.

The memory makes something lurch sideways in my stomach.

There may be more dinners with Warren when we get home. But every dinner will be followed, sooner or later, by sleep.

If I'm wrong, and Dylan is innocent, maybe I can just keep my dreams to myself. But if I'm right, and Dylan goes to jail, the dreams won't stop. They could get worse.

It's such an ugly possibility that I force it out of my mind, and an idea rushes in to fill the vacuum. I need to treat Dylan like exactly what he seems. To get confirmation one way or the other, I'll need to fool him, and even fool myself a little.

I haven't asked a single question about my long-lost brother. I must seem like the most self-centered girl in the world.

I ask, "How long have you guys been together?"

The conversation gets easier after that. Eliana has a funny story about how they met: she and her friend were on a hike, city girls limping up a mountain in the wrong shoes, and Dylan "saved their lives" by giving them water from his canteen.

"My big, burly mountain man," she says, nudging his shoulder.

Dylan finally starts talking. Maybe it was only the memory of our strange first meeting that made him shy. He gets more animated as he describes building scale models: manipulating tiny pieces of plastic and metal and wood, gluing and sawing them into shapes of bigger things. "Detail work," he calls it.

Yes, he's good at managing details. Dump sites, bloodstains, hairs and fibers. But no. Who knows if that even happened?

When I was little, I say, I craved a dollhouse like the ones in museums. I wanted to look down on a world exactly like the real one, but small enough to control.

"You should see the dollhouse he built Trixie," Eliana says. "Actually, why *don't* you go see it while I clear the table? In fifteen minutes this princess is going to bed."

We go upstairs to Trixie's room, which is painted violet

like the sky right after sunset, and look at the dollhouse. Dylan turns on its tiny lights for me.

It's not one of those Victorian mansions, just a little bungalow with two bedrooms. Every detail is perfect, from the tiny weave on the rugs to the white princess phone to the lettering on the encyclopedias in the bookcase. "How long did this take you?"

"Maybe ten months. A lot of it just *looks* real. The book spines are painted on, and the plumbing doesn't work."

He sounds so rueful that I laugh. "Why would you need it to? The dolls aren't going to be heeding calls of nature."

Dylan chuckles, too. "You never know."

"It takes so much patience to do this." *So much obsessiveness.*

But I have my obsessive side, too. Sitting in Trixie's room surrounded by stuffed animals, hearing splashing and laughing as Eliana gives her daughter a bath, I feel my fear giving way to a gentle buzz of familiarity. These sights and sounds are like my childhood. My home.

"Yeah, well," Dylan says. "Eliana has a different way of describing my 'patience.' She says I got the world's biggest stick up my ass."

"Focus is a good thing." When did I become his life coach? "Look at everything you get done that way."

Bathwater slurps down the drain, and Dylan stands up. "Bedtime."

I'm still staring into the dollhouse. On the tiny quilt in the second bedroom sits a fuzzy figurine of a white cat. "Sugarman," I murmur.

"Who?"

"Oh, nothing. I miss my cat back home." And I realize the dollhouse's immobile cat is the spitting image of my Sugarman, bright yellow eyes and not a spot of gray.

"Want a nightcap? Orangina?" Dylan asks when we return to the patio, where the mountains look bleached against the dusky sky.

"Sure."

But I don't feel like sitting down. When he disappears into the kitchen, I walk over to the far corner of the backyard, to the large shed made of grayish reclaimed wood. *The* shed.

No time to peek in now, though the door's not padlocked. My eyes go to the potted plants clustered on a low wall at the patio's edge.

Aloe, aloe—why do they all look like aloe? Why aren't my memories photographic? Why am I so dumb about plants?

I kneel and lift one pot of maybe-aloe, then another, then a third. A fourth—and I'm running out of aloes. No tiny silver key.

The door snaps open, and I rise as quickly as I can, teetering on my wedges, and reach out to take the bottle of Orangina. "I love your garden."

"Thanks." Dylan flops down at the table, raises a beer to his lips. "Eli does it."

I sit opposite him. *If you want to trick him into admitting something, now is the time.* I try to remember the plans I made on the drive today, but they all feel childish and transparent. "I want to go out in the desert," I say—the first thing that comes to mind. "It's so scary and beautiful, all that light. I want to walk in it."

"Well, Ma lives in the desert, pretty much. You'll see plenty of sagebrush at her place. I'll take you on a hike, too, if you want."

"Where?" My heart seems to suspend its beating, my throat taut. What if he takes me exactly where I was today?

"Chaco Canyon, maybe, or Sky City. Show you the Anasazi ruins."

Damn it. "I'm not so into tourist stuff. I want to walk out away from everything, like they do in *The Good, the Bad, and the Ugly*." (Old-movie reference courtesy of Warren.)

Dylan chuckles. "So what you're saying is, you want a parched throat and second-degree sunburn?"

Sounds like what I got today. I take a big swallow and almost choke, bubbles filling my nose. "Where do *you* go when you want to get away from everybody?"

"Me?" He chuckles again, two fingers loosely circling the bottleneck (*fingers that tightened on the neck of Kara Ann Messinger?*). "I just drive, mostly. The open road—that's where I feel free. But you know about that. That's why you came here, right?"

"What?" He can't be saying what I think he's saying—that I've been with him on the road in my sleep. That I know where he's been and what he's done.

I breathe again when he says, "I mean, you know what it's like to want to put home in your rearview and drive like hell."

"Actually," I say, "till a few months ago, I was scared to drive freeway speed."

"What changed?"

Why did I tell him that? Now I have to stick imaginary Jaylynne in Warren's place and explain how my friend taught me to drive with confidence. How she's more of a daredevil and a wild girl than me. I don't mention that "she" also taught me to shoot revolvers and semiautomatics.

"This Jaylynne sounds like a spitfire." Dylan's accent sneaks back as he downs the beer. "But I'm glad you're the careful type. That's safer, 'specially for a girl."

Wonder why that is?

"Being careful's kind of boring."

A new person is speaking through me. The same person who now grabs the beer from Dylan's hand, raises it to her own mouth, and takes a swig.

I hate the taste. But I like the warmth that blooms in my stomach as I take a second sip, Dylan watching me with a weird mix, I think, of curiosity and approval.

"You're not much of a drinker," he says as I slam the bottle down like Marion winning the shot-drinking contest in *Raiders of the Lost Ark*.

"How could you tell?" The choking and sputtering?

Dylan grins, and his cheekbones sharpen.

Then, just as quickly, it's like a cloud has covered the sun. When he looks at me again, his eyes are veiled, brows lowered. "I don't want you to Google our dad."

"What?" I never bothered to ask Becca my dead dad's first name, and since I met Dylan, finding out has been the least of my concerns.

He must assume I asked her, though—it makes sense to want to know how your dad died.

"His name was Stephen Dean Shadwell," Dylan says now, like he's figured out I'm not as curious about my birth family as I should be. He takes a long swig and slumps back on his elbows. "It happened almost eighteen years ago, so I'm not sure what's out there. But I don't want you finding out on the Internet."

"Finding out *what?*" I lean across the table.

Don't get too close, the old fearful part of me whispers. But Dylan doesn't scare me right now. His gangly limbs, his inability to sit still, how he stares too hard and then suddenly avoids eye contact—all these things are familiar to me. They *are* me.

I haven't seen his left eyelid twitch yet, but I know it does. I know how he's going to respond to things—like right now. He's acting like he doesn't want to tell me about our dad, but he will.

"He didn't just commit suicide," I say. *The sheet, not really hooked to an apple tree but to something Dylan doesn't like to remember.* "I mean, he did, but—"

Dylan nods, his eyes hooded now. "He killed himself in the joint."

That I suspected. "But"—and here's where my courage fails me, an eroded cliff crumbling under my hiking boots—"why was he there?"

Dylan closes his eyes. On the exhale he opens them and says, "Dad was convicted of killing his brother-in-law. His sister's husband. Shot him execution-style in his home."

My throat hitches, closes.

So maybe murder does run in our family.

I stare at the tabletop as my brother's voice goes on, "I should've waited for Ma to tell you. But I was worried you'd just run a search."

My dad is a killer. All I can do is nod.

"He confessed to it, premeditation and all. Only thing was, he told the cops and the court he did it to protect his sister from the rat bastard who was leaving her black and blue every weekend. Our uncle." Dylan clears his throat. "Our dad said our aunt tried to leave Uncle Rick three times, but he kept threatening to kill her. 'Couldn't reason with him. It was my last option.'"

What did Warren say about criminals? They always think they're right and the world is wrong.

"And was it?" I ask, raising my eyes.

"Was what?"

"Was it the last option? Was your uncle really beating your aunt black and blue?" I can't bring myself to say "our."

He releases the empty bottle, which nearly topples over. "Dad was the only person who said he'd seen these . . . beatings. My aunt's friends, they noticed bruises, but she said it was a lie. Said she never once tried to leave Uncle Rick, she bruised easy, and my dad was unwell."

Unwell. Where does that leave me?

"I've always wondered if they planned to whack that turd Rick together, Dad and Aunt Denise. Maybe she was supposed to back up his story, but at the last minute she wussed out."

"Maybe." I don't hide my skepticism. "But if your aunt killed her husband in self-defense, why would she lie about it?"

"Maybe she was worried about a jury not being sympathetic." Dylan sighs. "Maybe she changed her mind after she saw the body. Maybe she freaked. I wish I could ask her."

"Is she . . . ?"

"Dead, yeah. Took a bunch of pills two months after my dad killed himself. She left a note saying she couldn't sleep."

This is my family.

I feel like I've just watched five seasons of an intense cable drama, my jaw stiff from clenching. "It happened right around when I was born, didn't it? That's why Becca was having such a tough time."

"Rough time, yeah." Dylan rotates the bottle, tracing a half circle.

"You were six. Rough time for you, too."

"Bad Days," he used to call it. Are the Bad Days the key to understanding Dylan? Genetic mental illness, maybe, and then his uncle being ripped away, followed in quick succession by his dad, his aunt, and finally his sister.

TV reports on the murder, kids jeering at school, friends' parents not wanting him to sleep over. His mom bursting into tears at the slightest provocation. Babysitters, therapists, counselors up in his business. People dogging him and whispering.

It's all so vivid in my head, so real. And why shouldn't it be? Even if I can't remember, those Bad Days were my earliest ones, and they must have imprinted themselves on me, too. Days of the curdled aftermath of violence, days of ostracism and shame.

Warren kept asking me leading questions, digging for evidence of a long-buried trauma to explain my dreams. I thought he was a knee-jerk skeptic.

Maybe he was right.

"It wasn't the greatest time in my life," Dylan says, his eyes evading mine. "But after a while, you know, things settled down. Mom got a decent job. We lived out in the desert, and I collected tarantulas." He chuckles in his dry way. "We were doing okay. The only thing was, Mom wouldn't stop talking about you. Everybody told her it was for the best, getting you a new family when she couldn't hold things together, but she sure regretted it."

I nod, trying not to judge. Giving me up *was* for the best in the end, but I still don't see how Becca could do it.

"She tried." Dylan's hand darts out and covers mine. "I'm trying, too, Nina. With Trixie, I mean. I'm trying to step up, 'cause her actual dad isn't here like he should be."

I twitch away from him.

"Sometimes I worry I don't have the skills—not growing up with my own dad and all." His eyes are wet. "I just want to be there for that little girl like Mom and Dad weren't there for you. That means never doing anything that might land me where Dad landed."

Jail.

"Of course not," I say too quickly.

His eyes meet mine, widening so they stretch the pale skin. He looks like an owl, too alert. Almost like he's challenging me—or just like he really, badly, needs me to know he wouldn't do anything wrong.

"Doubt I'd survive in the joint much longer than Dad did," he says. "Some people, we need our freedom."

I blink hard. Could he be hinting . . . ?

No. He does not know. He does not dream his way into me. If he did, he wouldn't be treating me like his sister right now. I'd be dead, because I'm threatening his family and his freedom, the things he cares about most.

But I can't be sure of anything anymore, can I? And so I ask, testing the waters, "*Have* you ever been arrested? Or, you know . . . done anything?"

Dylan doesn't look startled or spooked, any more than he did when I used Jaylynne's name. "Arrested, no. Done some stupid shit? Yeah. Trespassing, shoplifting, joyriding—teen bullshit. Never got caught." He shakes his head. "Never tempting fate again. Straight and narrow."

He holds my gaze as he says it and raises his beer in a toast to lawfulness. I almost believe him.

· · ·

"When are you going to Arizona?" Dylan asks at the door. And, almost tentatively, "Could we hang out again? I've got a bunch of clients to see tomorrow, but the day after, I could drive you out to Sky City."

I told Becca I'd see her tomorrow, but I know now I'll need to postpone my visit again. If I can't get into the mine, I can at least sneak into that shed. "I'm staying a couple more days. If you need a sitter for Trixie, anything like that, I'd love to help out."

Dylan's eyes light up. "Our friends *are* having a barbecue tomorrow, and our sitter has a conflict. We could hang out afterward, bring you some dessert—"

He turns to pitch this plan to Eliana, who's tiptoeing down the stairs. Moving to make room for her in the narrow hallway, I find myself jogged up against a console with a lopsided ceramic bowl full of keys.

"What barbecue?" Eliana asks.

"Tomás and Marianne. You forgot?"

One key fob has a Toyota logo; that must be Dylan's. Angling my body to hide the maneuver—not that it matters, since Dylan and Eliana are glaring at each other—I reach in and close my fist on it. Soundlessly I slip the key ring into the loose pocket of my blousy top.

This could turn out to be a disastrous, boneheaded move. Or a useful one.

Dylan's saying something about seeing their friend Tomás before he goes to Europe. Eliana interrupts: "But Nina's on vacation. We shouldn't put her to work."

As I say, "I *love* kids," I register the tight set of her mouth and understand. Eliana wants to trust me, because Dylan does, but she's still reluctant to leave her child with a girl she just met.

I don't blame her.

28

parked around the block so Dylan wouldn't get a look at my car. Now I slide the Legacy up to the curb in front of his neighbor's house, giving myself a good view.

He and Eliana aren't asleep yet. The downstairs is dark, but blue TV radiance jitters in the master bedroom.

Could he try to slip out into the desert tonight? It's only eleven.

Then again, I've stolen his keys. Compromised his mobility.

The desert sun seems to have baked its way into my bones, making my eyelids feel as gritty as my nails, but I can't doze off here. I find a few more of my stolen Arizona photos and text them to Warren, Mom, Kirby. *We did Grand Canyon today. A-maz-ing. More soon.*

Warren's busy with the shoot; his one message today said they're working him *like a sled dog or a St. Bernard or some other dog that actually works.* Mom's asleep. Kirby writes back: *Awesome. Miss u.*

Houses go dark, porch lights clicking on all over the cul-de-sac. It takes about an hour, this conversion from a peaceful waking street to a peaceful sleeping one. Aside from the distant traffic, no sound but crickets.

Dylan and Eliana's porch light blinks on. About fifteen minutes later, the master bedroom goes black.

This is it. Either he'll slip out of the house and drive—assuming he has a spare key—or he'll go to sleep like everybody else.

I have no way of knowing when that will happen. But I'm ready. I scoop the heavy key ring out of my pocket and hold it in both hands so it catches the streetlight.

If he's inside my head when he goes to sleep, he won't miss the challenge I'm giving him, the red cape I'm waving. The question is, how will he react? Charge out of the house and confront me?

I'm not ready. All I can imagine is backing out, bolting for the interstate—and I don't know if I can even do that when my head feels so sluggish, my skin parched by the sun. But if the worst is true, I need to know.

I watch the dashboard clock. I wait. My tired eyelid twitches, but I force it open. If I can't see the keys, neither can he.

My eyes hurt from focusing, so I get out of the Legacy and

sit on the hood, playing with the keys. A hot tightness builds in my chest—I'm being ignored.

Fuck this. It's not working. I should go back to the motel, pull the covers over my head again.

Then I remember Dylan tearing up as he talked about Trixie—and the keys' sharp edges dig into my palms. Pain makes me light-headed. Who does he think he is playing, Father of the Year? How dare he?

He thinks I'm fooled. He thinks I'm scared. I'll show him I'm not.

I slide off the hood and stalk down the street into Dylan's driveway. Alarm bells sound in my head, but the house remains dark and silent.

Here's the Sequoia, sleek and black and enormous, and I have the key.

Didn't Dylan say he used to trespass and joyride? "Teen bullshit" was his phrase.

I press the button, open the door, and climb into the SUV, every tiny click and thud thundering in my ears. Each move into his space feels like a violation. Yet the cab smells familiar, like tobacco smoke and wood glue. Like home.

Here I am, in your private space. Do you see me? Do you care?

I wait, but nothing happens. So I turn the key.

The roar of the engine knocks me out of myself. I'm floating toward the roof of the SUV, my sore limbs left behind, like *him* after a kill. *If he knows ... I'll be the next one.*

Then I'm back in control, my head still light and humming, and the lit-up dashboard looks familiar, too, or maybe it doesn't. Warren would say our brains can convince us anything is familiar, and he'd have five links to prove it.

Screw his links. I remember how it feels to drive this thing—lofty. Powerful. Loud.

The house door stays shut, but my whole body thrums with the need to *go*. I creep out of the driveway and down the street, half expecting to see him looming in my path with a rifle leveled at the windshield.

Nothing. Once the house is out of sight, my limbs and eyelids feel heavy again. What's the point of running if no one follows you? After a few blocks, I pull the Sequoia into the empty lot of what looks like a preschool and turn off the engine.

The vibrating energy creeps back, making me drum my fingers on the wheel. *Here I am. Come and get me.*

This car has transported corpses, been a scene of death. It should smell wrong, feel wrong. Haunted. But, though I keep checking the rearview mirrors, the Sequoia itself doesn't scare me. Maybe the cigarette stink covers its sins.

The half pack of Marlboro filters I pinched from the Sands Café in Texas is still in my bag. I take one out and light it with the Bic from the glove compartment. *His.*

I've only smoked a couple times, with Kirby's brother after the support group, walking home down lonely, frigid streets. Last winter was so cold that lighting up was more about having something to keep my hands moving than getting a nicotine fix. When I try to inhale now, I can't stop coughing.

If Dylan's watching this, he'll laugh his ass off—until he realizes I'm in his car.

Check the mirrors. Just a parking lot, sodium lights on asphalt. I'm shaking hard now, not just from the coughing, and I can't bring myself to open the windows more than a sliver.

Maybe I should have jumped on the freeway and taken off. *Where are you? Don't you see this?*

He must not be impressed.

I stretch out my bare arm, sickly orange under the street-light. What if I burned myself, like the girl in support group who sometimes pushed up the sleeve of her fleece to show us raised circular scars?

That would get Dylan's attention. If he's with me now, if we're cursed to visit each other every night, then we need to stop lying. No more sibling bonding, no babysitting, no more of this "hanging out" BS.

Terrifying as it is to provoke him, pretending is worse.

I touch the cigarette to my arm, flinch as my nerves catch fire. *Feel that?*

But the pain yanks me back to myself, and I flick the butt out the window. I'm not hurting myself for him.

No movement in the mirrors. He's not coming. He's had plenty of time to chase me down the street. I jam down the window button, a chill tickling my shoulder blades, and start the Sequoia again.

I'll leave it a block from his house, easy to find. Hold on to his keys, dare him to ask for them back.

He can lie to me and himself. I still know.

29

When I return the following afternoon, the Sequoia is neatly parked in the driveway. As a glammed-up Eliana bustles around the house giving me last-minute instructions, I wonder if I imagined last night. Maybe I'm really losing it.

But no. "You *do* have your keys, right?" Eliana asks as Dylan holds the front door open for her.

Dylan looks blank for an instant, then annoyed. "You don't have to keep asking."

"Actually, I do, because this is your only set now, and you insist on driving." Eliana twists her arm around Dylan's waist, her expression half-teasing and half-annoyed, then turns to explain to me. "He must've dropped his keys in the driveway, because when we woke up, his car was gone. A neighbor kid probably took it for a joyride."

"I bet it was the Carson boy. That little no-good skater punk." A crease forms between Dylan's brows.

"But you found the car." Bland, innocent.

"Oh, sure. The pissant left it right down the street like he was jerking my chain. Luckily, I got a spare key." His eyes stay on me, narrowed.

But I see no personal reproach in them, no anger. If this was a test, he's passed it.

. . .

Trixie is one of those kids who absolutely, positively won't sleep while they can see blue sky outside, as if missing a single hour of daylight offends them. I remember my own childhood outrage at pre-sunset bedtimes. But I still tuck her into her pink-and-purple bed, arrange her stuffed animals in a protective encampment, and read her five storybooks.

She's almost drifted off when there's a *thwack* and a triumphant yell from outside—some damn skater kid doing a trick. Trixie shoots upright and asks, "Are bears ever scared of other bears?"

"What, honey?"

"I mean, a grizzly bear and a black bear are both *bears*." She illustrates this with two teddy bears that look identical. "But grizzly bears eat people, and black bears usually just eat berries. So if a black bear meets a grizzly bear, does he run away?"

"Probably," I say. "Grizzly's bigger."

"But they're both bigger than *people*."

I consider explaining that even animals of the same species

prey on each other, but Trixie seems too young to learn the brutal truths of the food chain. So I say, "Bears hardly ever eat people. They have to be really hungry. Anyway, *these* two are friends."

To illustrate, I make the two bears dance to a hummed version of "Don't Stop the Music." Trixie takes over, manipulates them through a series of sick dance moves, and giggles until she collapses. Fifteen minutes later, I creep out and close the door.

I checked: Dylan padlocked the shed before he left. But now I know where to check for extra keys—the ceramic bowl in the hallway.

I find three small silver keys and bring them out back with me. Sure enough, the second one fits the padlock.

Before stepping into the wood shop, I peer up at the purple scalloped curtains of Trixie's room. Sunset still splashes the western sky, and I hear crickets, no motors. But they said they'd be home "before ten," which could mean any time now.

Make it fast.

Here are the familiar smells of wood chips and epoxy. The place is much bigger than I realized—more barn than shed, lit only by a skylight.

I remember Dylan working on a lathe—that must be the steel monster barely visible on the central worktable. I find the main light switch, and fluorescents glare down on the plastic-wrapped bulk of the circular saw.

All basic wood-shop stuff, sights and smells I could've imagined. But I *knew* he worked with wood. I knew he made scale models.

Could our dad have been a carpenter, too? Maybe Becca took me into his shop, embedding these sights and smells in my preconscious mind.

No time to wonder. Cabinets stretch all the way around, and I bend and start opening them, favoring the crannies that are darkest and hardest to reach. Hiding places.

Here's a blue bucket stuffed with rags—stiff and gray, not blood-dark. Rolls and rolls of duct tape, but who doesn't have that? Stacked plastic buckets from Home Depot in two sizes, some blue and some orange, all empty.

One drawer holds a handkerchief dusted in reddish powder. My heart thuds wildly as I unwrap it to find a Boy Scout pocket knife so rusty it crumbles in my hands.

Was this our dad's? I'm wrapping it again when a motor rumbles up the street.

Shit. I shove the drawer shut, stumble to the door to cut the main lights. But the car passes the driveway and turns around in the cul-de-sac.

When I switch the fluorescents back on, it's harder to breathe. I mechanically open every aperture I can find; I even check behind the pegboard for secret compartments.

The pegboard. That's where he hangs his jumbo U.S. map and traces his routes with his index finger, tapping the paper for each kill. There are no markings, no pinpricks, but if you know where to look, you'll see the indentations of his fingernails. *Here's the hitchhiker—it was raining buckets that night. Here's that honky-tonk outside Amarillo—her blouse was so soft.*

Except there is no map.

I walk every inch of the pegboard. All I find are dangling tools and taped-up postcards of sandy beaches and Mount McKinley—places the Thief's never been, as far as I know. There are lighter marks from ripped-off tape, none in the right places.

I stand in the center of the shed, nails digging into my palm, and turn in a slow circle. Of course he *could* have taken down his map. But he loves being the only soul who can read its barely visible marks. That innocent, non-incriminating object is the closest thing he has to a trophy. It matches the map I use to track him—another connection between us.

It's gone like it never was. Just like the cave entrance.

And as I gaze around the shed, trying to match each piece to my memory, that memory begins to shift and sift and change like dust motes in a sunbeam.

· · ·

When Dylan and Eliana return at ten thirty, I'm sitting in the living room pretending to read a coffee table book about scale models. I refuse dessert and payment for my trouble. I'm beat, I point out, and Dylan and I will have a longish drive if we're still going to Acoma Pueblo tomorrow.

The truth is, I can't stand to be with this nice, normal family for another second. Her with her silk scarf, him with his button-down. I still smell of the shed and the desert and suspicion and lies.

Dylan walks me to the door. "That little bear cub didn't run you ragged, did she?"

"No way, she was totally sweet." I remember Trixie asking, *Are bears ever scared of other bears?* And my mind transforms the words into *Are psychos ever scared of other psychos?*

Unless I'm the only psycho here.

Dylan keeps on talking as I pause on the walkway, but I hardly listen. Something about how he missed knowing me as a kid, how he looks at Trixie and wonders if I loved animals, too.

"I used to imagine your life," he says, and that's when my mind switches back on. "I'd stand in the backyard and imagine what you were doing right then."

"Me too." But then I correct myself. "I would've done that, too. If I'd known about you."

On my way out of the cul-de-sac, I open the car window and slide Dylan's key ring as quietly as I can into the curbside mailbox, notch it closed.

I can't go back to the motel and lie in bed and watch memories playing kaleidoscope tricks behind my closed eyelids. There has to be one last way to test him.

30

Dark streets fly by, intersections and statues and parks. Before long I'm on the ramp for the northbound freeway.

I drive through Bernalillo, through Algodones, past the casino. On the dirt county road, I count two drivers passing in the opposite direction, five minutes apart.

Darkness closes in.

No more fast-food joints, streetlights, motels, housing developments. Just flat blackness and the occasional sign or cactus in my headlights.

After a few miles, even the double yellow line blurs, mirage-like. I could drive off the edge of the world. Every time a sign glares in the headlights—usually the name of a ranch—I feel a small stab of relief.

Stay awake a little longer, Dylan.

I'm going to his ridge, to his special place. If he sees me there in his sleep, he won't be able to deny the truth any longer.

Sometimes my eyes play tricks on me. I see taillights ahead, then nothing. The night's turned cool, yet sweat drips from my hair and trickles down my nose.

I drive half a mile too far and have to backtrack to the side road. Parked on the shoulder, I take deep breaths.

There could be snakes out there. There could be vagrants or vandals in the cabin—the road is scored with tire tracks, though I see no other cars.

But if I stay in the car, he won't know where I am. The last thing I want is to go back to that motel bed and let sleep take me. To give myself to a dream that feels too real, and then wake to a world where it isn't.

I'm done with these empty challenges after tonight. I want an *answer*. A confirmation, no matter how terrifying.

I count to ten, open the door, and step out.

Dry bushes loom in the flashlight beam—sagebrush? They look like pieces of a stage set, their shadows long and haggard. I feel the flatness stretching between me and everyone else. No protective hills, just sand and these ghostly bushes. Coyotes, rattlers, tarantulas. If Dylan were in the cabin or on the ridge, he'd see my light.

He's not. I got here first.

And besides, right now I don't care.

Last night when I slept, I was inside *his* sleep again. No dreaming, just slow and gentle breaths. Who knows if it was him or me?

Then I dreamed, but it was not his dream. It was mine.

I hike toward the base of the ridge, giving the cabin a wide berth. The moon's not up yet, so I use my flashlight, trying to keep it low and tight.

I dreamed I was in a cabin, not this one. The air was cold and moist, full of the eerie keening of spring peepers. In front of me on the rough boards, illuminated by a camping lantern, rested two corpses.

Mr. and Mrs. Gustafsson, in their pj's, laid out side by side as if for a funeral. Wrists still duct-taped. Faces pools of ghostly white in the darkness. Hair matted with gore. Eyes dead.

I did this. And it's not over.

I picked up a saw with a thin, serrated blade and a red plastic handle. I bent over the man and cut his wrists free. Got to work.

Me. Not me.

As I reach the giant staircase of boulders that leads up the ridge, my fear of this place begins to bleed away. Up here I'll be able to see someone coming from any direction. If he does show, I'll be ready.

I don't want to think about the next part of the dream. It was confused, wet, earthy-smelling.

All I know is that when I looked up from my work with that saw, there stood the Thief. Outside me. He saw what I'd done and nodded.

"This is good," he said. "You need to hide this. You need to hide what you've done."

But I didn't do it. My gaze crossed the distance between us, and suddenly there was no distance. We shared a space, our bodies overlapping like shadows.

"No," my brother said. "*We* didn't do it."

I woke, his words still echoing in my head. And I thought, *If we didn't do it, who did?*

. . .

All night is a long time to wait, even in June. I sit on a sandy patch of ground, my back against a rock, and gaze into the valley, at the road.

Waiting for headlights.

I watch the moon rise, the stars brighten and then slowly, slowly dim as the east pales. I hear birds call, tiny creatures squeak, distant bigger ones bark and howl. Sometimes I forget my promise to myself and drift off, but I never drift far enough to leave my own mind.

Dylan doesn't come, in person or otherwise. When the sun finally rises over the desert—that copper disc I've seen through his eyes burning through a swamp of pink haze, staining the chimneylike pinnacle to my right—I'm alone.

Maybe I always have been.

WARREN

31

The New Mexico sun feels like it could fry my eyelashes off. I gaze across miles of nothing.

From the plateau of Acoma Pueblo, scrubby grass and sagebrush stretch flat until a hundred-foot-high, salmon-pink highway embankment bars the horizon. The pamphlet I snagged at the welcome center says it's actually a mesa.

Above hangs a gigantic cirrus cloud that looks poised to slam into the earth. Nothing has reliable weight out here. Everything is half mirage.

Including Nina and Dylan Shadwell, who stand on the plateau's edge, about thirty feet away from me.

. . .

I first spotted them in the welcome center, where I'd just finished checking in with two stern guys in flannel shirts and showing them my permits to shoot in Sky City for the UNM film department. The letters requesting the permits were dated March, which gives you a sense of the place's level of security.

The head guy handed my documentation back when he was good and ready and asked to see the camera and monopod. When he'd inspected both, he said, "This permit is for the view *from* the plateau only. No shots of the residences."

"Got it."

My producer, the queen of anal, had already explained roughly a hundred times that I was to collect B-roll only from the southern and western walls, some of which I'd be allowed to reuse for my Chuckettes video. The views, she promised, were worth the hassle.

You can't just stroll into the city; guides bring you up to the plateau in groups. Waiting for mine to form, I listened to a guy chatting up the cute Native American chick at the gift shop counter.

"Your first time in Sky City?" she asked.

"I'm from another planet."

The girl giggled. "Where are you really from?"

"Vermont."

That made me turn around. The supposed Vermonter was young, lanky but muscular, with neat hair, spacy eyes, and nervous, tapping fingers. He struck me as a cross between the kind of dude who wants to talk about your spirit animal and the kind who tailgates you in his big-ass SUV.

A girl appeared beside him—black hair, white shorts, painfully familiar crooked smile. *Nina.*

In the instant it took me to recognize her, everything else snapped together. My memory matched the online photo of Dylan Shadwell to the stranger before me. My eyes registered Nina smiling and touching his arm like they were old friends.

My head pounded, and an emotion I couldn't name blurred my vision. I saw Nina sitting in the cedars behind the school, insisting she didn't know this supposed killer. I saw the text I'd received from her this morning: *Going to Painted Desert. Supposed to be surreal! Can't wait to see u tonight.*

We had plans: I'd check into our motel when I finished filming, and she'd leave Arizona late in the afternoon and meet me there. No more cinder-block dorm room reeking of gym socks. The gang was getting back together.

The world turned to a mosaic of bright lozenges as I waited for her to spot me, my breath coming short and harsh. If she did, though, she gave no sign.

Two can play that game. So I managed to gather my gear and drag it to the other end of the waiting area without attracting attention.

Since then, I've kept my distance, making sure to keep other people between them and me while I film. I don't know if Nina really hasn't seen me or if she, too, is pretending. I don't know how long she's been lying to me.

When I can, I watch them.

They've been talking for the past twenty minutes, leaning on the barrier. Their body language is eerily similar—awkward jabbing of their long necks, scratching of noses, bouncing on balls of the feet.

I can't hear a word they say, but I could swear they have the same Ray-Bans.

Sky City is really more of a village, or a fortress at the ass-end of nowhere. All the houses on the plateau are made of stone or adobe the same beige-pink as the dirt streets. Instead of interior stairs to the second story, rough wooden ladders poke the blue sky.

The tour guide has taught us that the Anasazi prefer to be called "pueblo peoples," and that they chose this desolate spot for a town so they could see enemies coming from all directions.

I empathize.

I adjust my focus and pan over to Nina and Shadwell, then zoom in. They're talking too quietly for me to hear, but Nina looks up at him with the weirdest expression on her face. It's like he's called her out somehow, and she's blushing. Like he makes her feel flustered and *guilty*. There are dark circles under her eyes.

What's he done to her—or what's she done to herself?

Shadwell shakes his head reassuringly, running a hand through his sweaty hair. He touches Nina's shoulder, and points, calling her attention to something out on the wastes. They hold still for a few seconds, watching. She smiles, and so does he—a crooked, halfhearted smile, weirdly like hers.

Then he raises his head to gaze along the parapet, straight at my camera.

I hastily pan away and zoom out again to get the landscape, hiding as much of myself as I can behind the monopod, which isn't much. Really, I remind myself, I've done nothing wrong. Who has the most explaining to do here?

I focus and refocus on sand, boulders, and mesa that I no longer see, my face burning behind my shades as I wait to feel her gentle hand tap my arm, to hear her voice tense with anger or alarm or apology. "Warren, what are you doing here? Why didn't you say something?"

When I finally look up from the viewfinder, they're both gone.

NINA

32

Warren shouldn't be here. Everything's planned out: I'm supposed to meet him at the motel and tell him about Dylan, and how meeting him *by chance* stopped me from going to Arizona. How I need to drive out there tomorrow and ask Becca Cantillo some questions, and he can come with me. Or we can extend our trip, add a few days in Albuquerque. Whatever he wants.

I was going to explain in careful stages how I think he was right all along and I was wrong. And yeah, maybe that does mean I'm a little crazy, but see how *rational* I'm being about it?

Now all that is wrecked.

Dylan grabs my arm, steadying me. "It's okay, Nina. Nobody lives here—it's just storage. The real homes are on the second floor."

He thinks I'm upset because we've ducked inside one of the adobe houses, which the guide proclaimed strictly off-limits. I followed when Dylan grinned slyly and swung open the window, because I needed to get anywhere away from Warren.

I don't see much in the dimness—stacked boxes, a picture frame. "What if they hear us?"

"They won't. Trust me." Dylan peels back the frilly curtain and peers out, his shoulder to the wall. "That kid was giving me the creeps."

I force myself to nod, though my next breath has died in my throat. "You mean with the camera?"

"Yeah. Didn't you see how he pointed that thing straight at us?"

My whole body's frozen. "That *is* creepy."

"Eh, maybe he just thought you were cute. Too many kids with fancy cameras these days. Anyway, now we can watch the tourists without them watching us back." Dylan beckons me over to the window with a conspiratorial squint.

He lifts the corner of the curtain again, and the desert sunlight bowls me over like a tiger leaping from a cave. "What's there to see?"

"Sometimes it's just fun to watch people."

Warren is gone, thank God. A middle-aged, over-tanned couple has taken his place, both of them snapping pictures with their phones.

"New Jersey," Dylan says. "Or maybe California?"

I nod, but I'm not looking at the people. The miles of flat dirt and sagebrush make me feel like I've reached a place where secrets and lies evaporate in the sun's glare. The mesas and plateaus aren't just random obstacles; their crags have collected the reverberations of religious rites, doomed expeditions, sieges, bloodshed.

I should've just gone and confronted Warren. There's no place to hide here.

"Think they're still into each other?" Dylan asks.

Who does he mean? Oh. The flashy tourist couple. "How would we know?"

"No touching or eye contact."

I shrug.

"It means something," Dylan says. "You gotta read body language—I learned that the hard way. When I was a kid, I couldn't read anybody. I didn't like to touch, so I thought the kissing and hugging everybody else did was for show, like actors in a play."

"Me too," I say before I can stop myself. I used to think it was bizarre when my friends' moms ruffled their hair, or their dads picked them up and twirled them. Not the love, just its oversized expression. Could they be faking?

He's still talking: "So I taught myself. I watched people in real life, on TV, and I learned to tell when they're for real and when they're not."

This sounds like something the Thief might confess: how he learned to imitate people, set them at ease, lure them into trust. But it also sounds like something a brother of mine would say.

How often have I had thoughts and feelings I couldn't express to anyone? How long have I been feigning normal ones?

I remember my dream—not the horrible part with the saw, but the part where Dylan and I became two halves of something, two overlapping shadows. We have parts nobody else does. What we form together is neither beautiful nor ugly; it's like one of those red rock formations jutting from the desert, jagged and brutal, complex and necessary.

I don't want to believe anything that would take him away from me. I just want to see his good parts match up with his bad parts; I want to know the story he doesn't tell anyone else.

That story has dark and sketchy passages, no doubt, just like my own does. But the darkness that's in him is in me, and I'm no killer.

Maybe there is no mine shaft in that ridge, never was. Only the imagined possibility. Maybe that's what I've been dreaming—possibilities stitched together from shreds of memory, distant smells and sounds and names.

Like Dylan's name. My mom has admitted that she never wanted to know too much about my past—and, growing up, I thought I didn't, either. But maybe some part of me disagreed, and it was that part that plucked his name from an adult conversation and stashed it away for future use. I may not have remembered who he was, but I remembered him.

And then, where my memories stopped, I started to invent him.

Dylan reaches into his backpack and pulls out a small, fat bottle. As he passes it to me, the liquid inside turns golden in the sun.

The label says Kentucky bourbon—a brand I've never heard of. Does he expect me to drink it?

"It was our dad's favorite whiskey. I got you a sample to drink when you turn twenty-one."

My face reddens as my hands caress the bottle's contours. It looks expensive. "But that's four years away. I'll see you before then." My throat goes dry. "I mean, I'll even see you on my way back through Albuquerque. My friend . . . I'll come back to pick her up, stay a few more days. Maybe you can take me out to the desert then."

"I'd love that," my brother says. "I don't know, it was just, I saw that bottle sitting in my shed, and—something moved me. I thought I'd give it to you now."

. . .

I don't text Warren; I can't bring myself to.

Instead, I go back to the motel room and crash on top of the covers, letting my throbbing joints and synapses rest. I've been awake all night, a boulder putting a painful crick in my back, and my throat feels scarred from the coffee I've drunk to conceal my exhaustion. My body doesn't care that Warren could burst in on me at any time, full of accusations.

At 6:20, I force myself up and pack for tomorrow's trip to Arizona. Call Becca to assure her I really *am* coming this time. Text my mom the daily update.

Mom's e-mailed me a long story about how Sugarman tried to assault a skunk and got a bath in hydrogen peroxide for his trouble, complete with photos of my seething cat, his wet fur in a full-body Mohawk. The last line is *Call any time.* I know she wants to talk daily, but she's trying to give me my space with Becca.

Kirby's been silent for a while. I almost text her, but then

I realize that to explain the situation with Warren, to get her advice on my next move, I'd have to explain too much else.

Before I can put down the phone, another name in my contact list catches my eye—Dory Biedenkopf.

Is Dory the one I should blame for all this? My mom chose to ignore my past, but maybe Dory read the files and paid attention to the news reports. She could have known all about my brother, my dad, the murder and subsequent suicide. When I was young, she visited us twice or three times in Vermont with her new family. Who knows what she might have carelessly said—not just about Becca and Dylan, but about the violence in my past. "Nina's so much better off with you," I imagine her telling my mom. "Sometimes I worry about the other one—that little boy."

Mom would have tuned it all out. But me—I might have listened and absorbed. Heard the note of warning in Dory's voice, known there was a terrible secret involving my brother.

And then, in the way kids do, perhaps I turned it all into a story I thought was about somebody else. A story that eventually inspired me to stalk my own brother, first online and then in person. A story that convinced me *he* was the killer.

It's after eight. Warren should be here—and suddenly I don't dread apologizing to him. I just want him close.

My hands shaking, I scroll to Warren's number. *I'm here. Where we planned. Plz come. Sorry.*

Long minutes pass with no answer. At nine, I start fidgeting. At 9:40, I consider reporting Warren missing. But that's ridiculous.

If this were yesterday, I might be worried about what I'd

see in my sleep if the Thief did something to Warren. Does something. Is doing something.

Today I know Dylan doesn't know about Warren and me. If he did, I'd have heard it in his voice when he called Warren creepy—there would have been an edge, a hint of something deeper than annoyance. Today I don't know if Dylan is the Thief, or even if there is one.

At ten, I open the bourbon Dylan gave me and take a swig. Disgusting, but it makes me feel light-headed, so I take another.

Inside my mind, of course, there is still a Thief. Maybe there always will be. But he doesn't kill people for pointing a camera at him, or for stealing his car or rifling through his shed. That would be unworthy of him. Too personal.

At 10:37, a key turns in the lock. I sit bolt upright. *Be Warren.*

It is. He's pulled a black jacket over the white T-shirt he wore in the desert, and his tan has deepened in the past three days, making his brown hair and eyes seem lighter.

I jump out of bed and almost hug him, then freeze when I see the hooded squint of his eyes and the line of his mouth. He's almost as pissed as a waterlogged Sugarman, though he hides it better.

I flop back down, staring at my hands on my knees. "You must be—I'm so sorry. I *never* thought you'd be there."

Warren tosses his jacket on the bed and throws himself down after it. "I'm beat."

"Me too." As if that's an excuse.

Warren's eyes slide to me, then away. All his movements are smoother, slower, less nervous than usual; has hanging out with college kids for three days changed him that much?

"He drove out where you said," he says finally.

"Who?" I whip around to face him, my own nerves jangling, but he doesn't even change expression.

"You know who. I tailed him after he dropped you off. He went north on Interstate Eighty-Five, past the casino, then off on that little county road. Then another turn, right where your logbook said it would be, but I didn't follow him. I waited for him to leave, and he did. About fifteen minutes before sunset."

I can't form words; everything's colliding. Dylan *did* go to the mine? Is that what Warren's saying? Dylan was where I was last night? But today, in daylight?

It doesn't have to mean anything. I've seen for myself there's nothing out there but sagebrush and graffiti.

Warren's staring at me the way Kirby did the first time she saw me fall apart and sob. Is that how I look now?

"Nina, are you drinking?"

"Only a few sips." As I point to the bottle, a chortling sound bubbles out of me, suggesting I've understated the case. At least I'm not bawling, though the sudden lump in my throat confuses me. *Too much at the same time.* "It was a twenty-first birthday gift."

"From him?" Warren asks in a neutral tone.

That's when I know he doesn't trust me. He's approaching me like the good cop approaches the murder suspect. The subtext of every word is *Go on, prove to me you're innocent, even though everything you say can be used against you.*

"Yes, from him. But it's not what you think."

Then it all comes out in a flood: how I had to see Dylan, who he is to me, everything I've learned about him, every way I've tested him.

"The more I think about it, the more I think you might have been right the whole time. About early memories. About just knowing things on a subconscious level. About my brain playing tricks on me. He's my *brother*. Of course I feel connected to him." I kick off my flip-flops, pull my feet up, and collapse on the bed beside Warren like he's shot me. "Do you hear what I'm saying? I think you were *right*. I'm sorry I had to lie to you to find that out."

He doesn't answer at first. I roll over to see him staring at the ceiling, eyes half closed.

"What about the Gustafssons?" he asks carefully.

My eyelid twitches. The images from that spring night are still too vivid; I shove them aside. "I don't know, Warren. Maybe it was a crazy coincidence. Maybe you were right about that slaughterhouse thing—I read an article about it, and their name stuck in my head."

"Have you asked your brother why he was in Schenectady that night?"

"No," I admit. It was one of the questions I meant to spring on Dylan, but the right moment never came. "But when we talked about back east, he mentioned he was in New York for a convention this spring. I checked—there *was* a scale-model convention in Schenectady. It was a week and a half earlier, but—"

"But he spent that week and a half at his friend's cabin in

Canada and then swung around back to Schenectady, even though it was out of his way. Right?" Warren folds his hands under his head. "Or did you not ask him about that, either?"

"How could I?" I'm stunned Warren even remembers my account of my night visions so well. "Anyway, you're the one who's been telling me it's all in my head, right?"

He props himself on his elbow and looks down at me. "It can't *all* be in your head. You told me the way to that dump site in the desert. I followed him there."

"There's zero proof it's a dump site. I told you, I went out there and looked for the cave entrance. Nothing." We've switched places, him suddenly hot on Dylan's trail while I hang back, and it's happened too fast. "Which means what I saw in my sleep was wrong. Which means you can't rely on me."

"But he was there today," Warren says doggedly. "Of all the places to go in the desert, he was *there*."

"So maybe I knew about that place—some way I don't remember. Just like the way I described his house—only I could've looked it up online, just like you did, and then forgotten I had. And his name. And Eliana."

I see it all like a movie. Me searching Dylan, learning his address. Memorizing his house. Watching his feeds, hearing about his Schenectady trip. I keep a logbook of his movements—how can I be sure at this point what I "saw" and what I researched?

"Maybe *I'm* the one who's been doing the stalking."

Warren's eyes fix on me, gleaming under the heavy lids. "Either you remember researching him, or you don't. Which is it?"

I pull my knees to my chest and hide my head in my arms. "I don't know. I don't know."

We stay like that for a while. Then the bedsprings squeak, and I peek through my fingers to see Warren scooting up against the headboard and leaning his chin on his bony knees. With my head inches from his hip, I feel his body vibrating, his breath coming quicker as he says, "I guess I never expected you to start—well, recanting. I'm confused. And honestly, kinda scared."

"*Scared*? What of?"

"Of him. Of you. *For* you."

"You need to stay away from Dylan," I say. "We can go out to the desert and search that place again if you want, but let me handle him."

I'm not sure anymore if I'm more worried about what Dylan could do to Warren, or vice versa. Who has the box of guns?

A snort of laughter, and I sit up to find Warren grimacing. "What?"

"I saw the way you 'handled' him today."

My face goes hot. "What do you mean?"

Warren's face is red, too, and the second derisive noise he makes is too loud. "The two of you, it was like you were flirting, almost. Or like you were desperate to impress him."

Blood still pounds in my burning temples, but it's so ridiculous I laugh. "He's my brother—seriously, *gross*, Warren."

Warren flushes deeper. "All I'm saying is, it creeped me out." He latches his gaze to mine, and I realize I'm not going to embarrass him out of this. "The way he was talking to you—it was like he was hypnotizing you, Nina. He kept getting closer and closer to you, like it was just you two against the world. Look, I saw him lie to a girl in the welcome center. He said he was from Vermont, and she believed him. Maybe he's manipulating you, too."

"You're jealous." It comes out before I can think.

"Jealous of *what*, exactly?"

Warren's eyes are too bright, like he's on the verge of tears, which tells me I'm right and should stop now, but I can't. "He gets me," I say. "In a way you never will."

Warren's lip curls as he backs away from me. "You told me he was a psychopath. You want to be one, too?"

I shake my head. What I do want crystallizes in my brain, clear as a constellation in the subzero sky.

I want a brother.

I want never to see another murder.

And somehow, in a way I don't understand yet, those two wants are connected.

Warren looks like he's about to ask another question, so I crawl to him and grab him by both shoulders.

He goes quiet. Right away. The power of my touch awes me a little—and then I realize I'm touching *him*, and I couldn't speak if I wanted to.

My hands slide up the hot skin of his neck where his pulse flutters. My fingers graze the high knoll of his cheekbone, the hollow under his left eye, the almost-invisible freckles on his nose. When I cup his face and pull him to me, he doesn't resist. He shuts his eyes and goes still as a mannequin, his lips dry and closed.

Then, all of a sudden, he gulps a breath and starts kissing

me back, his hands tangling in my hair. His mouth opens under mine, hot and wet, and I taste kiwi Life Savers as his tongue darts between my lips.

Here's that floating sensation I had when I started the Sequoia's engine, my skin getting tighter and hotter.

Because he isn't that middle school boy anymore. He's the lean, lanky boy whose face and chest show beautiful planes in the western sun. The boy who may already be making college girls fall hard for him.

And as long as we're touching, it's like he never asked me all those unanswerable questions.

Warren gasps, and somehow I'm on my back looking up at him. I forgot he's stronger than me.

His lips are moist and red. "You're crazy," he says between gasps.

His T-shirt hangs between us untucked, too loose, so I slide my hand under it, and he closes his eyes. "Nina, I'm serious," he says, but the words are broken up in the wrong places.

"You're serious what?"

Warren pushes me away and flops over on his back. His breathing is rough. "We can't," he says.

"Why not?" God, *why* not? I want to trace the muscles through his shirt—or maybe just pull it off him.

I touch his elbow, and he flinches. "Because you're trying to—I don't know what you're trying to do. This isn't you."

How's it not me? What kind of guy *stops* you? Bitterness creeps back into my voice. "Because you think I'm a bitch who's just using you?"

"I don't know." His voice breaks. "I don't know."

"Or maybe you think I'm crazy? Like you just said?"

"I didn't mean it that way."

Carefully, so as not to startle him, I prop myself up on my elbow. He looks so broken right now, and I want him to know this isn't fake.

It's a little too real.

"I think you should come with me to Arizona," I say.

He shakes his head. "You need to meet your mom, and you should be alone for that. I need to..."

I trace the line of his lips. "I don't want you to follow *him* again. I don't."

Warren frowns at me, his whole face going tight, suspicious. He's weirdly beautiful that way with his narrow eyes, so much more secretive-looking than mine. "If you don't think he's a serial killer, what does it matter if I follow him? I won't be in danger, right?"

"I don't know." I just don't like the thought of him skulking around Dylan's house, maybe getting caught and even dragged into the police station if Eliana's feeling especially protective. "You might do something reckless."

Warren sits up, and now it's me who backs away.

Only at first. When he leans against me, our foreheads touching, and kisses the corner of my mouth, I close my eyes.

I thought I couldn't have something like this. I dreamed of the Thief lying to his girlfriend, night after night, and I thought I'd never trust a boy.

But I do. "I want you to be safe," I whisper against his hair. Warren nods.

I hold his face between my hands again. I want to be closer

to him, want to feel the heat of the skin under his baggy clothes, want to kiss those vulnerable places on his neck hard enough to leave bruises, but first we need to settle something. "If you have to do it, Warren, promise me you'll be careful. Don't let him see you. No guns. And don't go near his girlfriend or the kid."

His eyelashes cast fluttering shadows on his cheek. "You think I'm going to terrorize innocent people?"

"I know you like those old Clint Eastwood movies." My blood pounds—not just with fear—as I imagine Warren as a gunslinger, lean and hard and pitiless, drawing a line in the sand with the Thief on the other side. "But in real life, suspects are innocent until proven guilty. Right?"

If it were you versus the Thief, Warren, a distant part of my brain says, *I'd root for you. But I don't know if I'd bet on you.*

Maybe there is no Thief, though, and anyway there's no room for him here, because I'm on my back and pulling Warren's shirt off, running my hands up and down his sides, tracing the grooves between his ribs. He gasps, and then his lips are hot on my bare stomach, his hands peeling off my own shirt, and I arch my back and let myself fall apart into fragments of heat and light, my fingers tangled in his soft hair. And when it's almost too much, blasting me like the desert at midday, I pull him up so I can kiss him again, catching his bottom lip between mine and releasing my hectic breaths into his mouth, against his neck, because I doubt too many things, but not this, not now.

His lips against my cheek form the words, "I promise."

WARREN

33

When I wake up, she's gone.

I'm alone in the wreck of a bed where we both spent the night, wearing my boxers, my mouth tasting like morning. The sky is barely blue below the blinds. The bottle of bourbon, three-quarters full, sits on the night table.

Think I had a few swigs, too, at some point.

All I have now is the memory of her head resting in the crook of my arm, my fingers tangled in her hair. Or is that something I dreamed?

No. Other memories flood back so fast I feel dizzy as I stumble across the room to pull back the curtain and feel the sun.

I shower quickly, dress, scrub my mouth with minty gel, and jog downstairs to the foyer where they lay out the continental breakfast. The Fair Trade coffee and croissants are in place, but Nina is not.

I spot her through the patio door—in a lounger by the pool, knees folded to her chest.

Please don't let her be regretting anything. Please don't let her have changed. It's not like I'm that asshole who just wants to score, but I don't want it to end like this. I want the next chapter where everything gets crazier, wilder, off the rails. I want my first time to be with her.

My first impulse is to rush out there, but *Don't be a dumbass, Warren.* I pour two coffees and fill a plate with pastries and grapes.

When Nina sees me, she doesn't wince, just slides her sunglasses down and takes a coffee. "Thanks, Warren."

Does she say my name differently now? Less of that *my pesky kid brother* lilt to it, and more huskiness, like *This is my man?*

I push the thought aside—this isn't about my insecurities. Before it all started last night, we were arguing about Shadwell—about her *brother.* I remember in a vague way how angry it made me to hear her changing her whole story, and then how worried, and then how scared, even though she was saying things I'd been saying all along.

I kept seeing the Gustafssons—their eyes on the MISSING poster, half imploring and half accusing. *Don't forget. Someone did make us disappear.*

Then I promised Nina something. What was it?

We eat and drink in silence, watching sun flood the deep end of the pool while the rest stays dark and still. Finally, I ask, "Did you see *him* last night?"

"I didn't sleep a lot."

That makes two of us. Too exhausted to move, too keyed up to sleep. "But don't you always see him?"

She doesn't answer for a second. Then: "He was asleep. At home. Not even dreaming."

"Do you think maybe you'll stop seeing things at night now that...?"

Now that you realize it was just your imagination. But has she?

"I don't know. It hasn't happened yet." She catches me with those bronze eyes—does *he* have them, too?—and reaches out to smooth my hair off my face. It's a casual gesture, yet I freeze, my mouth going dry with the need to touch her.

"I've had him with me my whole life, Warren," she goes on. "That doesn't just vanish."

I wish it would. I wish I were the only one you dreamed about. And then, I'm not sure how it happens, but we're sharing the lounger, her bare knees between mine. My arm's around her waist, playing with the edge of her shirt, and she grabs my other hand and interweaves our fingers and says, "Remember what you promised me."

Oh, shit, what did I promise? Something about not going near Shadwell's family—why would I do that? Oh yes, and guns. *No guns,* she said.

I copied the key to the UNM film department's van, and I'm pretty sure I can sneak it out—or just tell them I'm collecting more B-roll. They trust me, they're busy in their editing suite this weekend, and I think they've forgotten I'm under eighteen.

The just-in-case guns are locked in the Legacy. I can get my rifle out without her noticing, leave her the Sidekick. Maybe I'll even load the revolver for her—just the smallest precaution.

For the Gustafssons—and for *her* safety—I want to be sure.

I press my palm tighter to hers, kiss her knuckles, and say, "I remember what I promised."

No Wild West showdowns or shoot-outs. That should be easy.

"Thank you." She tickles me under my knee, and I try to bat her hand away with my other foot, which leads to us both tipping the lounger over, which puts me in a better position to tickle *her*.

"Oh my God, stop it, stop it!" she mock-shrieks, sitting up on the concrete.

I stop horsing around and cup her face in my hand. "This whole time I've been imagining you in Arizona with Becca, and you haven't even met her. Weird."

Nina drops her gaze. "I hated lying to you."

"It's okay. I get it. But now that you're finally going to see her, are you excited?"

"More like weirded out. And tired."

I lift her chin gently. "If she's related to you, she's probably awesome. Because . . ."

"Because why?"

Because you are. I squeeze her hand, so fragile in mine, and say teasingly, "Never mind."

She smiles, visibly relaxing. "Were you going to say I'm awesome? Because you can, you know. I might even say you're awesome back."

"I'm trying to think of a better word for you. 'Awesome' isn't scoring me any extra points on the SATs."

"Oh, you're scoring points all right," she says, smirking.

"Awesome," I say, and kiss her.

NINA

34

The woman who gave birth to me lives surrounded by birds and wind chimes.

Most of the wind chimes hang from Becca Cantillo's porch roof or dangle from the mangy trees nearby, which also hold dozens of bird feeders. As you step onto that porch, out of the hot breeze that scours the northern Arizona desert, you hear tinkling and plinking and clanging and other fragments of tuneless music, mixed with the cheeping, cawing, and warbling of the birds indoors.

Inside Becca's house, they occupy seven tidy cages—canaries and other songbirds and parakeets and a giant rescued parrot named Señor Bitey, originally from Argentina. Their music is tuneless, too, though the combination of all their voices with the wind chimes and the AC's hum can fool you into hearing a melody.

Dylan built the cages, Becca has told me. Most of the feeders, too—the tiny Taj Mahal, the replica of a Bavarian castle. Back when he lived with her, he spent every weekend hammering in the garage, making her something amazing, a handyman and an artist in one.

So far, the Dylan she keeps praising is the same one I know in the flesh. But if there's another side to him, a darker one, Becca must have seen hints of it. She raised him alone—how could she not?

After dinner, we sit on a patched-up leather sofa while the breeze blows the spindly trees in the bright vastness outside, and Becca leafs through a family album. The sun has just set.

Becca Cantillo is a large woman—tall and thick waisted, with a big head. Her hair is still black as mine, and she lets it fall to her elbows, held back from her face by a silver clip. I wonder if we have Native American blood, the two of us—and Dylan—and I ask her.

"Sure," Becca says after a deep chuckle. "My great-grandmother was Navajo, but around here, that's not exactly noteworthy, honey."

Boy-band faux rapping filters down from the second floor, where Georgia, Becca's eight-year-old daughter from her second husband, Edgardo Cantillo, is doing her homework. Georgia helped Becca make the peach crisp for our dessert and served it herself. She hasn't asked me any questions, only politely answered mine.

Sometimes I hear her sniping back and forth with her

six-year-old brother, Jackson. They were on their best behavior with me, a stranger.

Good kids, but they don't feel related to me. None of this feels real.

Hours of driving across the desert will do that to you.

I slept maybe two hours last night, drank sixteen ounces of coffee, forgot to put on sunscreen, and my skin feels tight and itchy. Not in a bad way, and not just because of the sun.

My skin remembers last night. When Warren touched me, he took away my old skin and gave me a new one that feels hot and snug and burnished, like a statue's bronze shell.

Does he feel the same way?

If I told Kirby about last night, she'd probably say, "He's hot, he's into you, and you finally did something about it. Welcome to the human race. What's the big deal?"

The big deal is, I started it. I touched him first, and I did it so he'd stop asking me about memories I can't make sense of anymore.

I never thought I could have someone in my life like Dylan has Eliana. I didn't think it would be safe to share a bed, or even a dorm room, because sooner or later I'd have to explain my nights.

Warren knows everything, and he hasn't turned his back on me yet.

I can't forget to call Mom when I get back to the B-and-B. I've been texting her too often; she deserves a full-fledged conversation, and I need to hear her voice.

Four days ago, when I was pretending I'd recently arrived at Becca's house—after my surprise-brother freak-out—I described Becca to Mom as "really cool" and "so incredibly nice," like she was a camp counselor. Partly because I had nothing better to say, partly because I wanted Mom to think that meeting Becca hadn't meant much to me.

Thing is, it did. When I finally walked up to Becca's wind-chimed porch and she dashed down the steps to meet me, I tried to shake hands. She threw her arms around me and drew me into her smells of basil and cinnamon, and I didn't pull away.

"Dylan told me you met," Becca said into my shoulder then. "I should've let you know about him, honey. It shouldn't have happened by chance."

Her voice betrayed decades of pain, and tears welled in my eyes, so I could only shake my head.

Mom doesn't need to know it felt good to be in Becca's arms. Familiar. Those feelings don't change my mom and me. They just are, like the desert spreading under the sun.

Now Becca is showing me pre-digital snapshots from the days when they lived in a trailer, just her and Dylan.

The Becca of those days matches up with the mom I remember from Dylan's early years: skinnier, almost gaunt, partial to tight Levis. Pretty. She often had a cigarette in her fingers—no longer.

I catch my breath when I see the first pic of Dylan as a kid—messy hair and those enormous, pale-brown eyes. In several shots, he's got his first BB gun.

And—oh. There's little Dylan beaming as he points to a house of cards—then, in a second shot, posturing like he's going to knock it down, a wicked grin on his face.

I remember a house of cards, don't I? But as I gaze at the photo, I'm not sure if I saw something similar in my night visions, or if I'm just telling myself I did.

"He could always make me laugh," Becca says, turning the page. "Honestly, when we were living out there alone, I don't think I could've survived without your brother. He kept me on level ground. It was the same when Edgardo and I split—Dylan came out here for a whole week. Cooked for me, took the kids to mini-golf."

I nod, remembering Dylan with Trixie. "He's good with kids."

At the same time I wonder why Becca keeps harping on the theme of Dylan's greatness. Is she just a proud mom, or does she feel like she needs to convince me?

"Oh yeah. I know it sounds strange, Nina, but I always wonder if Dylan relates well to kids because he didn't have a real childhood. Not like he should've."

"What about . . . his dad?" I ask. Unable to say *my dad*.

Becca flips more pages in the album and shows me a wedding photo. "There's me and Steve."

Stephen Shadwell, my biological father, was tall and lean with a crooked grin and a squint. He had Dylan's cheekbones. A very young Becca clings to him like he's a superhero who just saved her from a burning building.

"You look beautiful," I say, a lump rising in my throat, because I can't imagine being as sweet and innocent as she looks there.

Becca clicks her tongue self-deprecatingly. "Those were the days."

She points to another shot, a little out of focus: a shirtless young man with a gun slung over his shoulder, beer in hand. It could be Dylan, with those owlish eyes that seem to be accusing the camera, but it's our dad again.

"First year we were married," Becca says with a throaty laugh. "When Stevie and his buds got together and fired up the BBQ pit, it was redneck heaven at our place."

I don't want to hear Becca Cantillo lie, so I get in ahead. "Dylan told me."

"About our secret sauce recipe?" Her breath catches.

"About what Steve did. Dylan didn't want me finding out online. It was better just to tell me, he said."

Becca's hand clasps my knee as if to say, *Stop*. When I make myself meet her eyes, they're wet.

Mom doesn't cry, doesn't dredge up the past. "Water under the bridge," she always says. I learned from her to keep my brave face on, and then I learned from the Thief how to stuff my direst memories away in a dusty corner of my head. How am I supposed to deal with a mom who brings things into the light of day?

"I'm sorry," I whisper. "I shouldn't have ever... I mean... I know you..."

Becca's grip on my knee tightens, and her arm snakes around me like I'm the one who needs comforting. Me, who never even met my father.

Should I hate Steve Shadwell? He tore the family apart, and Dylan and I both still feel it in our different ways. But only we can take responsibility for the things *we* do.

"I'm the one who's sorry," Becca says. "No, maybe I'm not

sorry you already know. It would've been a hell of a thing to explain."

"Dylan pretty much explained everything," I reassure her. "And I understand a lot more now. About why—you know."

Why you gave me up.

My birth father ripping the family apart, then ripping himself away from us. He and my aunt and uncle, all dead in the span of what—a year? Handcuffs, courtrooms, newspaper articles, funerals. Grieving must have been practically Becca's full-time job, but still...

"You don't know, though, honey. You won't ever know." Becca speaks with no bitterness, still patting my knee. "Nobody ever knows till they've walked a mile down the same road." She laughs and wipes her eyes. "I'm brimming with life lessons, huh? Regular greeting card."

The woman who gave birth to me talks like a country song. She cries about stuff she can't change, she feels strange and familiar at once, and I like her.

WARREN

35

As I pull onto Piedmont Drive, I remember that night in Schenectady when Nina made me drive in circles for hours, searching for Dylan Shadwell's car.

That night I kept telling myself: *Now I know she's crazy. Next Monday at school, I'm not gonna look over at her in AP English and imagine running my finger along her dark eyebrows or down the nape of her neck. I'll just think: bitch made me drive around Schenectady for six hours.*

I'll be cured.

But I wasn't. Nina has set me adrift in a world where everything is a shimmer of disappearing water on the highway. All I can do is try to orient myself with good old detective work. No assumptions, just evidence.

I park the UNM van well up Shadwell's block and take

out my binoculars. First thing I notice is a house with a FORECLOSURE SALE sign, two down from Shadwell's with sight lines into his backyard.

I get out and dodge into the driveway of the foreclosure. A glimpse inside tells me it's been emptied down to the bones, so I walk around to the back patio, where I have a view of Dylan Shadwell whacking weeds in his backyard.

I duck behind a planter that must have been too heavy to move, take out my binocs, and watch him. After the weed whacking, he goes in the house and returns with a travel mug. Unlocks the shed and disappears in there. A few more minutes, and the whine of a lathe trickles outside.

Thrill a minute, this guy.

In the backyard to my left, a little girl has started splashing in a kiddie pool, so I keep low as I leave the foreclosure's yard and scuttle back to the van.

There I spend nearly two hours reading a Dashiell Hammett paperback and eating an entire bag of pretzel sticks and half a bag of licorice. When Shadwell finally backs his Sequoia out of the driveway, it's such a shock that I almost don't make it out of the cul-de-sac in time to follow him.

Maybe he's visiting a carpentry client. Or hitting up Home Depot for supplies. I can't wait to find out.

Anyway, he's leading me to the eastern edge of the city, where the streets grow narrow and curvy, closer to the Sandia Mountains. We leave the green suburbs and turn onto a two-lane that cuts through desert scrubland—houses bigger and farther apart, just silver grass and sand and coral mountains on the horizon.

Wind whistles in my ears and flattens my hair against my scalp. I never guessed the world had this much flat space open to the harsh blue sky.

As I tail the Sequoia, I imagine starting a new life out here. Renting a walk-up apartment, sitting by the window at night and listening to the groan of long-haul trucks on the freeway. Out here, where nobody knows my dad or my brothers, I could be whoever I want.

Then again, Nina knows my family, and she doesn't seem to mind me.

The road dead-ends in a gravel lot with picnic tables and hiking trails zigzagging toward stubby hills on the horizon. There are four other cars, so I figure it's safe to park and watch Shadwell leave his SUV.

He's acquired a huge backpack, like he's setting off on a day trip. But instead of taking a trail, he sits down at a picnic table, props the pack against it, and stays put.

Through my binoculars, I watch him slip a map from the pack and spread it out. More thrills.

Two cars arrive. One leaves. A group of college-age girls stake out the table beside Shadwell's, and he goes over to chat with them, pointing at his map. The girls flip their hair, consult the map, laugh, leave. One looks like she might be inviting Shadwell to follow, but he shakes his head.

More newcomers: it's a hiking hot spot. My target continues to study his map as kids with daypacks mill around him, their moms corralling them back to the group.

I return to my living-in-the-desert fantasy. Even if I can't afford UNM, I could probably get places on crews, working my way up from PA to boom operator to best boy. The student filmmakers made me work my ass off, but when they saw I was willing and able, they forgot I was a kid and invited me out for tacos and pitchers of watery margaritas.

I train my binocs on Shadwell again. The composite family group is gone, the kids straggling down the trail, and he's up. Map in hand, he approaches two newcomers: middle-aged women with fanny packs. The women both talk at once, showing him stuff on the map. He socializes for almost five minutes, then returns to his post.

The next arrivals are a hand-holding couple. Shadwell ignores them. A family with three screaming toddlers. Them, too. But when a lone blond woman wobbles her mountain bike over to the table, he pulls out the map again and makes his standard approach.

Twenty minutes later, the mountain biker waves good-bye. I hold my breath, waiting for Shadwell to follow her down the trail. But he's glued to that table. I check my watch—we've been here nearly two hours.

As two and a half more pass, the pattern repeats itself with uncanny accuracy. Whenever a woman or a group of women comes to the trailhead, Shadwell waltzes up with his map and plays Confused Urban Hiker. Smiling and laughing— Mr. Smooth. When they leave, he waves bye-bye and sits down to wait for the next comers. Any group with guys or children in it, he ignores.

What is he, a serial flirter? Or does he just really, really like the view from that picnic table?

A few groups of female hikers act especially friendly. Once

Shadwell follows two laughing girls down the trail, and I slip out of the van and glide across the parking lot, keeping him in sight—only to scramble for cover when he turns and heads back to that same damn spot again.

I've seen cats stare at mouse holes for hours. But when the mouse pokes its head out, the mouser generally *does something*.

Not this guy. When he finally folds up his precious map and rambles back to his Sequoia, I wonder if this is how voyeurs operate, getting a thrill just from being close to their targets.

Maybe these women aren't his targets at all. Anything seems possible. All I know is he has a lot of time on his hands.

And now he's spending it driving back the way he came. On the edge of the suburbs, he turns off into a dingy strip mall and parks in front of a Big Lots. So it's a shopping trip after all?

Or not. Because when Shadwell hauls himself out of the Sequoia, he's still harnessed into the megabackpack.

That seems odd.

I park at the other end of the lot and track him with my binocs as he trudges around the corner of the store. Then I dart across the lot to the building, flatten my back against the wall, and follow.

Beyond the loading dock and a ragged line of trees, the asphalt gives way to another wasteland of grass and sagebrush. There's nothing to block my view of Shadwell hiking his way across the scrub toward—what?

If I follow him out there, he'll spot me. But two of the low, bristly pine trees have limbs close to the ground.

I cross the loading dock and swing myself onto a bough, getting a faceful of chubby needles for my trouble. The bark is scaly, and the branches feel dangerously delicate, but I grit my teeth, brace my feet against the trunk, and manage to reach a decent sitting-fork about fifteen feet up.

There he is—his dark green T-shirt semi-camouflaging him as he strides rapidly among the sagebrush, heading for a cluster of piñon pines like the one where I perch. If he looks back now, he'll see me, but he doesn't look back.

Through the binoculars, I trace his route as a faint trail against the surrounding scrubland. Maybe those rec trails pass along the back of the strip mall.

Which means some of those girls from the picnic area could show up here. My nails bite my palm.

Shadwell disappears into the pines. I creep higher, giving myself a longer view, and wait for him to emerge.

What's he doing in there—lying in wait with his map? Picnicking?

But no: through the binocs, I spot movement among the spindly pines. A flash of silver rises, falls, rises, and there's a shudder in the air—the distant thud of steel on stone? Or my imagination? Wind catches the pine needles, tossing blinding sun into my eyes, and I feel dizzy and grab the trunk harder between my thighs.

Still the rhythmic movement out there. *Digging.*

If he turns around and comes back, I'll be ready to slide down the tree, sprint across the loading dock, hide in the van. But this time I won't follow him.

I'll go out there and see for myself what he's buried between the pines.

NINA

36

Vertigo tugs at my knees and throat as I gaze over the South Rim of the Grand Canyon. Below me stretch buttes and temples and spires, banded like the Kremlin in wine red, iris purple, velvet black. Coming from a landscape with only gullies and gorges, I've never seen the earth drop clean away before.

In the past few days, everything I thought I knew has dropped away, too. I should be grateful for the fresh landscape, but instead my head just keeps spinning.

I lay awake last night wondering how I could nudge Becca toward the subject of why she didn't tell me I had a brother. She won't say much about Dylan that isn't a love fest, I know now, but *how* she says it matters. If she won't meet my eye, I'll know something's wrong.

I just have to get up the courage to broach the subject.

"Why didn't you tell me about Dylan?" I blurt out, forcing my gaze away from the view.

Becca looks confused, with reason—she's already apologized for "accidentally misleading" me in her e-mails. "I thought I did mention him, hon, but I didn't say he lived in Albuquerque. I know now I should have."

I try to smile and look her straight in the eye, pinning her down, but it's harder than I thought. "You said you had three kids. You made it sound like none of them would remember me."

The abyss at my feet keeps tugging my gaze. If solid ground is down at the bottom of the canyon, where've I been standing my whole life? Maybe I've been living on a high, protected plateau like the people in Sky City, only I didn't know it.

I thought if I could catch the Thief, stop him, I wouldn't have to *be* him. But it's not that simple.

The rim feels safer. I'm glad we don't have time to hike to the bottom.

"Dylan was pretty young," Becca says. She doesn't add *when I gave you away*—doesn't need to. "Memories are weird at that age."

"You sent him my photo," I point out. "He recognized me from it. You never sent me a picture of him. And he says he remembers a *lot*."

What I really want to ask is "What do you remember about Dylan's childhood, Becca? Do you feel like you really know your son?"

Becca wouldn't protect a monster because he's family—I can already tell that about her. But if there's something even slightly off about her son, she knows.

I should be scanning her face for signs of denial or dishonesty, but I can't even look at her. Maybe I don't want to know anymore if something's wrong with Dylan. My own darkness is hard enough to face.

A heavy hand cups my shoulder—a mom's hand with experience in soothing freak-outs. "I'm sorry," Becca says.

This is her consistent MO. No excuses or drawn-out explanations, just *sorry*. How can I fight that?

Maybe she should be sorry, because she set me up for the sick terror of that moment in Home Depot when he spoke my name and everything started to unravel. But the terror itself came from inside me. From dreams and obsessions and memories that won't settle into consistent shapes.

Becca goes on talking while I stare into the chasm, tracing the distant flashes of the Colorado River. I force myself not to blink so my tears will dry where they are, unseen.

"I didn't want to overload you. The people at the agency, they say to take it slow with the information. You didn't even answer my letter at first. And Dylan—well, he has this idea that you're very important to him. I worried he wouldn't be able to give you space."

"He is . . . a little intense." I gaze at the darkness beneath our feet.

"I was afraid you wouldn't give him a chance. I'm so glad you did."

Not even a tremor in her voice. If she thought Dylan might

ever hurt me, she wouldn't be able to hide it. Not Becca, who expresses everything, and who knows how it feels when someone you love reveals an unexpected dark side.

She believes in him. Really believes.

"Becca," I say. "How did it happen? With my father? Did you know before the police did?"

Her arm leaves my shoulder and encircles my waist. "No, honey. It was Denise, your aunt, who called the cops. She told them what she'd seen, and then Steve confessed. He was a disturbed man, not a bad one. He thought he was protecting his sister."

Disturbed. A few chemicals out of whack in the brain, and—

My head and hands quiver like I'm grounding an electric current, and Becca lets her arm fall and steps away. Maybe she thinks she overstepped her boundaries.

"If you'd been the one to see the murder, would you have gone to the cops?" I ask before I can stop myself. "Or would you have protected Steve?"

Maybe she won't respond. Who asks that kind of question?

But my birth mother says in a lost voice, like she's floated to the bottom of the canyon and is calling back up to me, "I would have *wanted* to protect your dad. But . . . a mom thinks of her kids first. And I don't trust a man who's been violent once, Nina."

She would have turned him in. "Thank you," I want to say. "I'm sorry I ever doubted you."

Instead, I just clasp her hand.

WARREN

37

I take pics of everything.

The hiking trail winding behind Big Lots where I retrace Shadwell's steps after his Sequoia peels out of the lot. The grove of piñon pines from the inside, white light teasing the fuzzy boughs. The two boulders and the small, almost random-looking cairn of rocks between them.

I'm grateful to the student who thought to stow a spade with the other gear in the van. It's dinky, barely longer than my arm, but the hole isn't deep. Maybe six inches down, I uncover the bright blue lid of a five-gallon plastic bucket.

Even before I open it, I remember Nina saying the Thief made caches, burying his "supplies" in the middle of nowhere so he'd have them when he needed them.

I snap a pic of the contents once I have the lid off. And

later, once I've unearthed the bucket and lugged it back to the motel room, I slip on cheap rubber gloves, lay out each object on the desk, and frame and shoot them one by one.

A fancy rifle scope. Rounds for a .22LR. A suppressor, homemade by the look of it. A flashlight. Duct tape. Zip ties.

Everything you'd need for a murder.

No point in going to the cops. Maybe there are prints here—I didn't see Shadwell put on gloves. But unless somebody went missing within five miles of those hiking trails, the authorities wouldn't do much besides question Shadwell and keep him on the radar. *If* they believed me.

For now, all I have are shreds of suspicious behavior and buried tools. And, of course, secondhand "psychic visions."

Maybe he's one of those people who do weekend geocaching or live-action role-playing. But there's nothing pretend about the bullets.

I almost hit Nina's number, then stop myself. She doesn't need to know any of this while she's safe at her birth mom's place, well away from her brother, and I've got an eye on him.

I'll tell her when she comes back, but I'm already dreading it. I can see the anger and suspicion on her face as I confess I've been following her brother.

The only way to get through that conversation without making her wince and hate me is to gather as much evidence as I can. Enough to convict or exonerate him.

So I return to Piedmont Drive, which is starting to feel like my second home. I do some surveillance from the foreclosure, then sit in the van guzzling a sugary gas-station latte, watching Shadwell's house as the sky darkens and stars appear.

They grilled on the deck today. Shadwell chased the kid around the patio while she shrieked in that borderline hysterical, happy way kids have. Hot Girlfriend started laughing, too, and chased them both indoors.

TV glow bounces on the living room windows for an hour or so, then disappears. If it weren't for that bucket, I'd be almost convinced he's as normal as they come.

I'm about to doze off when a car door slams in the darkness.

I know that engine—the Sequoia. Shit. I need night vision goggles. He must've slipped out without making a sound.

I wait for him to reach the cross street before I start the van, my heart machine-gunning my ribs. Maybe he's going out in the desert where I saw him after Sky City, to the cabin and supposed dump site. Maybe he's going back to Big Lots to retrieve his cache. What will he do when he doesn't find it?

Whatever he does, I'll be careful. So careful. She can count on me for that, at least.

NINA

38

I lie in a frilly guest bed in Becca's house, listening to the drone of central AC and the faint singing of the wind chimes outside. The birds make no sound, their cages covered.

I knew Becca wanted me to leave the B-and-B and stay with her. The wish was in her eyes, unspoken, so I offered.

I text Kirby, and we go back and forth for ten minutes about the new guy she might be seeing, who is *older!!!! Like, almost legal drinking age!*

I try to imagine this older guy, but the only face I see is Warren's. *HS boys aren't so bad*, I write. *Srsly.*

I get a handful of kissy-heart emojis for my trouble. *Look at you! You are soooo falling for him. Adorable.*

I send a blushing-face emoji. *Stop embarrassing me! Okay, beddy-bye time. Miss u.*

The puffy white duvet feels like a cruel joke when the outside temperature hovers near eighty. Silk embroidery on the pillowcase scratches my cheek. Somewhere a real-ass cuckoo clock calls the half hours, breathily singing: *Whee-koo! Whee-koo!* Figures Becca would have one.

The smell comes up so quickly, filling my nostrils, that I almost moan.

Deep, dank, musty earth that hasn't been disturbed in ages. Soil hidden under the sand, rich with minerals, irrigated by hidden streams.

The duvet is gone. The AC is gone. The desert is still here.

The desert, still and always the desert. And now I hear a shovel biting the earth, hitting a rock with a dull clang. I feel the burn in my forearms as I fight the rock free and raise the shovel to toss a black heap on the growing pile beside me.

I'm digging a hole. He's digging a hole.

He hobbles with every step, his right knee sore because he missed a ladder rung on his way down and fell hard. It's his bad knee, the same one where he tore the meniscus after a run. But he keeps digging.

Timbers swing wildly in his vision as he turns back to the hole. The camping lantern brings out every crack and knot in the old wood. A blister is forming between his thumb and forefinger with a sweet, sharp ache.

He's skinning himself raw for this hole in the ground, nearly six feet long and going on five feet deep. The last hole he dug down here was pathetic, an act of desperation. The target had to be folded to fit. This one fits all the traditional requirements.

He did his homework this time, too—made sure the old gold mine didn't have a second level. He didn't want to dig himself through the floor and tumble into a shaft.

Luckily, this state is full of mining-history geeks. A book from the '30s taught him the Dennings-Goodman Mine was dug in this ridge in the 1880s, its main entrance dynamited shut in 1905. Just the three chambers, twenty feet at the deepest, plus the tunnel—more of a hopeful, exploratory dig than anything else. The vein gave out, and the get-rich-quick artists moved on.

Their loss is the Thief's gain.

His hole is a good hole. It will fit whatever it needs.

WARREN

39

My phone wakes me from a deep sleep, chirping like a mutant cricket, and I reach out blindly to squash it dead. Instead, I somehow connect.

Her voice, thready and tentative. "Hey. How are you?"

Hearing her makes me feel warm all over, and only part of it is guilt because I can't tell her where I was last night. "Hey *you*. I'm good. Just—kinda was sleeping."

"Oh God, I'm sorry. I know you like to sleep late."

"'S okay." My throat and nasal passages feel scorched, tender. I'm starting to understand why the old desert rats quake and drawl the way they do. "I like hearing your voice."

"Same here. We're going to the Painted Desert in a sec."

Ten A.M. already. I've been sleeping in my clothes, blinds open. I crashed here at seven after spending most of the night on the shoulder of that desolate county road, waiting for Shadwell to leave his desert lair.

When he breezed out of the house, I braced for him to return to Big Lots or the trailhead, but he headed for his favorite spot in the middle of nowhere. Staking out the mouth of the access road didn't make for a fascinating eight hours, but I could be reasonably sure he wasn't hurting anyone.

If only I'd gotten there *before* him, hunkered down, and found a place to watch. Maybe he would've shown me the way to the mine Nina keeps talking about. Cached murder accessories aren't evidence of murder, but a corpse helps.

Now Shadwell's back at home, sleeping the sleep of the unjust on his boring cul-de-sac. I made sure of that.

"Glad you called," I say. "Miss you."

Nina just breathes into the phone.

"What?"

"I had a bad dream." Softly, like she's apologizing.

"You mean . . . that kind of dream?"

"He dug a hole. Like a grave. I don't know anymore if it's real or not, but that's what I saw." On the last word, I hear her too-sharp intake of breath.

"*Like* a grave?" I keep my tone casual, but my heart is battering my ribs again. What if she somehow saw him burying the cache? "Was it, like, just a hole? Or six feet down and coffin-shaped and everything?"

"Coffin-shaped. Does it matter?"

I keep forgetting I'm supposed to be *discouraging* her delusions. "Where'd he dig this hole? In your dream, I mean?" I try to sound flip, skeptical, but my voice falters.

"In the mine shaft that probably doesn't exist."

So he was there. Adrenaline streaks from my kidneys to my brain to my fingertips, and I sit up straighter, not feeling the sand or the sunburn now.

A mini-movie blossoms in my head, all magic light and galloping strings. *The sun dips over the horizon, and the villain drives up in his Sequoia. He pops the trunk and yanks out a struggling figure bound with zip ties and duct tape.*

But who's that lurking behind a boulder with a bolt-action rifle? Our hero.

"It was just a dream," I say soothingly. "You know that now, right?"

My foot on Shadwell's back, my muzzle at the base of his neck.

Cut it out and get real, Warren—the situation needs a detective, not a cowboy. I have to find the mine entrance before he ever has a chance to use that grave.

"I hoped they would...stop," Nina says. "The dreams where he's hurting people."

"You're awake now. That's the important thing."

I'll find an army surplus store and blow my last cash on a cheap pair of night vision goggles, and tonight I'll go back to the desert. Get there first. I know where to hide the van now.

"I'm sorry to bother you with my weirdness," Nina says.

With each word comes a fresh twinge of guilt, but I brush my doubts away. Stay strong. "You're not bothering me. Ever."

For her own sake, she can't know. Not till I'm sure.

NINA

40

Becca says we're not lost in the Painted Desert, but I think we are.

This place is like a fever dream. No trail under our feet, just sand and dirt and dust. We passed two tiger-striped Egyptian pyramids a half hour ago, then skirted gravel heaps four stories high, then picked our way through a plain of cigarette ash strewn with black shards of petrified wood.

Becca treats these bizarre visions like landmarks on a map, saying things like "Only a quarter mile to the Lithodendron Wash."

And that, too, could be part of a dream. Any minute the pyramids and giant ash heaps will slide into rubble. The sky will go dark, and I'll lose the only thing I still recognize: the sun.

It's because of the dream last night, whispers the rational part of my brain.

After so many nights of peaceful, almost normal dreams—his sleeping mind, his breaths matched to mine—I thought maybe I was free of the visions. But last night's was as vivid as they've ever been.

Thank God for Warren's calming voice.

Every August, my mom and I used to visit the Great Vermont Corn Maze. There's nothing scary about corn until suddenly the world is *all* corn: a hissing green sea swallowing the horizon.

My dreams have conquered my brain the way corn took over that landscape. Only they're not dreams anymore, but waking visions that warp and fabricate memories. When Warren told me how he followed Dylan out to the desert, after Sky City, it was like my dreams had taken over *his* brain, too.

I'll call him when we're out of here, to remind him what's real. We can do that for each other.

If I ever do get out of here.

On our way around a hundred-foot-tall pyramid of shimmering, coppery something, we meet a family of backpackers. I fight the urge to ask them where we are. Becca's "Hi" sounds too chipper, and we all imitate her, echoes of the kids' shrill voices pinging off the monolith.

Then they're gone.

At the top of a rise, Becca stops to glug water. Sweat sheens her face as she takes sharp, staccato breaths. "I used to be able to do this hike in ninety minutes with Edgardo. Now I feel like we'll be making a full day of it."

"Are you sure we aren't off course? Should we look at the

map? Or my phone?" In a detached way, I hear the panic in my voice.

"No, hon, we're almost out. Your phone wouldn't work anyway." She wipes her face. "This hike is baby stuff, Nina. Nobody gets lost on the edge of the wilderness area."

"That's what hikers always say in the reenactments on *I Shouldn't Be Alive*. Then they end up spending a week in the desert drinking their own urine."

Becca laughs weakly. "You have to know the desert. Respect it. Too many tourists think it's just a big sandbox."

I remember how I wandered around looking for Dylan's mine, the sun beating on my head, and shiver.

The right ledge should have been so easy to find. I can close my eyes and find it now.

From outside, the crevice looks barely wider than a mail slot. You ease your knees over the rock lip and slide your pelvis in flat, then let go and jump blind, trusting you'll land on your feet. From the next sandy ledge, a wooden ladder takes you the rest of the way down. That's where Dylan missed a rung and hurt his knee.

Except there is no such place, I remind myself, and none of that happened. Just like the map in the shed. Just like the Gustafssons, who could be alive somewhere for all I know.

If I can't trust myself to sort out fantasy and reality, maybe I can trust Becca. She's so sure she knows where we're going.

We're back at the sandy riverbed Becca calls a "wash," though it looks like it hasn't seen water for centuries. "We're close to the parking lot, right?" I ask.

"Heading that way."

On the far side of the wash, I zigzag through a field of chest-high boulders, rusty and sulfur-splotched. One appears to be stenciled with a pale spiral—no, an ancient handmade doodle like I've seen on Warren's tourist sites. Petroglyph.

"Hey, Becca!" When I turn to survey the landscape, I see only boulders and a sky so blue it burns my eyes.

"Becca!" I scramble too quickly over the rocks, scraping my right shin when I fall and then my left forearm as I hoist myself up.

I leap off the last boulder and land practically on top of her. She's slumped in the grass, her back against a pitted boulder, her eyes closed.

"Becca! Hey!" I try to get water, but the zip of my pack catches, and I grab hers, pull out the bottle and shake it helplessly in front of her. How far away is that family?

"It's okay. Jus' tired." Becca opens her eyes.

She tries to drink, but the cap's still on, so I untwist it and raise the bottle to her lips.

"It's okay," I echo, more to myself than to her. "What happened? Did you faint? Should you be in the shade?" *Don't leave me here alone.*

Becca shakes her head, takes the bottle from me, and drinks for a while. When she finally lowers it, she says, "I lied to you."

"What?" Terror closes my throat. "We really are lost, aren't we? You don't know how to get back."

"No." She raises the water and takes another swallow. "I know exactly where we are."

"Then what?" I lean back against the pockmarked boulder, feeling its heat through my T-shirt. The sandy wash below us glares so hard I squint.

"I was here with your dad," Becca says, low. "We sat here with our backs against these very rocks. I think it was the same week you were conceived."

"Oh." I feel a little queasy. *No more trips down memory lane, please. Just show me the way out.*

"I lied." Her voice cracks. "I did have a reason for not telling you about your brother, but I thought you'd think I had a screw loose. Crazy lady with all the birds. You didn't hardly know me yet, Nina, and I didn't want you running for the hills."

I dig my hands into the dry grass, grinding sand into the tender skin under my nails. For a few seconds, I can't even speak.

Dylan is my brother. He loves me too much. She thought he'd spook me. That's all that's all that's all.

I ask, "What did you lie about?"

"I came here with your father," Becca starts, and then corrects herself. "With Steve. When we were sitting here, that's when he told me about him and Denise."

Denise. Dylan's aunt, *my* aunt.

"I don't want you thinking mental illness runs in your family. Steve was never diagnosed. And Dylan—he was a kid with an overactive imagination. His dad said something to him once, and he ran with it."

"Ran with *what*?" I drank an iced coffee on the way here, and it's curdling in my stomach.

"Steve thought he visited his sister in his dreams." A small voice, like she doesn't want anybody to hear. "Like he was inside her head."

Too late. All I can do is sit frozen, listening.

"Every night Steve would visit with Denise, no matter how far apart they were—that's what he told me, right here, like it was something normal between siblings. And one of those nights, Steve saw Rick—that was Denise's husband—knock Denise on the floor. Bruise her up, kick her bad."

My hand covers my face, protecting it. *Can't be.*

"I don't know if Rick really beat her. Denise and Rick lived in San Bernardino, and we were in Phoenix. We only saw her a few times a year. But Steve believed it."

My father had the same curse I do.

"That's why he killed Rick." My voice sounds tiny, childlike, helpless. Like my dad must have felt when his sister insisted that the scenes he'd witnessed were just his imagination. *Stop being crazy.*

My dad executed a man to protect his sister—to save her life. She didn't back him up. She denied his visions. She took her husband's side.

Becca's still talking.

Steve and Denise were always so close it was hard for them to live apart, she says. It practically killed Denise to testify against her brother, and maybe it *did* kill her, since she took her own life not long after Steve took his.

"Did she see the murder?" I whisper. Meaning: *in her sleep.*

But no. My dad was crazy. I'm crazy.

"When she walked in, Rick was dead on the floor, and Steve had the gun on his knee. He'd been waiting for Denise and said he could explain. That's what she testified."

I shiver, imagining my dad on his knees trying to justify a cold-blooded murder on the basis of a dream.

"That's why, after you were born—well, I went a little off the rails, Nina. I shouldn't have let it spook me. But one night Dylan started talking about seeing inside your dreams, and I couldn't help it—I panicked."

The too-bright sky lurches above me, pivoting into a new alignment.

No.

"I started worrying he had whatever his dad had. Schizophrenia, maybe. It started off innocent. But four nights in one week, something happened that chilled me."

"What happened?" My voice doesn't sound like mine.

"You'd be upstairs sleeping, and Dylan would pad downstairs in his pj's and say, 'Ma, the baby's awake. She's gonna cry.'"

Becca smiles like she can't help it, remembering six-year-old Dylan. "I'd say, 'Shush and go back to bed,' because it was crickets on the baby monitor.

"But then two minutes later, you'd be wailing. I'd ask Dylan how he knew ahead of time, and he'd say, 'I was with her in my sleep. She wasn't happy.'"

Becca breaks off, her dark eyes probing mine. "Nina, what is it?"

I can't breathe, my throat burning. Above Becca's head, two hawks—buzzards?—wheel in the sky.

Can't be true. Can't be.

Here she is saying it is true, not knowing her words are impaling me like a cold steel girder, because *I knew this I knew this I knew this.*

I just didn't want to know.

The water I just drank bubbles back into my throat, and I lean over and retch while Becca pats my back and throws an arm over my shoulder to bring me closer.

"Oh, honey," she says. "I don't think Dylan ever hurt you. I swear he didn't hurt you. I think he was just ultra-attuned to the sounds you made. But back then, I thought—I don't know what I thought. That he might be sneaking into your room, pinching you or something. Causing the trouble himself."

I shake my head. My eyes ache with unshed tears. No, Dylan never meant to hurt me, not physically.

This whole time, he's been inside my head, too.

Like Aunt Denise, but for his own darker reasons, he's acted perfectly innocent. Tried to convince me I imagined everything I saw him do. Succeeded.

What has he seen? What does he know? Why did he walk up to me at Home Depot and pretend nothing was wrong? Invite me into his house? Ignore all my tests and provocations?

Why *not*? I know how good he is at putting up a false front, at pushing ugly thoughts to the background of his mind. He knew I'd never beat him at his own game.

I used to go to sleep way earlier than he did—but not anymore, and certainly not on this trip. So he's seen me planning, plotting.

And then it comes to me: how my eyelid twitches, but only late at night. How *his* eyelid twitches, but not when we're face-to-face. Only when I'm inside his head.

It's not just a symptom of sleep deprivation; it's a signal. A warning.

Frantically I try to remember when I last had the tic. The night I spent on the ridge in the desert. Probably a few late nights in the car, driving. Almost definitely that night after Sky City.

Warren. He knows about Warren.

I free myself from Becca and rise shakily to my feet. "I need to make a call."

I turn my phone on; it searches for a signal. "Can we go back to the car? Right now?"

"'Course." Becca settles her daypack between her shoulders, her color healthier, like I've jarred her back from the edge of heat exhaustion. "We can make it in fifteen. Who do you need to call, sweetie?"

"My friend in Albuquerque. There's something important I forgot to tell him."

Her. I told Dylan my friend was a Jaylynne, and he may have told Becca, but I don't bother to correct myself.

As we clamber up the rocks, I try to think of an excuse for my sudden need to call, but I'm too focused on helping Becca over the tough places. Anyway, she's stopped asking questions. That's good, because I can't think of a way to tell her the truth without mentioning the part where her son is a monster.

In fifteen endless minutes, we leave behind the surreal world of giant ash heaps and anthills. We stagger across the lot to her truck, where I pull out my phone—thank God, bars.

My text looks like the handiwork of a drooling idiot: *Stay @ motell tonite, lck door. Dont go out, wait 4 my call. Pls.*

My hands shake too much to correct anything, so I just send. As soon as I'm alone, I'll leave voice mail.

If Dylan knows everything, maybe he's the one I should be calling and texting. But I *can't*.

He was digging a grave, but not for Warren. I would have known that. As long as he's busy with random "targets"—and I hate myself for thinking this—maybe we're safe.

Blood pounds in my temples as Becca pulls us out of the Painted Desert, switching off the radio. We listened to a country station on the way here and even sang together on a couple songs, our voices falling easily into harmony. She must know I'm in no mood to sing now.

The phone itches in my pocket, but there's no buzz of reply.

By the time we're back on the interstate, Becca's talking again, her voice riding nervously up and down. She's trying to explain something that makes her sound like she's fighting nausea. Like the words are rocks in her throat.

"I could've brought him to therapy. I should've had him evaluated. But I was just a kid myself, and I was scared stiff to find out craziness ran in the family. If my old man hadn't been a raging boozer, I'd have brought you to my folks' house, Nina. But I couldn't think of anywhere safe.

"Getting Dylan out of the house—I thought about it. I imagined Child Services taking him away. How he'd look when they put him in the van, his eyes like his dad's—his eyes pleading with me. No."

"It's okay," I whisper. She doesn't seem to hear.

"You were an adorable baby—who wouldn't want you? But Dylan was almost seven, with scraggly hair and missing teeth, and I couldn't give him up. He'd go from foster family to foster family. That was my reasoning—no, it was panicking, Nina. But I didn't know; I wasn't *sure*—"

On and on like that. On and on, till I stop whispering and start practically yelling: "It's all right, Becca. It turned out okay. I'm okay. Dylan's okay—and you needed him. You don't have to explain."

She stops talking.

We're not home yet, haven't swallowed enough miles of asphalt and sand and sagebrush that all look the same to me now because—

Warren. He has to get safely back to the rolling green hills and valleys of home. It's all that matters now.

Nothing on my phone.

"After I left," I ask, "did Dylan still say he was inside my dreams?"

Becca just grips the wheel. Then, as we hit our exit ramp, she starts talking again. Like I've turned a faucet in a long-abandoned house, and all this gunk comes pouring out.

She describes the drive from Phoenix to the detention center in San Bernardino to visit my dad. Hours of crossing the desert, first when she was very pregnant, and later with me wailing in the car seat and Dylan doing puzzle books beside me. He was so good. He tried to distract me with songs and games. Becca didn't dare leave us at her parents' house, and her friends had gone weird and distant after the sentencing.

The visits were hard, too, because Steve was "unquiet in his mind," Becca says. He wouldn't stop talking about his sister and her husband. "That man was poisoning my sister's mind, and she was poisoning me," he'd say. "He would have killed her in the end, and that would kill me, too. The nothingness, Becca. Every night, the nothingness."

Becca started spacing out her visits. She always came back from the penitentiary wanting a stiff drink or several.

When she heard Steve was dead, she blamed herself. She'd never wanted to visit him again, and he'd made her wish come true. For us.

I shake my head, *It wasn't your fault*, as Becca turns onto the long dirt driveway leading to her house.

After Steve hanged himself in jail, Becca passed out drunk two nights in a row, leaving Dylan to put me to bed, which he did with no mishaps whatsoever.

Then she got dressed and brought me to Child Services.

She did it for Dylan. She believed he'd return to normal, and she was right (*she thinks*). She did it for me.

And yes—because Becca is finally answering my question, as we sit stiffly in the parked truck, not looking at each other—yes, for a few years after that, Dylan talked about seeing me in his dreams. Becca let him, because it made her feel better to pretend she believed what he was saying. Sometimes she caught herself believing it for real. "False balm for the heart of the wicked," she says and laughs.

Dylan described me sleeping. Full, warm, contented under soft blankets. He described the mobile hanging over my bed. The sun shone through its cutouts of tigers and starfish, and they chimed sweetly.

As she says this, I hear the chiming. I see the starfish,

marigold yellow with pink stripes. We took the mobile down when I was eight, but it was exactly as Dylan described it to Becca.

And one day when he was nine, Becca says, Dylan stopped talking about me. He never mentioned his dreams again.

Like me, I see now, he kept silent out of love. I wanted my mom not to think she was second best, so I stopped talking about the boy in my dreams. Dylan wanted his mom to know she hadn't made the wrong choice in protecting him.

Two people can be a family, as strong as any. And that's why I can never let Becca know what she was really protecting when she kept her son by her side.

. . .

When we finally leave the truck, there's only one thing in the world I want to do, but I still take time to hug Becca.

I hug her on the porch while the wind chimes sing and ping around us. She flinches at first, but then she lets her head droop on my shoulder, her broad arms tight around my waist.

All the time my mind churns, like Dylan's mind when he kisses Eliana. *I have to convince her everything is okay with us. So she'll never suspect that Dylan and I didn't turn out okay after all.* She's punished herself enough for giving me up; she doesn't need to know the rest.

Dylan must have started deceiving his mom early. He told her about his dreams as long as she needed reassurance, and then he stopped. He learned to hide, to have a secret life.

In that secret life inside his head, our family was still intact, just a little discombobulated. Brother and sister saw each other every night. Our dad lived in Dylan's dreams, too, under the apple tree. He would never die because Dylan controlled death. He decided when it would happen.

My eyes are still wet with tears I don't remember crying as I lock the upstairs bathroom and sink down on the fluffy white bath mat to call Warren.

Still no new texts. No calls. I leave a message, keeping my voice level: "Warren, it's six thirty. I need you to stay in the motel room—no, wait. Go somewhere public, like the pie place, and text me. I'll meet you tonight. I found out something new, and he could"—I swallow hard, can't expel the dry knot from my throat—"be dangerous after all. He's probably seen your van. Wait for me. Just trust me. Call me, and I'll try to explain."

Steve explained his dreams to Becca. That helped a lot.

The call ended, I sit for a minute taking in the bathroom's soothing orderliness: the pink, blue, and mint-green toothbrush holders perfectly match the towels folded on a shelf. My brain roils in sickly circles, still stuck on *This is not happening*.

Becca tried. With her color-coordinated bathroom, her photo album, the birdcages Dylan built for her.

I dig my nails deep into my palm and hit Dylan's number.

What will he say? What will *I* say? How can I tell whether he plans to hurt the boy I think I might love? How can I persuade him not to?

It doesn't matter, because he doesn't answer.

WARREN

41

I t's nearly seven when I reach the access road, well before sunset.

My phone keeps searching for a signal, draining the battery, so I turn it off after I've parked a half mile past the turn-off, in a packed-dirt pullout screened by piñon pines. Then I hoist my pack on my shoulders and get going.

The shortest way to the ridge is straight across the desert, through the purple clots of shadow cast by sagebrush and creosote bushes. Where the ground softens, I pause to scuff out my prints. Blue drains from the pale-rimmed bowl of sky. Lizards dart out of my way, but otherwise I could be the only thing alive for miles.

Here's the cabin Nina described—and here's where the tire

tracks end. No one's parked there, but I get low and skulk from bush to bush.

From the parking area, the natural path up the ridge is east. West for me, then, where the ridge deteriorates into head-high boulders and ledges sloping toward the desert floor. There's no trail through this mini badlands, and that suits me fine.

I climb to the top and then explore the ridge face, looking for the mine entrance. Today I researched abandoned New Mexico mines—coal, gold, uranium. Some are flooded; some are radioactive; some could collapse at the slightest provocation.

I find bare reddish rock face and a few ledges where a person could almost sit concealed from the valley. But no gaping chasms in the hillside, no railroad tracks or rotting timbers, nothing to suggest the ridge is hollow.

Damn it. But Nina said the cave was tricky to find. And if she didn't imagine it, I *will* find it tonight.

Back on the ridge's western approach, I hunker down between two red boulders, one a seven-foot standing monolith and the other half sunken in sand. Here I command a view of the cliff and cabin but can still duck out of sight.

The rifle's been weighing on my back. I take it out, load it, chamber a round, and strap it across my chest. Easy gestures, long practice.

If anyone asks, I'm hunting. What do people hunt out here?

The night vision goggles go around my neck. Water bottles and protein bars by my side.

I was always a whiner during deer season. Marines, my dad would tell me, carried five times the gear I did over ten times the distance without bitching or moaning.

Was Shadwell a marine? Am I well and truly screwed?

The night vision will give me an edge, and the moon won't rise till after midnight. But I'll need to be still. The ridgetop is less than fifty feet away, and the desert amplifies the sound of every falling pebble.

I eat a protein bar, rehydrate, and watch the sun slip down the sky. The bookmark from Rivendell Books flutters from my torn Dashiell Hammett paperback and skids to the sand.

My hometown feels even more than two thousand miles away.

Clouds sheen the horizon, then the whole desert catches fire. New crannies and protuberances appear in the boulders like they're aging before my eyes.

The sun slides under the earth, and in a blink, all the colors change again. The fire melts, leaving healing-bruise purples in its wake. The sand goes beige; the sagebrush and pines turn to inky pools.

Birds cry, scurrying rodents rustle. Shrieks that I recognize as hunting owls set my teeth vibrating.

It takes more than an hour for darkness to fall.

I prop my feet up and watch the nightly show. Mice venture from their burrows, owls scream, light hangs lurid in the sky. No one to witness it till now—except Shadwell, I suppose. I've stumbled into a fairground that's been officially shut for years, yet every night the midway still lights up; the roller coaster and Tilt-A-Whirl still run, their hurdy-gurdy music hectic on the breeze.

I see why he comes here.

Best-case scenario: I stay out of sight and obtain crucial

intel to supplement the contents of that blue bucket. Worst-case scenario: he comes with someone. A captive. A girl.

The .30-06's got a decent scope. I might only have one chance to take him at a distance, but my hands *would* be steady.

Worse worst-case scenario: he comes with a body.

That won't happen. But I think of the Gustafssons buried in a cold hole. Missing until the news reporters got tired of a story that never changed.

Back in Vermont, Nina was scared shitless of Shadwell. Back then, she didn't care that we didn't have a shred of evidence. Now she's doubting herself. Letting him win her over.

She may be confused, but she's not on his side. The way she kissed me, touched me—it was real. Awkward. Messy. More importantly (though my body tells me nothing's more important than that night), Nina made me promise not to confront her brother. She tried to keep me safe, just like I've tried to keep her safe by not telling her about the cache.

I hate keeping secrets from her, but that won't last much longer.

The eastern sky turns slate blue; the stars evolve from etchings into tiny headlights. The western sky bleeds light. The fairground is shutting down, the ghostly carnies flitting back to their graves in the sand.

I watch long-legged birds fight over a patch of dust.

A hundred years ago, maybe more, someone dug a mine in this ridge. Grizzled men dueled with six-shooters, squabbling over gold. Maybe bones were left to rot. Maybe ghosts return by night to lament fortunes never made, coasts never reached, friendships betrayed, treasury notes buried in the desert and never found.

As the cabin in the valley disappears, I close my eyes and try to imagine home.

Mom's washing the dishes, Aretha Franklin bawling in the background. Outside lurks Vermont's June gloom, gray clouds racing above pale green maples. Upstairs, my dad hunches over the computer, a finger flicking across his lips.

My mom dreamed of college, never made it. She says I should be a professor, probably imagining me with a flock of adoring students and a leather couch in my study. In New England, of course. If I stray too far, it'll be a desertion, a betrayal.

Yet here I am.

The ridgeline blackens against the sky. The Big Dipper blazes. The rest of the desert might as well be the bottom of the ocean.

I put on the goggles, adjust the strap, and practice walking, getting the hang of navigating without depth perception. The range is only fifty feet in "stealth mode," but it should be enough.

The sky stops changing. Still I wait—for moonrise. For him.

Wouldn't it be fucking hilarious if he didn't show?

Five or six cars have passed on the county road since I hunkered down. Each time, I crouched and got a good grip on the rifle, but they all sped on.

Now a motor does slow. Idles. Turns.

The tires kick up an invisible veil of dust as the car rambles up the side road toward the cabin.

For a second, I can't get the night vision goggles back over my head. My heart pounds against my chest like a clapper in a bell.

The engine sputters, goes silent. The desert's tiny sounds become deafening.

I creep to the edge of my retreat, brace myself on one knee, and get a look at the Sequoia.

In the eerie, green-limned world of night vision, the SUV's driver is a moving blot. He's unloading another blot, nothing too heavy, because his gait is normal. He shuts the car and disappears behind the cabin.

Where behind the cabin?

Screw the fifty-foot range and the flattened green outlines. I wrench the NVG onto my forehead and stare into pitch black, my heart still hammering.

Too dark. I could be in a cave.

I force my throat muscles to relax so I can *breathe, Warren, breathe. If you don't breathe, you can't aim.*

With painful slowness, my eyes habituate again. The ridgeline emerges against the starry sky.

Light darts in the cabin. A flashlight.

He's there. I breathe evenly like you do when a buck enters shooting range.

The flashlight disappears, and I will my ears into superhuman sensitivity. *The door. Is he opening it?*

Wind. Insect drone. Two witless shrieks from the clumped sagebrush. Thanks a shitload, Mr. Owl.

Or is the owl warning me? Did Shadwell startle it?

Without the flashlight inside, the cabin is barely

visible against the sky. I steel myself and clamp on the goggles again.

It's like snorkeling, your breath tinny in your ears. Gazing into the underwater world, I see no one by the cabin or the car. No one coming up the rise toward me, or on the ridge. No one behind me in the rubble.

Where the hell is Shadwell? Why's he sitting in the cabin in the dark?

Could he be on the phone? Is his signal stronger than mine?

I resist the urge to remove the NVG and check for telltale blue LCD glow. The cabin window's too small, anyway.

He can't have slipped up the ridge. There's no route that doesn't take him into my sightlines. Besides, assuming he doesn't have his own NVG, he'd need the flashlight. No matter how well he knows the path, it's treacherous.

No smoke from the cabin. He's not using the woodstove for light.

My breathing shallows as I open my ears to the minutest sounds. All I hear is blood pounding in my temples and my inner voice screaming at Shadwell: *Asshole, will you just leave your little hidey-hole and hike up the ridge already?*

It's okay, Warren. Calm down. Breathe from the diaphragm.

A man doesn't bitch and moan, my dad would say. A man waits patiently for his game, hours if need be. A man doesn't complain that his legs are cramped or the desert night is surprisingly cold or his rifle is heavy.

If Shadwell popped out of that cabin and made a beeline for me, what would I do? Aim for the center of mass and then tell Nina, *I shot your brother 'cause, well, he was there?*

Even with night vision, he couldn't see me in my hiding place. Yet a shiver slithers down my back as I imagine his eyes (bronze like Nina's) narrowing as they zero in on me.

This isn't Shadwell's property. He's no cop. I've got as much right to be here as he does.

Am I really prepared to shoot him? What if he's exactly what he appears to be—good with his hands, nice to kids, served our country, likes to grill corn on the cob?

Anger at Nina whips through me like a gust of desert wind. Before she changed, *she* convinced me Shadwell was America's greatest unsung serial killer. She dreamed he was digging a grave, for God's sake. If I'm here for nothing—

As blood starts its drumbeat in my ears again, I hear something else.

Rock hitting rock, a percussive *snap*.

Too loud for the wind or a critter. Out there on the sloping plain between me and the cabin.

The *empty* plain.

My eyes scan the flat green field of my night vision, back and forth, back and forth, willing the device to improve its range. Could he be in front of the cabin? Behind the Sequoia?

Again: *crack*.

An impact, pebbles sliding in its wake. A footstep?

It's no more than ten feet from my hiding place. I lower the rifle at sagebrush, finger on the trigger, *breathe, breathe*, only there's nothing to aim at; the bush is too small to hide anyone—

"Hands in the air."

A crisp voice, barely raised. Behind me.

Suddenly, the desert is full of light, the shrubs casting shadows.

I'm so confused I almost fire into the sagebrush where he should have been, where he isn't.

"Hands in the air."

Exact same intonation. No wasted breath, like a cop or a soldier following protocol. No emotion.

I wheel to see him standing five feet up the rise.

A faceless figure and a blazing headlamp illuminating the fat barrel of a .40-cal carbine. Steady as they come.

It's as clear to me as the desert swimming in his beam that he doesn't think he's confronting a prowler. He tossed stones over my head to confuse me. This is an ambush.

I raise my .30-06 to aim, willing my hands still because this is my last chance.

"I got no problem killing you," the dead voice says.

NINA

42

The drive back to Albuquerque takes four hours, and every ten minutes I hit REDIAL.

Every time it's the same horrible, generic message, not even Warren's voice. *The customer you've called is currently unavailable. . . .* And I cuss and fiddle with the car's AC. Outside, the sunset makes the west glow nuclear before it all fades to black.

When I came out of the bathroom, back in Arizona, Becca was warming up canned soup. I couldn't remember anymore whether she thought my "friend" back in Albuquerque was a boy or a girl, so I just said, "My friend called. There was . . . a mugging. I have to get back right away."

"I'm so sorry, honey. Your friend's okay now?"

"Yes." *I hope.* "Just scared."

Then Becca's eyes filled with tears. "I was afraid you might leave after I told you everything."

"Oh, God, Becca, it's not that, I swear. I don't *want* to leave you." This time I wasn't lying, and I threw my arms around her, muttering, "I swear I'll come back" into her shoulder, a ragged pulse throbbing in my temple.

"Okay," she said, patting my back. "You go be with your friend, Nina. I understand."

When we said good-bye, the desert shadows stretching long, I let Becca hold me longer than I should have. I'd miss that house, its birds and wind chimes, its pastel bathroom that strove in vain to deny the past.

The whole time I was waiting for the fateful sign, the twitch of my eyelid. *Can Dylan see this? Is he inside my head?*

I can't reach him, either. Not the normal way.

Not now, I tell myself for the hundredth time as I gun it toward Albuquerque. When it happens, I'll know. And that won't be for a while, because Dylan keeps vampire hours.

Except those nights when I staked out his house or his hideout—and now I know why he was all tucked in by midnight. He suspected I was watching him, and he wanted to be sure.

As I cross the New Mexico border under the darkening desert sky, a passing car blinds me, and shivers cascade down my spine. The Legacy floats toward the median—have I lost control? No. A twitch of the wheel rights me.

A twitch. Dylan knew the whole time. He knew when I was in *his* head, too—he must have figured it out at some point—but he kept the awareness from forming into telltale thoughts. He repressed, he compartmentalized, so all I sensed was the faintest anticipation, like something bright flickering at the corner of his vision. *She's here.*

God, I hope he didn't see me and Warren in the motel room when we...

How did my dad and Denise stand it, knowing about their connection the whole time they were growing up? And that makes me wonder—if I'd been raised with Dylan, would things have been different?

If we'd grown up together, I'd have agonized during his tour of duty, checking on him every night in my sleep, terrified of losing him. After he killed the old man in upstate New York, I would have had to choose. By now, one of us might be dead or in a cell. Or worse: I might be keeping his secrets.

I don't want my eyelid to twitch; it'll mean he's in my head or looking through my eyes, polluting me. And I do want my eyelid to twitch, because then I'll know he's asleep and Warren is safe—for now.

Call me, Warren. Text me. Do it.

• • •

Still no calls when I hit the city limits at eleven thirty, so I race to Dylan's house first.

Piedmont is as placid as ever. Eliana's Civic sits in the driveway, but the Sequoia is gone. Where is he?

No way to know. I head to our motel, forcing myself not to run the last red light. *Be there be there be there.*

The window's dark. I catch the seat belt in the car door,

let it go, dash up the stairs so fast my eyes tear and my heart hammers in my ears.

Be here anyway. Be sitting in the dark watching a marathon of a stupid cop show, surrounded by empty bags of Funyuns. Look at me like I'm nuts. Ask me, "What are you freaking out about now?"

I fall into the room. Empty except for his stuff.

I grab a T-shirt Warren left crumpled on the bed and bring it to my face, breathing him in. He was here this afternoon after the bed got turned down. Where did he go?

Then I spot the blue plastic bucket wedged under the motel desk, and I already know what it is, and I groan aloud.

I've seen buckets like this before. I don't have to open it to know what's inside—flashlight, restraints, ammo. I don't even have to read the Post-it stuck to the lid, but I do anyway.

It says in Warren's neat handwriting: *Watched DS cache this in piñon pines behind Big Lots. Bring to PD.*

Instructions for me, I suppose, if I don't find him. Without a word about his current location.

He didn't expect me back tonight. He was probably hoping I'd never read the note at all.

Dylan couldn't have come here and taken Warren—he'd have spotted the bucket and grabbed that, too. Maybe Warren meant to hide the evidence later. But he went out somewhere—for junk food, probably, or to case Dylan's house—and then . . .

I collapse on the bed like a puppet with cut strings. I need to get up and drive, but my exhausted brain tells me, *Too much. Too much.*

Maybe Warren didn't go out to the desert. Maybe he's eating pie right now.

I clutch his shirt to my chest and pull my feet up on the spread, Chucks and all. I'm only resting here for a moment, enough to get a second wind, and then I'll go downstairs to the car.

After all, I can't *make* myself sleep. No matter how helpful that might be.

Back when I was trying to pull all-nighters, before I got the pills, all my straining to stay awake just made my vision blur and my body go heavy like I had the flu. I remember how my head fell back, how I'd trace circles on my palms, how I'd pinch myself or pull my hair just to hold myself fast in this body a little longer—

Yes. Like that—and I force my eyelids open. I need to stop letting myself slip into this grayness, I need to be alert, I need to *go*—

Behind my drooping eyelids, I'm still awake enough to see a tiger-striped pyramid rise from the desert floor. Becca appears beside me, tears in her eyes. "It's okay," she says. "I know the way out."

My eyes snap open. There's my childhood mobile with its clinking tigers and starfish, sun from the window setting them afire. Tiger stripes on the desert. Tigers, tigers, burning bright.

I'll get up. I'll go.

I don't feel my eyes close this time. Shapes flit in the dark like stray radio signals, parts of my brain that haven't shut down.

Then, without warning, light.

I'm in a dark place staring into the glare of a flashlight.

My chair is straight-backed, uncomfortable, and I'm facing somebody else in a chair, only he's not sitting alert like me.

He's slumped, bound. *Dead weight.*

The angled light glints on the duct tape that covers his mouth and, above that, on his glazed eyes. Half-open. One lid puffy. The cheek below it is bruised and swollen, too, so it takes me a second to recognize Warren.

Oh, God. Where are you?

But Warren can't hear me.

I recognize that chair. The one in the cabin.

I feel the crick in my back—*Dylan's* back. The knee aching where he banged it climbing into the cave. I feel his body's determination to sit here as long as it takes with his eyes trained directly on the boy slouched in the chair, still breathing.

Breathing.

The boyfriend. A skinny kid playing with a man's tools. Disgust mingles with pity in Dylan's mind, and we don't want to look, but we have to.

We'll sit here as long as it takes, waiting for the twitch.

The hole in the ground is ready. Deep.

Don't think about that.

Dylan's eyelid twitches, and then he knows. He doesn't mask or muffle his triumph this time as his eyes—my eyes—slide down Warren's body and fix hard on the white thing pinned to his army jacket. A sheet of drugstore notebook paper with words scrawled in black Sharpie. Not as neat as Dylan would like, because his hand quivered as he wrote the message to his sister. He may be the Thief in the Night, he may control death, but he can't always control himself, and right now he's a bit pissed at her. Prepared to forgive, but still annoyed, because she could have prevented this. None of this should have happened.

The paper says: *Text yes if you know where. Before sunrise. Bring anyone, he dies first.*

WARREN

43

He stares at me.

I have to let my eyes drift to the side. Sometimes I close them—anything but return that gaze.

The headlamp he placed on the ground is angled up at me, so his eyes are just glimmers of reflected light. It could be worse—the glare is a small price for not having to see the expression on his face.

Things that couldn't be much worse: my zip-tied hands going numb behind my back. My ankles duct-taped to the metal legs of the chair. Breathing through my nose and knowing the tape on my mouth is gonna hurt like hell when he rips it off.

Knowing he may never rip it off.

He's going to kill me.

This is not speculation. The way my captor looks at me, for him it's a done deal. In his mind, I am not breathing laboriously through my nose, *in out in out*, smelling the gluey fumes of duct tape and wondering if I will get high on them. I'm silent and still.

When he puts me in that hole, will he remove the duct tape and zip ties? Or will he let me stay like this, shackled, till I turn to black goo and only noxious plastic remains?

You have to fight *before* they tie you up. Every kid who's ever watched TV knows that. Once you're tied up, it's curtains, baby.

I fought. In my mind I'm still out there on the ridge, fighting him.

. . .

His first blow catches my chin, stops me from pulling the trigger. When he twists my arms behind my back, I kick him in the balls and jab my elbow in his ribs.

The second blow makes the world into a carousel, my stomach dropping.

I don't remember a lot between that and being plunked in this chair. A glimpse of the dark ridge against the stars (no moon yet). Scrubby grass casting enormous shadows as I gaze down from a height, blood rushing to my head. His hand probing the cabin floor, finding a crack between the boards and pulling.

A trapdoor.

The cabin has a cellar. Nina didn't mention it, so she must not have known. Not that there's much to it—a musty hole furnished with this shitty chair and another chair where he sits, staring at me.

After he trusses me to the chair, I learn to breathe again and watch him rifle through the stuff in my backpack. He hasn't gagged me yet—no one in earshot.

Breathe, breathe, breathe.

Shadwell's headlamp washes the cellar, and I see how the sandy hole narrows into a burrow, a blackness the headlamp doesn't penetrate.

The cabin can't extend that far. A passage?

He must see me looking, because he takes off his headlamp and aims a flashlight into the darkness. Packed-earth walls, reinforcing timbers.

"It's a bootlegger's hole," he says.

His first words since he's ambushed me, his voice no longer dead but normal, almost impersonally friendly. Like he's giving me a tour.

I take a deep breath, ready to force out words, but only a laugh emerges. More of a grunt, really.

Shadwell keeps talking. Bootleggers in the '20s built their still in the cabin and used the cellar tunnel as an escape route. When the five-o closed in, they'd scurry through the underground passage into the abandoned gold mine, where they kept their overflow stock of gin until the state dynamited the main entrance shut.

"There are two exits. One behind the ridge, outdoors. One in the old mine."

I register this info like I register the itch of toothed plastic on my wrists and the throbbing in my throat and left temple.

313

That's how he ambushed me. From the cabin, he used the passage to slink under the ridge, crept up behind me, and tossed stones over my head.

"There's evidence," I croak, trying to save myself. Draw a deep breath, swallow, remembering I left that damn bucket in the motel room, practically in plain sight. If he goes back there, he may find Nina—

He doesn't seem to be listening, though. "Password?"

He jiggles my phone irritably in his palm, trying to unlock it. I shake my head.

"What's your password, kid?" His voice returning to that dead level.

"No real service out here anyway. Tried. Call her yourself. Or were you not smart enough to buy a burner?"

Dylan Shadwell looms over me, all six feet plus of him.

Out on the ridge, his dead voice vaporized my last doubts. When he restrained me, more businesslike than brutal, I knew he'd tied people up before.

His other victims must have realized what they were dealing with, too, right before the end. The animal part of us recognizes a predator, just as that predator knows its prey.

But he *is* still human, isn't he? He has motivations deeper, more gnarled and perverse than hunger.

He doesn't bother asking for the password again. I don't bother shaking my head.

Instead I say, "You're not gonna make her come here. You're not gonna hurt her." *Not while I can do anything to stop you.*

Still he stares down at me, letting me feel the silent threat. I shake my head and shut my eyes, bracing for a blow.

None comes. When I open my eyes, I'm looking down the barrel of a rifle—not the .40-cal he used to scare me earlier, but a slim little Remington 597 with a fat suppressor like the one I found in the bucket.

Nina said he did Mr. Gustafsson with a .22-LR like this one. His kill weapon. A plinker, more than adequate to put holes in my head. Which is where—in the middle of my forehead—the muzzle is lodged.

I swallow, and something like a moan slips from my mouth. *Not now. Not like this.*

But if I tell him my password, Nina may get texts from a dead guy asking her to join him in the desert. Urgent texts, and she'll speed to my side.

She knows I love her. And she—maybe a little—loves me back.

One last look at the half-lit cellar room and the blurred barrel of the .22 and Shadwell's finger on the trigger. *Dying won't hurt. I won't even be here.*

I shut my eyes again, visualize the desert stars, shake my head. The gun moves with me.

Then it withdraws, and I brace myself, thinking he's setting up a kill shot he likes better.

Instead, footsteps kick up pebbles. I open my eyes and find Shadwell pacing the length of the cellar. My breath returns when I see the 597 propped against the wall.

His mouth contorts in a cartoonish grimace. He doesn't look at me—I'm still dead to him. Still, seeing him pissed off makes me less scared and more angry.

"She'll never come here," I say. "Not unless it's with the

cops. You better hide me somewhere else, good and deep, because she'll bring them out here to dig up this whole place, and she knows all your dirty secrets, and you'll be fucked, you—"

Shadwell stops pacing at the word "knows." I halt in mid-sentence, wondering why, and that's when he gags me.

. . .

That all happened an hour ago. A half hour? Fifteen minutes? Ten?

Since then, he's been staring at me like a cat at a mouse hole, while I twist and flex my wrists and ankles and read and reread the sheet of paper he pinned to my jacket.

I feel like a slow kid on a field trip whose mom labeled him with his home address. It takes me a while to grasp that he actually thinks Nina's going to read that. Through his eyes.

He believes in dream telepathy, too.

Just as I figure it out, he slumps to the side, his gaze leaving me. His phone pings, signaling an incoming text.

I try to send her my own message with sheer force of will: *Don't. Don't. Don't do what he wants. Don't come alone.*

I know it's too late.

NINA

44

The first few miles are fine, because I'm going to kill him.

Resolution pumps in my blood, depressing the pedal for me as I gun it to eighty, eighty-five, ninety, my fears of dark freeways as distant now as childhood snapshots.

Warren left me the key to the box in the trunk, and in the box are guns, and I'm going to kill him.

Dylan. The brother who calmed me on long desert drives to the penitentiary. The boy who's shared my dreams since I was born.

I feel no fear for the first few miles, no doubts. Just the bright, metallic taste of knowledge in my mouth.

He's asking me to kill him. No, he's *begging* me. Like he knows it's better for Becca that way, better for Trixie, for Eliana, for all of us.

He didn't call me. He waited to contact me in the way only he can. Now, if I shoot him and bury him deep in the abandoned mine, nothing will incriminate me but a one-word text.

If Warren and I die tonight, no phone record will incriminate Dylan, either. I left a note on my bed in the motel: *If I don't come back . . .* Then the address of the cabin in the desert, or as close as I could get. Then Dylan's home address. At the bottom I wrote: *Ask him about the Gustafssons. Take fingerprints from the bucket in the closet.*

Voices of reason are starting to chatter in my head. *Call the cops now. Let them handle it; they're trained for these situations.*

That's what Mom and Kirby would say. Warren, too. They don't know my brother. When he says he'll shoot a hostage before the cops have both feet out of their patrol car, that's what he'll do.

Bring anyone, he goes first. The word "first" is key to the message. If the cops drive up, Warren will get the first bullet, Dylan the second. He won't be taken alive.

Near Bernalillo, the fuel gauge dips into red, and I screech into a rest stop for gas and coffee, rapping on the steering wheel and hissing to myself: *Soon soon soon.*

I want movement, asphalt blurring in my headlights. Out of the car, I can barely walk, barely stand, barely speak. The minimart's stainless-steel counter bloats me like a funhouse mirror.

Dylan felt so powerful at the midnight rest stop, flirting with Jaylynne, luring her to his car. I feel limp, adrenaline draining from my veins. I need to be *there now.*

A dollar eighty-six. Two quarters, three dimes, one nickel, one penny. I had two singles; why am I counting change?

Warren could be dead now. Warren could be dead over and over.

A scaly, furtive thought rears its head through storm-wrecked earth. Why should Dylan keep him alive? He knows I'm coming.

Don't think. The coffee sloshes. The parking lot is endless. *Turn the key.* There will be no choking, no sputtering. No crisp *click-click* of a busted starter like we heard on the way to Schenectady.

Oh God, Warren.

You're the Thief's sister. Stop being afraid. Be like him. Think like him.

The engine roars to life, and I hit the gas. The Legacy eats up desert highway.

Dylan wants something from me. Warren is a hostage, a means to an end, not disposable yet. But he won't let Warren go.

Not a fear but a certainty, a sickening pattern emerging in my mental wallpaper. A broad-shouldered troglodyte looming over the swamp. No, Dylan won't let Warren go. Why would he? How could he?

When he needs to cut loose ends, he doesn't hesitate.

He may feel a wisp of sadness. He cares about me, and he knows I care about Warren. Remove me from the equation, though, and he'd press the trigger like he crushes a cigarette.

Flat miles pass too slowly. I take another gulp of coffee that tastes like burnt plastic. Check the odometer. Gun the gas. Repeat: *I'm gonna kill my brother.*

Walk straight up and shoot him? He wouldn't expect that, would he?

My son. Your brother. Becca's voice now, and I feel her arms around me, her steady breaths in my ear. *Calm down, Nina. No one has to get shot. Make him be his best self, his other half. He won't hurt anyone in front of his family.*

Maybe that's true for Becca. Dylan can't let his mom know he was swamped by the rage and terror that took his father. He might kill her before he showed her the truth.

Me, though—I've seen it all. He knows it.

Blurred asphalt, mile markers, billboards, distant street grids. Warren's glassy eyes. At last, the county road.

Hang on. I'm coming.

The secret is more important than anything. Dylan has to hide his other life from those he loves. He needs them, and that makes him vulnerable.

My skin's an itchy clay shell. The coffee has soured my mouth, and the base of my spine throbs.

I pass the side road with the numbers. Metal glints in my headlights to the left. There's a van half-hidden in the pines— Warren's loaner.

When the engine dies, the desert silence rushes in. No, not a silence but a rhythm: the booming of my heart.

A tapestry of stars seethes above me as I open the trunk. The half-moon drowns its corner of sky in milky light, and the pines and sagebrush cast baleful shadows across the sand.

This isn't real. I'm not unlocking the box to realize the rifle is gone—surely because Warren broke his promise to me and took it. I'm not unwrapping a heavy, wadded-up bag from Hunger Mountain Co-op to find the Sidekick, the first gun he ever handed me.

320

"It's a semi-antique shitkicker," Warren said as we stood in the mountain pasture, showing me the name etched on the barrel between straight quotes. "Working-man's gun, durable. Ugly as sin, but I got it for next to nothing."

"Does it have a safety?" My first question about every gun he showed me.

"Nah, it's a revolver. You just gotta pull the hammer back. Then forward to cock it."

The hammer's back now. I push in the pin and swing out the cylinder. Everything's heavy and sticky, like the gun needs oiling, but it's loaded. Nine rounds.

I hold the Sidekick at arm's length, muzzle pointed into the desert. It's been weeks since I held a gun. Warren spun the cylinder like I would spin a coin, the gun an extension of his hand.

I practice a stance, feeling Warren's hands on my arm and the small of my back. "Be ready to absorb the kick," he warned. "Don't limp-wrist it, or it could jam."

His life shouldn't depend on me.

· · ·

The Sidekick sits beside me in the passenger seat as I backtrack to the gravelly rut of the access road. There's the Sequoia, snagged in my headlights.

Like someone flipped a switch, everything changes. The desert glares under the moon. A distant charge in the air makes my ears ring.

I brake beside the Sequoia, turn off the engine. *Breathe.* My hands are not okay with this pause. They dart out, grab the

Sidekick, and thrust it into the waistband of my shorts. Cover it with my shirt.

Madras plaid shorts. White smocked shirt. I'm terrifying.

Should I have cocked the gun first? How much time will I have?

A tap on the window, and before I can stop myself, I lurch wildly away from it, straining against my seat belt.

It's him.

My brother wears a faded denim shirt. Nothing in his hands. He steps back, his face one big apology, and gives me space to step outside.

What's he sorry for?

My shoulder hurts. I must have banged it when I tried to bolt from the locked car like a startled animal. The Sidekick feels enormous, cold against my bare skin. I'll never be fast enough to surprise him.

"Mom said you were going to the Painted Desert," he says. "How was it?"

"Where is he?" My voice comes in a croak. "I want to see him."

Dylan nods, like he doesn't need to shift gears from *Hi, sis* to *Here's my hostage*. "In the cabin."

We cross the sand together, silent. The cabin is dark and stinks of smoke. When Dylan sets down his flashlight and squats to raise a trapdoor in the floor (*I missed that*), the light spills across the boards, and everything in me screams *now*.

I tug the Sidekick from my waistband and cock the hammer, my hands shaking so hard I almost drop it.

The noise makes Dylan raise his head, but his face doesn't

change. He nods, acknowledging that I am aiming a gun at him. "I'll go first."

"Don't pick up anything." My teeth are clenched so hard, he may not understand the words.

He nods again and disappears down the stone steps, asking from below, "Can I at least get the flashlight? It's dark down here."

"Right here." I kick it toward the hole in the floor, and his hand comes up to grab it—a white, spidery hand, unexpectedly vulnerable.

He lights my way down the stairs, then swings the beam around the cellar room, which smells like chalk and mold. "Shit."

Something's scrabbling on the floor.

I dart away, pulling the heavy Sidekick close to my chest to stop it wobbling, and retrain it on Dylan, who gazes down, shaking his head.

It's Warren, tied to the chair where I saw him in my sleep.

The chair's been overturned in the dirt. My breath stops.

But no. No blood. The flashlight spears him where he twists and flails, his face red with effort. I want to run to him, shield him, peel off the duct tape.

"Aw, kid," Dylan says, shaking his head with mild annoyance, like Warren borrowed his car and left the tank empty. He turns to me. "Okay if I pick him up?"

"What you are going to do"—*deep breath*—"is untie him."

Dylan looks at Warren, disgust growing on his face. Then he turns to me and holds out his hand like he's done with this charade. "Give it to me."

The voice of authority he used on the Gustafssons. *Now or never.* I aim.

But the trigger resists, sticky or just heavy, and my index finger is still forcing its way through that friction when his fingers close on the barrel.

He yanks the gun up and away in one easy motion, jerking me sideways with it. The next instant, I'm sprawled on the earthen floor staring at my empty hands.

Warren bellows through his gag.

That easy. That quick.

My shoulder hurts, my vision turning to watercolor. They must be tears of pain, because I haven't given up yet.

Dylan gives the Sidekick a curious glance and aims it at me. He looks embarrassed, almost sheepish—for me or for himself?—but his gun hand is steady. That's when I notice the long rifle leaning against the wall.

He thought I'd go for that, mapping my next move before I could. How many points will he earn this time?

"Okay if I get the stuff in your pockets?" he asks me with that same ridiculously pained expression. "Your phone? I'll give it all back later."

Later when? There's no later anymore. I hand over my phone, a stick of gum, and a movie ticket stub and turn my pockets inside out. I didn't even think to bring my Swiss Army Knife.

All his victims had a moment like this. When they'd exhausted their options and couldn't face what came next, the end of the story he'd written.

Warren is still squirming and trying to talk. Not giving up.

"Thanks, Nina," Dylan says. "It's gonna be okay. How about we go outside?"

He bends to grab something, his eyes and the gun still on me. A metal toolbox. "Just making sure the kid can't get hold of anything he'd hurt himself with," he says.

It's gonna be okay. Did he tell the Gustafssons that, too?

. . .

As we leave the cabin, Dylan shines his flashlight back inside and says, "Look."

He's set the Sidekick on top of the woodstove, beside the toolbox and my phone.

He raises both hands, then his shirt, so I can see he has no weapon. "Neither of us need that."

I wonder if he knows I know he has more guns inside the mine. *The mine*—does it exist after all?

The sand sinks under my feet with each step; the distance between us keeps increasing. When he turns to look back at me, the moonlight makes his features ghoulish.

I can't breathe, can't count my footsteps. There's no plan because every second is the last second, or every second of my life at once. The half-moon glares on us as we climb the ridge, the other half of the sky black between the teeming stars.

He hangs back now and makes me walk first, his flashlight beam guiding me over the jagged rocks. "How's Mom?"

"She's not my mom."

"I bet you like Becca, though. Everybody likes her."

"I like her." *Where are you, Nina? Come back. Find your way into his head, it's your last chance. Where are you going? What does he want?*

"I like Warren," I say, hardly able to get his name out. "I like him a lot."

Dylan laughs—not an evil laugh, or even a snarky one. It's the guffaw of a brother ribbing his kid sister after he sees her making out with her boyfriend, and that's worse.

"I know how much a lot," he says.

"I wish you hadn't seen that." *Don't think of that night. The look in Warren's eyes as it dawned on him that this was really happening and I wasn't just kissing him by accident.* "I didn't know you could."

"I didn't know *you* could see me, either. Not till I saw you on the road, driving to Albuquerque. Dad told me it went one way. He said God arranged things so he could keep an eye on his baby sister."

"I used to try to send you messages. But it doesn't work like that, does it? When you went inside my head, I must've been asleep."

"Not this week," he says.

"No." We've reached the ridge's highest point, and when I see a flat stretch of rock like a surfboard, gleaming in the moonlight, I know where we are.

"You came here," he says. "Did you spend the whole night?"

I nod, plunking myself down on the too-familiar seat without waiting for his permission. When I extend my right leg, toe pointed, I feel the edge of the ledge that should have been my way into the mine. "I couldn't find your place."

Dylan sits down beside me, and I force myself not to edge away from him. "I hid it."

Of course you did.

"I always wondered," he goes on. "I mean, the map on your wall. The way you were scared to sleep. And how your left eyelid twitched, just like mine at night. But I didn't know for sure till one night I went to bed and there you were, driving through freakin' Oklahoma. Your friend was driving, actually, and scarfing White Castle, and the radio said something about Bernalillo. You said, 'So *that's* how you pronounce Bernalillo,' and all of a sudden I could see everything, clear as crystal. How you planned to drive out here and explore a cave and catch some...monster. Which was me."

Focus. The key is to pretend to see him the way he sees himself. Not a monster, but a boyfriend, a son, a brother who just happens to kill strangers now and then.

Warren is not a stranger.

"So you threw me off track," I say. "You almost convinced me I'd imagined everything."

"I wasn't going to come out here at all. Not at night. Not as long as you were around." A half chuckle. "I didn't think you'd steal my car."

Pretend you're giving him what he wants. I try to laugh, too, like we're reminiscing about a kooky stunt a normal girl might pull on her brother. It won't come out. "Yeah, I tried everything. That poker face of yours...it worked."

Dylan leans back against the ledge, barely nods.

"But something changed after I went to Arizona. Digging that grave—did you do it for me? So I'd see and tell him? So

327

he'd come out here?" Something bitter lodges in my throat, but I can't say the words: *So you could kill him.*

He shakes his head firmly. "Nah. I wasn't gonna hurt the kid. But the way he tailed me in that van, it was like he was daring me to. When I went to check on my cache today and it was gone, I knew who had it. After that, I had no choice."

My throat closes tighter. "It's my fault. Everything he knows about you, I told him."

I pulled Warren into this. I am his real killer-to-be.

Something shrieks in the desert, an unearthly sound, and I jerk upright. Dylan pats my back. "Just an owl."

It's all I can do to keep my voice level, a sister talking to a brother. "We can get rid of that bucket. Nobody will ever know."

Silence.

"He won't talk if I tell him not to." I press my nails deep into my palm.

Still no answer. I draw my knees to my chest and look past him toward where the owl cried—willing it to cry again, to rupture this sense of unreality, to shock me into action.

"So?" I ask at last.

"Only one of us can leave this place. Me or the kid."

I shake my head.

"You brought him into it. You need to be the one to choose."

"Choose?"

He takes my gun, then pretends to offer me a choice. *Remember Kara Ann Messinger writhing in his grip. Remember the old man's skull cracking. Remember Mrs. Gustafsson.*

My voice starts in a whisper, gets stronger. "I chose a long

328

time ago. You forced *my* hand. By...doing those things. By being what you are. So if you're giving me a choice, well, why don't you just kill yourself? Because that's what I want."

The words come out in a rush—too harsh, too honest, all wrong. I bite my tongue.

He just looks at me, and when he speaks, his voice is so sad it makes something ache in me, a twin vibration. "I wish it weren't like that."

"Me, too," I say before I can stop myself.

"Yeah." He draws the word out, kicks the ledge with his boot heel.

Our eyes meet in the darkness, and I remember how he brought me into the adobe house in Sky City and showed me his view of the world. He must remember, too.

"Maybe it doesn't have to be this way." The words catch in my throat, muddy trickle in a drought-year streambed. "I care about him like you care about Eliana. What would you do if she found out? What choice would you give *yourself*?"

Dylan shakes his head, and there are too many words in the gesture.

"You'd kill her." A word he hasn't used yet.

"No." He sounds so awkward, almost shy. And then he points his index finger at his head, mimes a shot. Bullet No. One for Dylan.

He'd kill himself before he'd kill Eliana. But can I be sure I know what we're talking about, even now?

I've wrapped my arms so tight around my chest, my breath comes short. I still feel the Sidekick's weight and solidity at my hip like a lost lover, and then I feel Warren's fingers in the same

329

place. Time is a conveyor belt slipping away too swiftly—*think think!*

I can't jump off the ridge; it's too high. If I run, he'll catch me. Somewhere below us an underground passage snakes to both the cabin and the mine, but I've never been there, not even inside his head.

"I can keep Warren quiet," I lie in a whisper. "I swear."

Silence. Above us the Milky Way blazes, half drowned in moonlight. Sagebrush and yuccas cast gaunt black shadows. I rub my goose-bumped arms. *Hold on, Warren.*

Dylan sighs. "I'm sorry, Nina."

He sounds so genuinely sorry that my eyes fill with tears. When he looks at me, moonlight shows me the painful squinch of his eyes. "The joint's a shitty enough place to visit when you're a kid. I don't plan on seeing the inside in my lifetime. Or letting it wreck my family."

What about the families of those people you killed? Maybe they're not people to him.

He covers his face, scrubs his fingers all the way to the hairline. "Look, I told you I never wanted to hurt your friend."

"But you're going to."

He was always going to kill Warren, ever since he guessed Warren took the cache, but he needs my blessing. That's what he means by "choice."

To erase a person, don't you also have to erase the memories? The grin, the narrowed eyes, the ridiculous appetite for junk food, the detective-speak, the fingers tickling under my knees. No, that's not possible.

Dizzy fatigue sweeps over me, and I let my legs dangle

down to where the mine entrance should be. My heels swing back and forth and find—

A gap. A slot in the rock, just wide enough for a slim person to slip through.

The mine entrance. Dylan must have filled it with debris to hide it, then cleared it out again. Warren said he came here the day I went to Arizona. Then, last night, he was in there digging the hole.

If I wedge myself into that cave, maybe I'll never get out. But—there are guns in there. An entrance to the tunnel leading all the way to the cabin.

Dylan wants me to say it's okay to kill Warren. Those are my words to speak. He must think I'm like him underneath, a cold-headed, coldhearted butterfly struggling to burst free from its chrysalis of normality.

I remember the dream that terrified me: how he watched approvingly as I picked up the saw to dismember his victims, who'd somehow become mine.

Those dreams and doubts are an icy weight on my chest, a magnet pulling me toward him. *I killed the old man. I strangled Kara Ann Messinger. I saw it. I did it.*

"I'm sorry," he says now. "Sorry I screwed up your life, Nina. Sorry you saw things you shouldn't have seen."

Even now he won't confess, won't name the things I saw. Won't, can't. But I know.

I gaze into the moonlit waste that dwarfs us both. The weight in my chest dislodges itself, and a trancelike lightness replaces it.

We are not the same. Kara Ann Messinger's desperate

struggles were my struggles. I rooted for Mrs. Gustafsson to escape. I don't even want to see *him* in pain.

And I will never, ever make the choice he wants.

I bump the crevice with my heel and think again of the tunnel, the guns resting so close below us.

Dylan rises and stretches the kinks out of his arms and legs, gentling his sore right knee. The one he banged climbing into the mine. "I told you," he says. "One of us leaves here—me or your friend."

With the moon rising higher, he's abandoned the flashlight. My hand darts out and closes on it; pulls it behind me as I get up, too. I shuffle, testing the surface of the ledge. Narrow but level.

"If I don't have a gun, I don't have a choice," I say.

My voice is steady now, because my mind is focused elsewhere. I edge sideways so Dylan can't face me without turning his back to the drop-off.

"I can't give you a gun."

His form blocks the moon, top-heavy with its sturdy shoulders and long, skinny legs. He's sure-footed, but the cliff edge is inches from his heels. "What if I asked you to kill yourself?" I say. "Would you?"

My brother nods.

"You're full of shit."

He touches my arm, his fingers simply pressing their warmth into my skin. "No. I mean it. But Nina, there's something you should know. If I did kill myself, you'd be alone."

I force myself not to yank away. Eyes darting to his right

knee, gauging a trajectory. "I've lived seventeen years without you. I can manage more."

"I mean at night. Mom told me our aunt Denise killed herself because she couldn't sleep after Dad died." His voice quivers, and he pauses. "I think she saw our dad at night, just like you see me. When he was gone, she saw...nothing."

I scrub my free hand over my eyes and find them wet, remembering what Steve kept telling Becca in jail. "Nothingness."

It would be strange to fall asleep alone—like missing a routine you've had forever, a beloved pet, even a limb. But I don't think it scares me.

I let my body sag against his arm. "I can't let you hurt Warren. Nobody can die tonight." Tears blurring my vision, *blink hard*. "Nobody."

Dylan's voice goes big-brotherly, reassuring. "It'll all work out."

Sure it will. I raise my wet eyes to him. "Yes. Okay. No more fake choices. Please?"

"Okay," he starts to say, when I whip the flashlight sideways and bring it down on his right knee.

He yelps and hops. Before he can regain his footing, I jab my heel viciously into that same knee. Then I lean forward and use my weight to topple him off the ridge.

Already unbalanced, Dylan tries to grab my shirt, but it slips through his fingers as he falls, twisting in midair. An instant of flailing, and he's gone. Rocks slide and grind.

A groan from below.

Get to the cabin. Run for it.

I head for the way we climbed up—but there's scrabbling behind me, movement. I dash back to the edge of the precipice and peer over.

The muddle of struggling shadow turns into Dylan on his knees. One foot braced on the sand, he's getting up, nothing broken in the short fall. By the time I get down there, he'll be back at the cabin waiting for me. Or maybe he'll decide I've already made my choice and—

I need to lead him away from Warren. Or if it's a race to the cabin, I need an advantage. A weapon.

No time to fear the dark. I'm already down on the ledge and then on my belly, flattening myself to slither into the mine.

. . .

The first drop is the hardest, backward into blackness. My Chucks smack sandy rock, and I gasp and nearly drop the flashlight.

Yet it's all familiar. I could do this with my eyes closed.

I switch on the flashlight, praying for it to work. A wobbly circle of radiance shows me the ladder flush to the rock wall and the chamber below.

Any second Dylan could scramble his way up the ridge. In here, I may not hear him.

After the first three rungs of the flimsy ladder, my toes find nothing to hook into, and I grunt and jump.

I'm prepared for the impact, my knees bouncing. The flashlight jitters on rusty rock.

Now to find that tunnel.

I sweep the light over the wall. Warren is immobilized, no threat to anyone. Dylan will come after me.

I've rejected his choice, refused to play by his rules. Before, he wouldn't hurt me. Now I don't know.

The beam catches the ancient bench. I kneel, grasp the splintery seat, and hoist it up to reveal the hollow compartment beneath.

The long metal box. My hands shake so much I can barely unlatch it.

His rifle's gone. Maybe it's the one I saw in the cabin. But the compact black Beretta is exactly where he left it, wrapped in a blue velvet scarf.

I scoop up the heavy chunk of metal and plastic in my free hand, stagger upright, and run for the jagged opening that leads into the second room, the one where he dug the grave. I know where the hole is before my beam jogs the dark lip of disturbed earth. Still empty.

Light darts from wall to wall, my hand unable to steady its source. The mouth of the tunnel must be in here, or else the entrance to a third chamber. But I see only sandy rock, support beams, and a cluster of rotting wooden barrels.

Behind them. That's where the passage must be.

Something echoes above me, boot on rock.

I flick the light off and scuttle behind the barrels, my dad's Beretta pressed to my chest. Last option. Last chance.

So dark. The air is moist, heavy, nothing like outside. The wall against my back feels solid—am I trapped?

Think. Think. I blink, willing my eyes to adjust. Dylan reloaded the Beretta after he cleaned it. Did he chamber a round?

Rack the slide, quick. At worst you'll waste a round, says Warren's voice in my head.

"Nina?"

He's close but still above me. Maybe on the ladder.

I squat and fumble with the pistol, willing myself to become the Thief. Letting him fill my mind. He can chamber a round in pitch-dark. He's shot hundreds of rounds from this gun.

"Hey, Nina." He doesn't sound angry, just dog tired. "My knee hurts like hell. You got me good."

Light bounces off the walls of the first chamber. Of course he's got another flashlight down here. The Thief is always prepared.

I'm tugging on the slide, and it isn't budging. Obstinate metal, reminding me I'm not a gun person, not a killer. Not even in self-defense.

"That was a pretty bad-ass move, actually." A chuckle that sounds like grudging admiration. "You keep surprising me."

My palms are suddenly so moist I have to wipe them on my shorts. He thinks I'm out of options. He thinks he's in control.

I shift my grip, pull again, and something catches. Metal slides, lovingly lubricated by Dylan's own hands. Snaps back with a satisfying click.

Footsteps, light sweeping the doorway. Did he hear that?

I have five seconds before he reaches me and wrenches the Beretta from my hand. This time I can't just point it at him. He does not fear this pistol like Kara Ann Messinger did.

I rise to my knees behind the barrel farthest from the

entrance, watching his dark shape appear. His light arcs over my head.

My brother, holding only a flashlight. Unarmed.

The Beretta shudders so hard I almost let it go. I vise my trigger hand with the free hand and steady it. *Nice and easy,* Warren says. *Get everything lined up. No limp wrists.*

"Nina?"

You can do this.

Dylan pauses, doing another flashlight pass, and Warren says, *Don't wait.*

I pull the trigger.

The crack deafens me. The gun kicks hard; the casing tinks. *Oh God, oh God, easy, easy, hold on. Don't let it drop.*

The pistol's wobbling. I must've missed. He's still coming— brisk, businesslike steps. Now he knows where I am.

Two seconds till he gets the gun. I stagger to my feet, clamp my trigger hand, and brace myself against the wall, smelling a century of decay. The sweat of miners and bootleggers embedded in the timbers. One last chance for Warren.

"Stop," I say.

When he freezes, just for an instant, I shoot. The sound cracks the space between us wide open.

This time I don't hesitate. The slide racks itself back, beautifully efficient, and I pull the trigger again, barely sighting now. Again.

Still my brother comes toward me, a dark mass outside the flashlight's circle. He lurches against the barrels and shoots out an arm, trying to grab me or steady himself. His fingers graze my blouse, and I skitter sideways.

He sits down heavily on the floor. "Shit."

I edge along the wall, the Beretta still tight to my chest, ears ringing.

"Shit," he says again, his voice guttural. And then he laughs, or maybe coughs. "Pretty bad-ass, Nina."

I dart forward and snatch the flashlight he let drop. Raise it.

His posture is too loose, his head drooping. Darkness spreads on his shirt.

How many times did I hit him? I flick the flashlight from side to side, looking for something to restrain him with, not wanting to turn my back.

"Nina. I'm gonna move."

I pull the beam back to him, the Beretta with it, my voice harsh with terror. "Stay."

Now that I'm no longer just a sighting eye and trigger finger, I seem to be drifting off in several directions. My gaze hovers somewhere in midair, my heart bounces from wall to wall of my chest, my legs are lead.

Dylan raises both hands, pale and spectral in the light, and that's when I start shaking so hard I have to lower the gun.

His face is paper white. Bloodless. He's changed.

"I'm gonna scoot over here," he says in that thick voice— and, before I can lift the gun, he crabwalks to the hole in the ground, his mouth writhing with effort.

The grave. His legs dangle in it.

"Now," he says, each word coming like sludge, "you can put one in the back of my head. I'll fall in there, and you fill it in. Nice and easy. No worries. No one ever finds out."

Without warning, I'm sobbing aloud.

I see Dylan's eyes meeting mine at the Home Depot cash wrap. His wide grin as I swiped his beer bottle on the deck. His sly smile as he ducked into the adobe house in Sky City.

My mouth makes senseless sounds as I mourn the brother I almost had.

The whole time he stays still.

Steady. Focus. Could he be tricking me after all? Playing more wounded than he is?

"Please," he says. "Do it now. Make me disappear."

I circle the grave till I face him across it. "No."

I want to see justice done. Real, molasses-slow, deathly boring, humiliating justice—the kind our dad got, not the frontier kind.

"It's easy. Nobody will ever find me here. Leave the Sequoia at the airport. Make it look like I skipped town." A long, rasping breath. "It's a gut wound. It could take me days to die, Nina. Infection. Nasty shit."

"You won't be here. You won't die." Back in the cabin, I will call nine-one-one. The cops will follow on the paramedics' heels.

He must know I won't shatter his skull and silence his brain, its sanity and its insanity. At the thought of extinguishing everything he is—every hair, gesture, impulse—something buzzes behind my eyes, and I taste bitterness, my fingers slack and slick on the gun.

But neither can I rely on people who don't know him, people who will shackle him to a table in an interrogation room and serve him coffee and danishes and fumble clumsily around in his head. He doesn't owe those people anything. He won't tell them anything. He owes the victims. He owes me.

And he will escape. Rather than take their deal and tell them where to find the bodies of Kara Ann Messinger, the Gustafssons, and the rest, he will imitate our dad with a bedsheet or a razor or whatever comes to hand.

I believe it. He will do whatever it takes to make sure Becca doesn't have to visit her son behind a soundproof barrier, and Eliana and Trixie will never know.

The detectives can't promise him what he wants. But I can—if he doesn't rip the gun away and kill me first.

He wants silence. He wants me to choose him.

"I never wanted to hurt you," I say. "I won't hurt you now. If you'd confessed to me sooner, told me everything, maybe it would be different."

It wouldn't. I know all I need to.

"Sorry." He grunts, coughs, his body so still—yet I know how fast he can move.

He knows I'm boxed in. I can't kill him, not like this. Can't just hand him over, either.

I fall to my knees beside the dark trench, still keeping a careful grip on the gun. "I like Warren. So much. But he can't ever be as close to me as you. You've always been there."

Dylan speaks like it hurts him. "You should've thought of that before you shot me."

"I can't stand this," I whisper.

I'll let him think I fear the nothingness, the long nights without him. But it's not that I dread. It's *now*, watching him bleed and knowing I'd shoot him again to save myself, to save Warren.

Do I want to take it back, to will the bullet out of his tender flesh? Maybe I do, just enough to make him believe it.

"You don't have to die," I say, very low. "We can find help for you. We can . . . explain."

Dylan stares at me, but I can't see his expression. "We," he says.

We. Not me and Warren. I mean you and me. The word hangs in the air between us, as I add the explanation with my eyes. I remind myself that no cell will hold him, that he won't confess to anyone else.

"I can't lose you." The words will barely come. "I don't know what that means, Dylan. I don't know what we'll have to do."

Still he stares with glassy eyes. "Your move."

And I raise the pistol to my own head. "Tell me where you buried the Gustafssons, or *this* happens. Warren will get free and call the cops, and you'll spend your life in jail with your head full of nothingness every night."

Is he still strong enough to get up, kill Warren, bury me? If so, all this is for nothing.

Wordless horror flickers on his face, as if his pain-fogged mind needs time to process my new tactic. Then: "Why do you want to know where they are?"

"Because I have a right." I wedge the barrel against my right temple, my hand steady at last, finger on the trigger. "I was there with you when you did it—did you know? I have a right to know." *And so do their families.*

"You won't do it, Nina."

341

"I will." I'm threatening everything that scares him most: not death but exposure, discovery, being paraded all over cable news and the crime blogs—just another cautionary tale, another bogeyman. "Or maybe you want to be famous," I say. "Maybe you want everybody to know how smart you are, how cold, how people are just things to you. Maybe you don't care if Becca knows. Or what it does to her."

"You can't do that to me." The defiance has bled out of his voice.

"I can. I will."

He spits words at me that sound like curses at first, but they aren't. "It's a road, a road—Lone Spruce. Off One Forty-Six. Three-point-five-four miles up, there's the cabin. Inside."

He remembered down to a hundredth of a mile. I will, too.

I keep my voice as cold as the gun barrel resting against my temple. "And Kara Ann Messinger?"

"County Road Sixty-Eight A. West from the turnoff, five-point-nine miles. Up the bank to the left, between the scrub pines and the cliff." His lip is bitten white as he raises his eyes to me. "Between us."

"Yes." I lower the gun slowly to train it on him again, and hear him release a long, wheezing breath. We're both bone-tired. "It stays between us."

The flashlight beam bobs on the lip of the grave, leaving his face in darkness. I swipe my eyes.

And that's when he reaches across the space and grabs the gun.

This time I fight. I hold on. He's not as strong as he was, but he's strong enough.

Almost. And he's balanced awkwardly on the edge of the hole, his face catching the light and contorting with pain as he forces himself upright. "Damn it," he says, yanking me toward him. "Damn it, *help me.*"

As he says these words, an image blooms in my mind, clear as HD. With my eyes open, my mind alert, I dream a last time:

I'm in the dingy red-vinyl seat of an old car. Yuccas fly past outside. A baby bobs in a car seat, fretting, her face red and wet. I (*but it's not me*) hold out a stuffed cat, tickle her with its tail. I hum a song I just made up that goes, *Don't be such a brat, bee-na good, Nee-na.*

Not me—him. His memory inside me.

My fingers loosen, and he wrests the gun away and raises it to his own temple.

"No!" I scream.

I'll always love you.

His thought, not mine, as he pulls the trigger.

WARREN

45

When the shots split the night, they come to me distantly, reverberating in the earthen walls.

A weapon fired underground. In the freaking mine.

I find the strength I need, finally, to wrench an ankle from the tight layers of tape and kick the other free. Skin goes with the tape, but who gives a shit now?

He didn't shoot her. He wouldn't.

I knee the chair viciously away from me and loop my feet through my bound hands like a contortionist. My hands are still zip-tied, but now they're in front of me, and I can use them to ease the tape off my mouth.

Hurts like a mother. Any second I could hear his shuddering footfalls on the floor above.

No. Because that would mean—

I stumble up the stairs, mouth and ankles stinging. Here's my Sidekick on the woodstove, clear as day in the moonlight spilling through the door.

What time is it? The night feels endless.

Revolver in linked hands, I limp out of the cabin into the night. To the east, the sky is just starting to lighten, black turning to slate blue.

When I hear another shot, I run.

The sound guides me to the mine entrance, though I fall twice and scramble up with imprints of jagged pebbles in my forearms. The eastern light is dimming the moon when I slide my head through the crevice into blackness.

"Nina!"

Heart thudding, I withdraw my head from firing range, brace my back on the ledge, and roll on my side so I can aim the Sidekick into the hole. I'll let him think I'm bumbling in unprepared.

"*Nina!*"

Silence. Smells of earth and mold. He's down there with her, and she—

A shiver on my nape makes me spring erect and scan the rocks. He could be coming at me over the ridge from his secret tunnel.

As I point the gun around wildly, seeing only the dark blue sky and sinking half-moon, a voice speaks softly from the dark below.

Her voice. My name.

. . .

She helps me down the ladder, then finds a knife and severs the zip tie. Her face and hands are smudged with dirt, her eyes huge in the flashlight beam. And the whole time she's helping me, she clutches a pistol in her free hand. A Beretta.

"I'm sorry," she says. "How long has it been?"

I don't answer. I'm busy looking.

Shadwell lies six feet down in a trench of dirt, his open eyes staring up. A bullet hole just north of the right one.

It takes me a few seconds to register that he's not looking at me, not blinking. Gone.

It doesn't seem real. I still see him pacing the cabin, telling me the story of the bootleggers' passage. All his weird tics engraved themselves on my brain while I watched him like a wounded, frozen piece of prey.

"He did it," she says, probably seeing the question on my face. "I think I let him."

. . .

Dawn comes. We figure it out, sitting in the dark with our heads on our knees.

Her plan is to bury him right here in the grave he dug, along with the Beretta emblazoned with her fingerprints. Hide the evidence like she's guilty.

Maybe in her mind, she is.

For a while, I try to make a case for going to the cops. But, as Nina points out, the evidence doesn't favor our story.

When she gets up and starts tossing dirt on her brother's

corpse, I gently take the shovel from her. "You said there might be other people buried here. Victims."

"At least one."

"I want to know."

Despite the exhaustion, digging makes my adrenaline flow. I brutalize the earth with the shovel while Nina gathers her brother's stuff. The 597 she places in a metal box, along with the Beretta that killed Shadwell. The box goes in his grave, along with the headlamp, tools, and duct tape.

"What are we gonna do with the Sequoia?" I ask. "Drive it into a swamp like Norman Bates?"

We decide that after dark, we'll drive Shadwell's Sequoia to the bus station. We'll use his credit card to buy a ticket in his name—to LA, maybe. Or Alaska.

When that's done, she'll use his phone to text his family. *I love you all, but I've decided I need to seek my own path.* Some vision-quest bullshit.

"Honestly," she says, "I don't think they'll look too hard for him. His whole life he's been taking off whenever he felt like it. He's the type of person you expect to disappear."

My shovel strikes something solid— probably just a rock. I bend again, my back protesting, and scoop dirt out of the hole as fast as I can.

"What?" she asks.

I stare for a few seconds before I say, "Come look."

NINA

46

Together we gaze at the remains of the homeless guy.

He was a corpse over Dylan's shoulder when I met him. An unwieldy weight that had to be levered between the rock ledges and allowed to tumble to the mine floor.

How or where they crossed paths, I will never know. My brother was bursting with pride that night because he'd used his .22 in the city—albeit in a run-down, poorly populated neighborhood—and, damn, did the homemade suppressor work. Barely a pop. Half his thoughts were about his skills and his gear. The victim was almost an afterthought.

The homeless guy still wears a navy jacket with a faded gas station logo on the pocket. He no longer has a face. In two years, whatever lives in this dry soil has shaved most of his flesh neatly from the bones.

Does he have dental records? Maybe somewhere. Maybe he has surviving relatives, people who'd want to know. Kids.

After the first shock of uncovering a desiccated skeleton, Warren sits back on his heels, his eyes glittering. "It's real."

I wish I could give him the satisfaction of following through on his detective work, delivering this evidence to a forensics team. But I've made a promise and sealed it in blood.

Not to Dylan. To Becca and the other people who loved him.

"Now you have your evidence," I say, then clear my throat. "We're going to bury him. Rebury him. Then . . . the other one."

Warren looks at the skull, still patched in places with salt-and-pepper hair. His jaw tightens. "People should *know*," he says softly, like he's already given up this fight.

He knows my fingerprints are all over the gun. Maybe he even thinks I made the head shot in cold blood to put my brother out of his misery.

It was almost like that. I let go of the gun. Knowing exactly what Dylan would do, I let go.

I walk over to stand at the foot of Dylan's grave, while Warren faces me at the head. My brother's body between us. "Yeah, they should know. And they will. He told me where the Gustafssons are."

Warren skirts the grave and grabs me in a clumsy hug. His skin is warm, and a pulse beats under my hand as I let my head rest on his shoulder. "You did the right thing—the *only* thing," he says.

I hope I am doing the right thing—for the other family I almost had. For Becca.

Warren picks up the shovel and drops a soft load of dirt on my brother's face. The wound I made disappears.

Good-bye.

I take the shovel from him and finish it myself.

WARREN

47

planned a trip to the desert, and somehow I got the coast into the deal.

It's nearly sunset of the following day when we roll into San Diego in the Legacy. There's an exit for something called Pacific Beach, and that's what we want. More specifically, a Pacific pier.

Nina sits up beside me. She'd been cat-napping all day while I drove through the desert. "Where are we?"

"Lost in suburbia. You missed the scenic part."

"I've seen enough desert," she says.

Last night, after we finished burying the bodies and cleaning up the cabin and ditching the Sequoia and returning the van, I insisted on crashing in our motel room. We both needed sleep almost more than air.

At five A.M., Nina woke me. Our bags were packed, and the shadows under her eyes made her face look hollow. "You sleep while I drive," she said.

"Drive *where?*" The only place I could imagine going was home.

She explained, and I protested.

In the end, though, my aching muscles and bruises won out, and I collapsed in the backseat and lost consciousness within five seconds.

When I opened my eyes, we were parked beside a little white house with wind chimes hanging from the porch. Morning sun slanted over acres of yellow desert, so we couldn't have gone that far.

I sat up and blinked my vision clear, groaning as all my pain receptors reignited.

Somebody knocked on the window, and I jumped. It was Nina and a lady wearing a flowy dress, her long black hair held back with silver barrettes.

"Warren, this is Becca. Becca, this is my boyfriend, Warren."

The instant Becca saw my bruises, she started clucking over me. She shepherded me out of the car and into her house, where she sat me down and fed me coffee, bacon, and pancakes while asking a million questions. Was I sure I didn't need medical attention? Had I made a police report?

Apparently I'd been mugged in Albuquerque the night before last. Hence Nina's abrupt exit from Arizona, and there were further bogus explanations I didn't bother to register.

We buried a guy in an abandoned mine, and we're letting his mom serve us pancakes. That's where my head was at the moment.

Most of the time, though, I simply shunned coherent thoughts. Under the stiffness and pain, my body felt warm, almost glowing.

She called me her boyfriend.

. . .

And that is how I came to drive nearly eight hours more across the desert to the Pacific. The sun beat down on Nina dozing beside me in the passenger seat, and she kept stirring, waking, and saying, "Let me take a turn."

I shook my head. "I can tell you didn't sleep last night. I got this."

Pacific Beach turns out to be a funky surf-bum town, full of bars with goofy names and little stucco houses. I park a few blocks from something called Crystal Pier.

The sun paints the west a riot of colors as we reach the sand. The thin strip of beach lined with hotels stretches as far as I can see. The ocean is as flat as the desert. People with surfboards and romping dogs stand out against the fire on the rim of the world.

"Wait here," Nina says, gesturing at the pier. "I need to do this alone."

I shake my head. "I'm in this with you."

High above the waves, the pier feels miles long. We pass tourists, patient fishermen, and even a motel built precariously atop the wood struts. When we reach the end, I look down and see surfers carving the foamy swells, staying just ahead of the turbulence that will wipe them out.

"All done," Nina says.

I didn't see her send the text message or toss Shadwell's phone in the ocean. It doesn't matter, though—like I said, we're in this together.

We bought him a bus ticket to San Diego, and that's where the last trace of him will be found. From there, his mom and girlfriend can imagine that he hitched to Alaska or Mexico or boarded a freighter bound for Asia, never to be seen again.

Nina seems to like this idea.

"I'm starving," I say as the sun slips below the horizon.

She jabs my shoulder playfully, then apologizes when I wince. "Of course you are. We can grab something on the way back to Albuquerque—I'll drive."

"You're kidding, right? It's eleven hours." At least, I hope she's kidding. Now we've come all the way here, I want to spend some time on the beach.

"I'm totally rested."

"No, you're not. You need a full night's sleep that's not in a moving car."

"No, really," she says. "I'm good. We'll drive back tonight, and I'll sleep tomorrow."

Is she worried somebody will see us here and connect us to Shadwell's disappearance? That's a long shot, and I've got no intention of letting her get behind the wheel.

To buy time, I steer her to a Denny's a block from the beach, where we both order huge breakfasts in defiance of the dusk outside.

The adrenaline of the trip has ebbed away, and I'm so tired

I can barely see straight or keep my head upright. Nina looks worse.

"We need a bed. Mattress. Pillows," I say. "Maybe we can get a spot at that tacky motel on the pier before we pass out."

She shakes her head, and I realize that she's clenching her fist, digging nails into her palm.

I take her hand, coax it open. The other diners, broad-backed tourists and goateed stoners in surf gear, fade into a blur and hum around us.

"What's wrong?" I ask.

She just shakes her head, and I pull her against me.

Her head stays on my shoulder, her breathing evening out, while people come and go. I finish my giant breakfast and some of hers. The waitress brings the check and asks if my girlfriend is okay.

"She hasn't slept for a while," I say, and ask for another cup of coffee.

Ten minutes later, Nina wakes with a jerk. She sits up, rubs her eyes. "I'm so sorry. You should've woken me."

"It's okay. You needed it."

That's when I notice her eyes are bright with tears. She takes both my hands and says, "I didn't want to sleep after sunset."

"Why?" Finally it dawns on me. "That's when you saw *him*."

"When I fell asleep. After dusk. Only then."

I don't believe in an afterlife. If Shadwell's spirit *did* end up anywhere, I don't want to know where that is.

"It's okay," Nina says, folding my hands against her chest.

She blinks the tears away and smiles. "He made me scared of the nothingness, but it's fine."

"It was nothingness?" I ask cautiously.

She nods. "But it doesn't make me want to kill myself. It's not like that at all."

"Jeez, I hope not. It's just like not dreaming, right?" I disentangle one hand and wrap my arm around her. At least I'll be with her tonight, and tomorrow night, and for as many nights as I can manage.

"It's like—for a second he's with me. But not in a bad way. Maybe it's just a memory. Then he slips away, and it's like I'm looking out at the desert or the ocean at night."

When she wakes, I'll be there. I'll be there when she mails the letters to the police departments in Schenectady, New York, and Hereford, Texas—letters we'll print in a shop in San Bernardino and fold and seal into envelopes with gloved hands. Letters we'll drop into two random mailboxes off random exits as we make our way back east. Letters that will uncover corpses while leaving their killer an enduring mystery for crime hounds to speculate about on message boards until one day he's forgotten.

Maybe someday we'll start forgetting him, too. I draw her close, knowing that day can't come soon enough for me.

NINA

48

"Nina—hey, Nina! Didn't you hear the bell?"

Kirby leans over my desk, brows hoisted, hair straggling out of her ponytail. Behind her, beyond the classroom window, scarlet leaves drift from sugar maples in a hazy blue sky.

It's a perfect October day. Why am I in this stuffy room? What class is this again?

Oh, right—French. Madame Verger was explaining the subjunctive when my left eyelid twitched, and I forgot where I was for a while.

No, I knew exactly where I was. Back on that ridge in New Mexico, under the stars, having a conversation that never ends.

It doesn't have to be this way, I beg.

It does, he says. Over and over.

Kirby raps on my desk, her enormous shoulder pads making

her look like a Reagan-era secretary. She's been dressing in hipster vintage ever since she started dating her SAT prep tutor, a nineteen-year-old Brown sophomore.

"We're gonna be late for English," she says. "Did you finish your college-app essay?"

"Uh, almost." The one where I write about my trip to the desert, but *not* about rediscovering my birth family.

Warren appears in the classroom doorway, making *c'mon, let's go* gestures. I go to him and slink my arm around his waist, trying to ignore the din in the hallway, sneaking my fingers under the hem of his army jacket to feel the heat of his skin.

Kirby says, "You guys are so cute you're giving me a sugar rush."

Warren whispers in my ear, "Outside. Need to show you something."

"See you in English!" I call to Kirby—who shakes her head in mock exasperation—and follow him out the side door just as the bell rings.

In our old spot in the cedar grove, Warren takes out his phone. My limbs go heavy when I see the cued-up video with the WRGB logo.

"They finally found them."

He nods. "Took them long enough. Or maybe the cops were making the press sit on it till now."

Together we watch as a blond, bug-eyed anchorwoman announces that the remains of Ruth and Gary Gustafsson have been identified using DNA. We see jerky footage, taken from a distance, of cops behind yellow tape.

In the background, I spot that cabin, too familiar, its

slanted roof weighed down with blackish moss. I shudder, and Warren pulls me against him so I feel the beating of his heart.

The Gustafssons' grown son talks to reporters. "A very sick individual is still out there," the Schenectady County district attorney proclaims next, his mouth an unforgiving line.

I tremble so hard Warren stops the video. "This is *good*, Nina."

"It's not enough."

We stay there for a while, my face in the hollow of his neck, his pulse to my ear, till he says, "We've got Calc coming up."

"Screw Calc." I want to stay outside under this blinding blue sky, watching the airborne leaves, feeling the last balmy breezes before winter sets in. *He* could never stand to be inside on a fine day.

Then I nod, defeated. I have to maintain my GPA so we can graduate and go to college together in California. Warren finally told his mom he wants to study film at USC, and she's half-reconciled to it. We'll get jobs out there and spend our days in the sun, forever and ever.

That sun won't dispel the night in my head, the night that closes over me every time my eyelid twitches. Not the real night where I lose myself in unconsciousness, but the night that exists only in my waking imagination, because he's gone.

We dawdle back into the building, the noise melting away around us, because I'm already somewhere else.

He's not gone entirely. Never gone. Every time I read a headline about someone who went missing without a trace, he stands beside me and says, *There are so many more you don't even know about. People no one will ever miss.*

You aren't there, I tell him back. *I don't miss you.*

That's okay, he says. *I'll be waiting for you on this ridge when you need me.*

I'll never need you. I tug Warren closer. A few girls at lockers eye us briefly and look away.

This conversation is over, I tell the imaginary person in my head. *Over, over, over.*

Someday maybe it will be.

I'll wait for tonight—for the nothingness that he feared and I don't. My sleep will be a blackness like the abandoned mine. His step will never be heard there, his headlights won't sweep the dark away. The night goes on without him.

ACKNOWLEDGMENTS

This book was born one winter's night as a disturbing idea; a raft of intrepid readers helped make it a reality.

My tireless agent, Jessica Sinsheimer, read with an editor's eye and contributed invaluable elements to the story. Thanks to her, I will never be able to shop at a Home Depot without noticing all the sharp objects it contains.

Laura Schreiber got under the skin of this story and helped realize its true potential. As someone who understands the challenges of editing, I'm deeply grateful for her patience and vision.

Jody Corbett kept me honest with her eagle-eyed reads of the book; Maria Elias gave it a gorgeous presentation. So many thanks to everyone else on the Hyperion team.

Nicole Lesperance was the first reader of this story and

offered astute critique and encouragement in equal measure. Many thanks to her and to my other friends at Absolute Write.

Thank you to my colleagues at *Seven Days* for teaching me the useful investigative principle of JDLR ("just doesn't look right"), and for your patience and flexibility.

Thank you to my dad, Harvey Sollberger, for raising me with books, scaring me with tales of the lost mines of the Southwest, and exploring New Mexico with me.

And to my fellow hardworking members of the Deadbeat Club, Sophie Quest and Eva Sollberger: thank you for being there, day in and day out.